POWER OF ETERNITY

Krystal,
Sláinte!

POWER OF ETERNITY

DRUID DUO BOOK ONE

SECOND EDITION

CARLY SPADE

POWER OF ETERNITY

DRUID DUO BOOK ONE

1

"SPEAK NOW OR FOREVER HOLD your peace. I am two seconds from clicking the purchase button." I hovered my finger over the mouse. My best friend for as long as I could remember, Phoebe, clutched her hands under her chin, squealing like a little girl.

"Do it, do it, before I change my mind," she screeched, closing her eyes and turning away.

I closed one eye and clicked the mouse, watching the confirmation page light up on the computer screen. My hair flew over my shoulder as if a sudden gust of wind blew through my apartment. I flattened my hand on my desk, slowly turning in the swivel desk chair.

I waited for her to say something about the mysterious wind. We stared at each other before she squealed and pulled me from the seat.

Burying my petrified face against her shoulder, I joined her in a bout of circular hugs and screaming while her fiery red hair slapped me in the face. Her hip bumped into the nearby table housing most of my potted plants. I gasped, grabbing the corners before one or all crashed to the floor.

Phoebe clapped her hands over her mouth. "Sorry, Abs. Did you—get more plants since I was last here? It's starting to look like a forest."

A warm smile tugged at my lips as I smoothed a leaf between two fingers. "I can't always get out to the woods, so I figured I'd bring it to my apartment."

"And you call *me* weird." She gave my shoulder a playful shove. "I can't believe we're going to Ireland, Abby. And for three weeks. Who's going to water your plant friends?"

I'd been half-listening to her, eyeing my computer desk quizzically, noting the vent on the ceiling directly above it. It wouldn't be the first time the AC vent went wonky in this apartment. It had to be a random draft—plain and simple.

"My neighbor Sylvia said she'd do it."

Phoebe frolicked to the kitchen only to return with a green bottle of liquor and two shot glasses.

"I'd say the occasion calls for a celebration shot. Jameson, of course." She set the shot glasses down with a clank.

"Okay, but only one. I have a date with Bruno in the morning, remember?"

"Oh yes, we mustn't negate Bruno. He'd be furious." She handed me a filled whiskey shot with a sidelong grin.

"Cheers." We clinked glasses.

"*Áthas,*" Phoebe replied in Gaelic—a language she often used to drive me crazy for she knew full well, I didn't understand a lick of it. Her grandparents were straight off the boat from Ireland and had taught her the ancient language since she was old enough to speak.

We both tilted our heads back, consuming the amber-colored liquor. We'd been planning this getaway for years, and it was finally about to happen. Bruno would be sad when I told him the news.

As I dipped my feet in the water, I pulled my hair into a low ponytail. Sinking to my collarbone, I winced when the familiar furry face poked from beneath the surface, spraying water.

"Well, good morning Bruno." The river otter shoved his face into mine, his whiskers tickling against my cheeks in excitement.

"Oh, I'm happy to see you too, Bud. But, as much as you hate weekends, trust me, I need them."

Dr. Lewis created The Lewis Conservation and Rehabiliton Center as a means to preserve, protect, and help animals in need—any animal. After a fishing boat killed Bruno's mom, he arrived at the center pre-maturely born. We'd tried to free him several times over the last year but he kept coming back. Now he called the center home. Bruno took to me immediately. I always liked to think it was because we both lost our birth parents to unfortunate accidents. That and I also loved the water.

He swam circles around me, and I removed the digital thermometer from the zipped pocket of my wetsuit. Obligingly, Bruno rolled onto his back, floating as he rested his paws atop his belly, cocking his head to give me access to his ear.

"You're such a good boy," I cooed, taking his temperature

and smiling as the desired degrees displayed on the screen.

"Good morning, Abby," a familiar female voice said.

"Good Morning, Dr. Lewis. Just the usual with Bruno this morning."

Dr. Lewis peered over the edge of the tank, watching Bruno swim his underwater dance. "He seems extra chipper this morning."

"If only we could all be this energetic on a Monday morning."

Bruno's head popped from the water, and I puckered at him.

"Whenever you get a chance, Abby, if you could check on Delilah, it would help me out a great deal today. I'm absolutely swamped with regular check-ups."

"Delilah? Is something wrong?" I winced, water splashing in my eyes.

"Not physically, at least the last time I checked. She's seemed depressed. She's eating less, not socializing like she normally does, and hasn't been in the wading pool in over a week."

"That *is* strange. As soon as I finish up with Bruno, I'll check on her."

"Thank you. Duty calls." She patted the rim of the tank.

Bruno floated on his back, his whiskers twitching. "Now, Bruno, I have to tell you something. Very soon, I'm going to be gone for a little while, but I'll make sure Bernice comes to play with you and keep you company."

Bruno stuck out his small pink tongue and slapped his paws over his face.

I bit back a laugh. "Oh, she's not that bad." He continued to paw at his face unappreciatively. I reached behind me for the container of small fish and held one to his nose.

"Will this win me back some brownie points, Bud?" Bruno's nose flittered back and forth. His round eyes popped open, and he greedily grabbed the fish with both paws, giving it the tiniest bites. With his lips curled, it looked like he was smiling at me. "Glad we're back on speaking terms." I patted his wet head and left the tank.

Approaching the elephant enclosure, I looked for Delilah. She was one of the zoo's younger elephants, which made it odder she felt anti-social. My first instinct said she might have been going through an adjustment period to a life in captivity. Her instincts would have to be fulfilled in other ways here, much like her instincts for avoiding predators or searching for food and water would be necessary in the real world.

Hm. That gives me an idea.

I grabbed a couple of lettuce heads.

Keeping a watchful eye on Delilah, I buried the heads of lettuce in two separate areas. One under a bit of dirt and the other within a bush. I walked to the elephant, reaching my hand out.

"Hey, pretty girl." I calmly stroked her trunk. Her head perked up, sniffing my hands, detecting the traces of lettuce leaves. Her large brown eyes blinked before she pushed to her feet. Her trunk began to work its way around the exhibit, excitedly searching for the hidden greens. It didn't take her long to find them and her ears flapped with each crunch as she ate her lettuce reward.

"How on earth did you manage that?" Dr. Lewis asked.

"I had a hunch she wasn't feeling useful. So, I gave her a

purpose, an achievement to gain," I said, grinning. Delilah picked the second head of lettuce up and slipped it in her mouth, flapping her large ears.

"You know, I'm happy you're finally going on a vacation, but I'd be lying if I said us and the animals wouldn't sorely miss you."

"I'll miss all of you too, Dr. Lewis."

Delilah's tail swayed. She decided to drop a rather fragrant load three feet away in the large amount that only an elephant could muster. I grimaced, and Dr. Lewis placed a hand over her mouth, holding back a smile.

"I will *not* miss that."

We both shared a laugh.

With international travel looming and all the stress that went with it, I ventured to the one place I could always rely on to relax me—to clear my head and give me clarity.

The forest.

The sun beamed through the canopy of autumn leaves—vibrant red, yellow, and orange. Hugging my jacket tight over my arms, I stood alone with my eyes closed, listening to the wind rustle the trees. Songbirds spoke to one another from above, the occasional woodpecker knocked on a trunk in the distance, and grass shifted as squirrels chased each other.

I'd always believed if I stood perfectly still—nature would calm itself around me. Welcome me into its embrace as if I were one of its own. Being outside, in the elements, felt more like home to me than any New York apartment could offer. Serenity trickled through my chest until my feet molded with the dirt beneath them.

The wind shifted, and a dense chill filled the air. Leaves prickled almost as if whispering to me. Nature always had things to say when I took a moment to listen, but this was different. Never before had the communication sounded so—human.

I opened my eyes, craning my neck back to squint at the trees. The wind swirled, kicking up a coil of leaves, shifting past me before trickling to the ground.

"What are you trying to tell me?"

Branches rattled. Birds chirped so loud it became deafening. The woodpecker's thuds timed with the beat of my heart like a rampant bass drum.

I whirled in a circle, expecting someone or something to appear.

And then the world fell silent—deadly silent. The kind of quiet that set eerie unrest crackling through your bones. The calm before the storm.

I tugged on my jacket sleeves, pulling as much as I could over my chilled hands. "I suppose I should thank you for the warning?" The wind only answered with a light passing breeze. "Could be a bit more specific next time," I grumbled.

A snapping twig jarred my attention, followed by a light whimper—a sound synonymous with a stressed animal. I moved toward the sound, with cautious steps, avoiding sticks that would make a loud crack beneath my boots.

A puppy cowered behind a bush, curling its long tail around itself, trying to keep warm. A pit bull puppy, judging by the shape of its head and paw size.

Slowly crouching to one knee, I held my palms up. "Hey, little guy. I'm not going to hurt you." I kept my tone soft and inviting.

The poor thing shook uncontrollably and leaped to its feet, backing away.

A pickup truck pulled up on the dirt road leading through the clearing. Grey smoke plumed from its tailpipe, sending the surrounding trees in a rustled fury.

The puppy scampered into the bush, shaking so uncontrollably it made the branches vibrate. An animal control officer slid from the truck, his portly belly hanging over his belt as he adjusted it. With the waddle of a walrus and mustache to match, he walked straight to the bush, a noose-styled leash in hand.

"Please stand back, miss. I wouldn't want you to get bit," he said, motioning for me to step away.

I didn't budge. "I'm an assistant zoologist. I know how to handle animals. He's scared out of his mind. The only thing he's bound to do is piss on you."

"Miss, this dog escaped the pound. I need to take it to the shelter immediately." He swung the leash into the bush, latching around the puppy's neck.

It yelped and cried. The birds squawked from branches above.

The dog was a pit bull. There was a great possibility he'd be euthinized at a shelter. An orphaned child is forced to go to a place people wouldn't love it—a similarity that hit far too close to home.

"Stop." I took one step forward.

The man's hand shot to the black holster on his hip. "Miss. I'm going to need you to step away."

My knees shook, but I made all sense of fear melt from my face. "What if I adopted him?"

The puppy cried louder as the officer pulled him toward the truck, his claws scraping the dirt.

"He's not up for adoption. Go about your day, miss."

A lump formed in my throat. They *were* going to kill him. I looked skyward as if the clouds could make the next decision for me.

The sound of the truck's rusted door slammed shut sprung me to action. I bolted, and as I neared the car, I dropped to a crawl to avoid the mirrors as much as possible. The officer had his head down, busily scrolling through his phone. I pressed my back against the truck, reaching for the handle, praying the guy didn't lock it from the inside. Even with the door shut, the rust build-up made the latch faulty, and I didn't even have to pull on the handle. The door groaned as I eased it open, and I froze, pinching my eyes shut.

As the surrounding birds chirped louder, I yanked the door open, curled the puppy into my jacket, and ran for the woods. Finding a tree trunk wide enough to hide behind, I pressed my back to it and tried to steady my thumping heart. The dog whimpered before popping its head over my collar, and we stared at each other. He canted his head from left to right and gave one tiny lick to my chin.

"You're welcome," I whispered with a smile.

The truck peeled away, none the wiser the puppy was no

longer inside. By the time he'd notice, the puppy and I would be nothing but a distant memory.

The puppy wiggled in my arms, desperate to move, but I kept him pinned to my chest, glancing around at passersby as I waited for Dr. Lewis to answer her door.

When it flew open, I plastered on my brightest smile.

"Abby?" Her eyes fell straight to the roiling bumps under my jacket. "What is that?"

There wasn't any fooling Dr. Lewis.

"Can I come in?" I raised my brow, wincing as one of the puppy's claws dug into my chest.

"Uh-huh." She gave a wry grin as she stepped aside.

As soon as I was in the living room, I pulled the puppy from my jacket and held it up.

"A pitbull puppy? What in the world are you doing with one?" Dr. Lewis held her fist out to the puppy, letting him sniff it.

"I may have possibly stolen it from Animal Control." I winced.

"Abby." Her tone was that of a scolding mother.

The dog wagged its tail, letting his large tongue hang from the side of his mouth. "I know. I know. They were going to kill him, and I couldn't let that happen."

"Why bring him here?"

"My apartment doesn't allow pets. And he's a pitbull. I know it'd be hard to put him through adoption, but I thought maybe you would know someone who'd want him?" My brow pinched together.

Dr. Lewis sighed and scratched the dog's head, studying his reaction and behavior.

I'd be lying if I said I hadn't planned to take advantage of Dr. Lewis's weakness for endangered animals. I couldn't whisk off halfway around the world without knowing the dog would have a home.

She held her hands out, and I passed the puppy to her. The dog rolled onto his back in her arms, letting her scratch his belly. "Alright. I have a friend with a farm. They'll more than likely be interested since he seems pretty friendly. I'll foster him until then."

Tears stung my eyes, and I shrieked, giving Dr. Lewis a side hug. "Thank you. I saw him out in the woods alone and then dragged to that truck and—" A lump formed in my throat.

"Say no more, Abby. Go on your vacation. Have a ball. Rest assured he'll be safe." She squeezed my shoulder.

After thanking Dr. Lewis another dozen times, I left with the relief of knowing he'd lead a better life than the one dealt for him. Standing on the stoop of her house, I let the sun warm my cheeks. The trees must've been trying to warn me about the puppy.

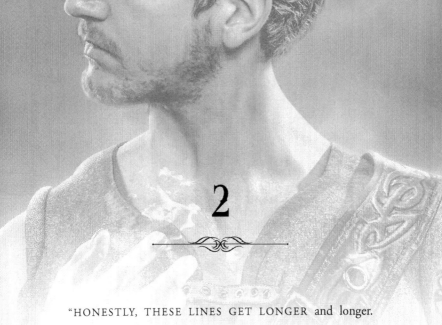

2

"HONESTLY, THESE LINES GET LONGER and longer. We're going to miss our flight," Phoebe complained, impatiently tapping her foot and looking at her imaginary watch on her wrist three times.

"Phoebe, seriously relax. Our flight doesn't leave for another four hours." I watched her in amusement, attempting to hide my smile by biting the inside of my mouth.

"And you made fun of me when I said we should get here *extra* early."

"You were so right, Phoebe," I replied monotone.

We went through the usual gate security routine of throwing our belongings on a conveyor belt and waiting to be scanned. The agent waved Phoebe through the metal detector first, her red hair bobbing up and down, practically skipping her way through.

"We're going to Ireland," Phoebe shouted at the agent.

The agent, an unenthused middle-aged woman, cocked an eyebrow. "Oh yeah? Know what island I'm going to?"

Phoebe's eyes widened in anticipation.

"Staten. Retrieve your bags, please, miss," the agent deadpanned.

Phoebe scrunched her face and continued to gather her things from the belt. The agent waved me through.

"Sorry, she's excited. I hope your shift is over soon."

"Well, I appreciate that. I'm used to it. All day people are coming and going. All part of the job." She gave a tired smile.

I turned to gather my bags, eyeing Phoebe jumping up and down. I was going on vacation with a pre-teen.

"Abby, quick. We can still make Happy Hour." She pointed at the airport bar called O'Malley's Pub.

"Since when did you become a drinker?" I asked, doing up the laces of my sneakers.

"Since we decided we were going to Ireland. Building up my tolerance." She gave an exaggerated grin, causing all her perfectly white teeth to show.

I snickered. "You're crazy."

"Would you have me any other way?" She pulled me into a side hug, her eyes brightening.

"You're right, Phoebs." She never failed to make my life interesting. Well, she and Bruno, anyway. I couldn't imagine life without her.

"Now come on. I'll buy ye a Guinness." She recited the words in a perfectly impersonated Irish accent.

She dragged me into the pub, and we each took a black leather stool. Patrons nursed their drinks, eyes on their phones. Television monitors were in every corner, each playing a different sport.

Did pubs look anything like this in Ireland?

"What can I get you, ladies?" The bartender asked, his voice rich with a New York accent.

Phoebe whipped out her credit card with a bounce on her stool. "Two Guinness, please."

"Sure thing. Eight dollars."

Phoebe handed him her card. "We're going to Ireland." She grinned, tapping her fingernails excitedly on the wooden bar top.

I held my head in my hands. The bartender chuckled, handing Phoebe her receipt and a pen.

"Oh yeah? Getting used to the pub scene, huh?" he asked as Phoebe proceeded to scroll her elaborate signature, replacing the last "e" of her name with a heart.

"Absolutely." She handed the receipt back with a bow.

He placed our two perfectly poured and foamed pints of Guinness in front of us. She lifted her glass, and I followed suit.

"To having the absolute best time in the world for two chicks that completely deserve every minute of it." She toasted, lifting her chin into the air.

I laughed. "I'll drink to that." We clanked glasses and took our first sip, relishing in the stout's earthy, rich, and delicious flavor that only a Guinness could give.

"I couldn't help overhearing you're goin' to Ireland," a man sitting next to Phoebe said, his back to the bar top, elbows propped up as he leaned toward us. Either he was mocking the fact that we were going to said country, or he was Irish, given the accent. He had blue eyes, terse, dirty blonde hair mixed with flecks of red, and when he smiled, the most prominent dimples I'd ever seen on a man's cheeks appeared. He wasn't unattractive by any means but had more of a boy-like charm about him. Phoebe would eat him right up.

Phoebe turned to look at the stranger. Her finger traced the rim of her pint glass as she absently licked her lips.

Here we go.

"Well, you heard right. I couldn't help but overhear your amazing accent. Are you from the motherland?"

I somehow avoided an eye roll and stuck my nose into my glass, taking a long swig.

The man's smile widened, turning his dimples into craters. "That I am. Flyin' back in a few hours."

Phoebe's jaw dropped as she turned to slap me in the shoulder. "Oh my gosh, we are too. We must be on the same flight."

I rubbed my shoulder, frowning at her.

"Luck 'o the Irish, indeed. My name's Patrick Callahan." He extended his hand in greeting.

"Phoebe O'Connor." She shook his hand far more enthusiastically than necessary.

"Ah, so you *are* Irish. I didn't want to assume," he said, taking a small lock of Phoebe's red hair and letting it run through his fingers.

And now he invaded her space. I reached past her and stuck out my hand. "Abby Weber. And it's perfectly fine if you assumed I *wasn't* Irish." Given my dark hair and olive complexion.

Patrick shook my hand with a curl of his lip.

"Say, you two should let me be your tour guide. I can show you places you won't find in any tourist brochure. Far more interestin' too." He glanced between us.

"Oh, that would be amazing. How nice of you." Phoebe bounced on her stool.

I cinched my brow, grabbed the sleeve of her T-shirt, and yanked her toward me. Dipping my head low, I whispered, "Phoebe, we don't know this guy."

"That's what we're doing right now, isn't it?" she countered, and I reluctantly let go.

Call me paranoid, but I had no interest in being the next victims Liam Neeson had to save in *Taken 12*. I concentrated on my beer, keeping an open ear to their conversation.

"Where will you two be stayin'?" Patrick asked.

Surely she wasn't so smitten over this guy to divulge *that* information.

"Oh, it's this super cute bed and breakfast called Lucky Cove, right in Dublin."

My head whipped in her direction, eyes ablaze. This is where assumptions got you. She was ready to give this man her social security number if time allowed.

"Oh yeah, I know that place, it's…" Patrick started to say before I quickly pounded the rest of my drink and grabbed Phoebe by the arm, interrupting him.

"We should go to the bathroom before the flight, Phoebs."

"But I haven't finished my drink."

I grabbed her nearly full beer, tossed my head back, and drained it before letting the pint glass slam onto the bar top.

Phoebe's eyes widened, and she let me yank her off the stool.

Patrick beamed. "I'll see you two in Ireland."

I forced a smile and half-waved over my shoulder at the

creepy Irishman.

"Since when can you pound a beer like that, Abs?"

I let go of her arm in a huff. "Since you decided to share all of our travel information with a complete stranger. I want to return from this vacation alive."

I pulled my airplane ticket from my pocket and checked the gate number. Phoebe folded her arms.

"What?" I snapped.

"You're adorable when you're all paranoid. Patrick wouldn't hurt a fly."

"He wouldn't, huh? Did you suddenly become psychic?"

"Of course not. I have a good feel for people."

"Oh, you mean like Stalker Stanley?"

"He sent me a few e-mails, so what?"

"He sent you over two hundred e-mails of his naughty bits, Phoebs." I stared at her as if she were growing a second head.

She shrugged.

"Or what about that guy who stood outside your window for six hours straight waiting for you to acknowledge him?"

"In his defense, he did leave after I said something."

I blinked and turned for our gate. "Phoebe, do me a favor. When we get there, we're going to avoid Mr. Patrick Callahan completely, just in case he's one of your infamous weirdos."

"Aww, but he was so cute!"

"I'm sure you'll find plenty of cute Irish men *in* Ireland. I'll steer them at you in droves if you want."

As we approached our gate, I eyed the display screen stating our flight was on time.

"You can be such a party pooper sometimes, but I still love

you." She elbowed me in the ribs.

"Yeah, yeah. Love you too, nutcase." I nudged her with my shoulder.

We flopped into seats in front of our gate, waiting for the boarding announcement. I dug out my phone to flip through article suggestions, most of which involved Ireland, considering how much I'd looked it up the past few months.

Phoebe flipped through some teeny-bopper magazine she bought from the gift shop with exaggerated licks of her finger with each page turn.

I paused on an article titled "The Monster of Muckross Lake." A survey group doing sonar scans claimed something blocked the reading...and it was the size of a two-story building. Huh.

"Hey, you ever hear about a monster in Muckross Lake?" I asked Phoebe, squinting at the photos of the article.

"Some superstitious rumors like the Loch Ness monster in Scotland," she replied with a flick of her wrist. "Okay. I'm going to ask you some questions, and you answer the first thing that pops into your head."

"Oh, boy." I continued mindlessly scrolling, preparing myself to humor her.

"Physically, what's the first thing you notice about a guy?"

My first instinct was their ass. "Eyes."

She made a buzzer sound. "I know for a fact you look at a dude's butt."

"That's shallow, Phoebe. Come on."

"There's nothing wrong with noticing a man who puts dedication into his posterior, Abby." She scribbled on the page.

"Where would be the hottest place for a guy to have tattoos?"

"Arms." My stomach flipped at the thought of previous sleeve tattoos I'd seen.

"An honest answer. I'm shocked." Scribble. Scribble.

Giving up on distracting myself with my phone, I threw it into my purse and concentrated on the planes wheeling about the tarmac through the window.

"What would be the preferred occupation for your guy?"

I blew out a breath and folded my arms. "Should I be saying pediatrician or something?"

"No, because that'd be you thinking of what this quiz *wants* you to say. First instinct."

"I don't know. Something outdoors, I guess? Uses his hands. Makes calluses."

"That's definitely you." She jotted it down and chewed on the pen. "What is your go-to flirting style?"

I rolled my eyes and crossed my feet at the ankles, stretching my legs in front of me. "I don't flirt."

"Sure, you do. You're extremely sarcastic and play hard to get."

My jaw dropped. "I am *not* a tease, Phoebe."

"St. Patrick's Day 2017."

"Is that supposed to mean something to me?"

She tapped the pen against her lips. "Ryan Schmitt. Met at the bar. Persued you all night."

"That's called not recognizing a dead end."

"You admitted you liked being chased."

Sulking in my chair, I glared at her.

"Your ideal shoes to wear." She dropped her gaze to my

boots. "Combat boots."

"I don't *always* wear boots."

She set the magazine in her lap. "Oh? When don't you?"

Squinting at her, I bit down on my lower lip. "Bowling."

"Do you expect chivalry?"

I let my head fall on the back of my seat. "What kinds of questions are these, Phoebe?"

"Answer. What else are we going to do?"

"Not entirely, but it'd be surprising, refreshing even if he were a little bit."

"Another honest answer. I'm so proud of you."

A group of women stood in front of the digital New York to Ireland flight sign, taking a selfie together as they made duck faces and flipped peace signs. When I'd asked Phoebe to go to Ireland years ago, it wasn't just because of her heritage. I'd also felt this cosmic pull. There were plenty of countries I had an interest in visiting, but something about The Emerald Isle begged me to come.

"Where do you typically meet guys?"

"The internet."

She cackled and slapped her knee.

"Got a problem?"

"You lie to yourself way too much, Abs. You tried online dating for like an hour and deleted your account."

"All the guys contacting me were skeezballs."

She nudged my shoulder. "The right answer? Bars. You met all of your exes in bars."

"Perhaps I should re-think my strategy."

She stuck her tongue out the corner of her mouth as she

scribbled away.

I pinched the bridge of my nose. "How many more questions are there?" Bouncing my knee, I glanced at the clock.

"Two more."

A groan escaped my throat.

"Cars or motorcycles?"

"Cars."

She made that damn buzzer sound again.

"I've never even been on a motorcycle."

"You want to be, though. Do you not remember our Sons of Anarchy binge session? Tell me what you wouldn't give to be nestled behind Jax Teller on a bike?" She cocked an auburn brow, challenging me to deny it.

"Fine," I said through gritted teeth.

"And finally...where would your first ideal date be?"

I gazed out the window at the familiar surroundings of New York. So much hustle and bustle. So many people and little lands left to explore. "Absolutely anywhere I've never been already."

"Yup. Knew it."

I snapped out of my daydream. "Knew what?"

"You attract bad boys." She flipped the magazine around and shoved it in my face.

"You had me take a 'Do You Attract Bad Boys' quiz?" I pushed the magazine down, cocking my eyebrow at her over the top of it.

"All in good fun," she beamed.

"We will now start the boarding process," the gate agent announced.

We gathered up our things and eventually made our way onto the plane. As per our usual traveling arrangements, I took the window seat, and she took the middle. It was always a game of crossing your fingers as person after person shuffled down the aisle and you prayed no one sat in the empty seat.

A familiar red-headed Irishman made his way through the rows of seats, and Phoebe elbowed me.

"I see him, Phoebe. We already knew he was on our flight, remember?"

She gasped. "Oh, my God. What if he's in our row?"

"He better not—"

Patrick paused by our row, glancing at his ticket to the numbers attached under the overhead compartments. "Wow. Uh. It looks like I'm your row mate, ladies."

Unbelievable.

"Can you believe it? How crazy is it that we all ended up in the *same* row?" Phoebe bounced in her seat, grinning at Patrick.

"Small world," Patrick said.

I looked at him just in time to see him dimpling at me. "The smallest."

If there was ever a moment I wished I'd spent time developing a very particular set of skills like Liam Neeson, it was right here and now.

Luck of the Irish my left foot.

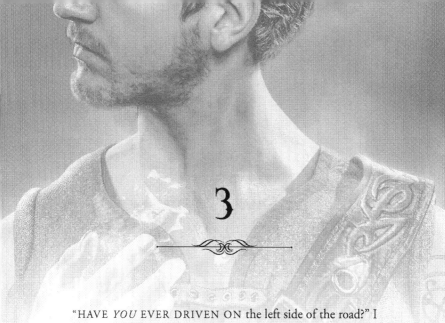

3

"HAVE *YOU* EVER DRIVEN ON the left side of the road?" I stood in front of a car rental kiosk in the Dublin airport with an eager beaver known as Phoebe.

"No, but how hard can it be?"

I ignored her ignorance and turned to the attendant. "We'll get a taxi, thank you."

"Suit yourself," the old man behind the counter answered.

I extended the handle of my suitcase, ready to wheel it to the exit.

"Or I could give you a ride," Patrick's familiar voice said from behind us.

"Or Patrick could give us a ride," Phoebe beamed.

Damn. I thought we'd lost this guy during baggage claim. "That's very nice of you, but we wouldn't want to impose."

"Nah. Impose on me all you want," he said.

"Abs, let's impose." Phoebe clapped her hands together.

I looked between the two of them before I let out a long, audible sigh. "Fine. Lead the way."

Patrick motioned for us to follow.

I pulled Phoebe aside, grasping her shoulder. "If anything feels off, the first traffic light we stop at, we bail. Keep your suitcase with you."

One finger at a time, she pried my hand away. "I seriously worry about you sometimes." She did a hitch-step to catch up with Patrick.

I growled under my breath and picked up the pace. We reached Patrick's car, which looked about the size of a clown car from the circus. I canted my head to the side as Patrick popped the trunk.

"Are we going to all fit in this thing?" I asked.

Phoebe stared daggers at me from over her shoulder.

"Oh yeah, don't you worry. This be a Fiat. Plenty 'o room," he said, lifting his chin as he whisked my suitcase from my grasp before I had a chance to protest.

Okay, no big deal. I had some clothes in my carry-on bag and a few other essentials. I could survive without my suitcase if need be.

Patrick opened the doors for us, like the upstanding gentleman he claimed to be. I immediately reached for my seat belt, my body stiff with tension. Patrick got into the driver's seat in front of Phoebe. When he started the ignition, I heard the locks on each of the back doors slide into place. I frowned and pulled on the handle. Locked.

"Child safety locks," Patrick said with a smirk, watching me pull on the handle one more time for good measure.

I tapped the window with my knuckle. I could kick the window out. Actors did it in movies all the time. Phoebe's hand patted my thigh, her smile not reassuring my nerves.

"Off to the Lucky Cove we go, ladies," Patrick said, pulling out of the parking lot.

As we drove, I took in the sights. I couldn't wait to explore more of the countryside, see the rolling green hills and the ancient castles—I wanted to get lost in the fantasy of it all. That is if Patrick didn't turn out to be some psycho serial killer. I eyed my knees pushed up against the front seat, and stifled a grumble.

"Behold your home away from home," Patrick said.

We sat in front of a simple building that looked an awful lot like a bar. A quaint, slightly disheveled concrete building painted bright yellow with black accents. "Phoebe, please tell me you didn't book us a room in a pub."

"I didn't think I did. Are you sure we're at the right address?" She scooted forward, reaching her arm between the seats for the directions.

"The Lucky Cove is above the pub. Quite convenient if you ask me," he said with a snicker before exiting the car.

Phoebe smacked her lips together, pretending to look anywhere else but at me. She had one job, and she booked us a room above an Irish pub. I couldn't be mad at her. We *were* in Ireland. We'd spend most of our time outside of the room, so who cared? I eyed Patrick making his way to the back of the car, and to my relief, he opened each of our doors. Perhaps he wasn't a serial killer. He waited with my suitcase, handle extended and all.

"Thanks," I said a bit sheepishly.

"O'course."

When we walked inside, the sounds of fiddles and Irish

pipes flooded my ears. The darkness outside made the candles at each table brighter, and the flames danced in time with the music flowing from the band's fiddles in the corner. A patron occupied every other seat at the bar and most of the tables. Phoebe jumped up and down, breaking into a quick jig that looked like 'The Chicken Dance.'

"If you ladies want, I'll take you to a real pub tomorrow night. The pubs in Dublin are so bleedin' cliché it makes me mad as a box o' frogs," Patrick said.

My mouth formed a small oval shape, stunned by his comparison.

"Oh, yes, please. What time?" Phoebe asked.

"Say, I pick you up 'bout seven?"

"Perfect! We'll be ready, right, Abby?" Phoebe finally acknowledged my presence with a smile.

"Fine by me. About the only touristy attraction I was interested in seeing while here was the Blarney Stone."

"Ah, seekin' some eloquence, are you?" Patrick asked, scanning me.

I raised a brow. "Do you believe in all that?"

"Do you not?"

"Of course...not." I scrunched my nose.

"Interestin'," was all he said.

What was that supposed to mean?

I opened my mouth to question him, but Phoebe interjected.

"Let's go see our room, Abs."

Patrick's lips curled before he gave a flourished bow. "Have a lovely night, ladies. I'll see you tomorrow."

"Night, Patrick." Phoebe grabbed my hand.

Patrick winked at me before exiting. He may not have been a serial killer, but he was definitely…something. I took a moment to survey everyone, considering most of them would undoubtedly be a floor below us nearly every night during our stay. Many of them stared back, not bothering to look at their pint glasses as they brought them to their lips. The bartender, a short, portly fellow with bright red hair, mutton chops, and plaid suspenders, absently cleaned the inside of a glass with a rag.

"Come on, slowpoke," Phoebe said, jarring me from my perusal, and I allowed her to drag me to the stairs.

A tiny sign hung on the wall reading, "Lucky Cove," with an arrow pointing up. I glared at it before we ascended the stairs—all thirty of them. Our suitcases made loud thumping sounds against each one. The steps creaked so loudly I feared my foot would go straight through. I let out a breathless huff once we reached the top—a confined space with a desk nestled in the wall.

Was this supposed to be the lobby?

Phoebe slapped her hand on a small antique bell. We jumped when a silver-haired head popped up from under the desk. I clasped my hand to my chest while Phoebe let out a yelp.

"Top 'o the evenin' to you! Welcome to The Lucky Cove! My name is Iris." The older woman greeted us with such enthusiasm I wondered if her accent was real.

"We have a reservation? Should be under Phoebe O'Connor."

"Yes, let me see 'ere." Iris pushed the round, wire-rimmed glasses up her long, pointy nose. She grabbed a large book from behind her and let it slap onto the desk, sending plumes of dust and debris. I coughed, and Phoebe waved her hand.

Iris opened the book, its pages yellowed and stained. As she flipped through it, I thought pieces would start to crumble in her hand. She reached a page that wasn't as aged and dragged her gnarled finger down the calligraphy written list. She stopped and poked her finger to the page, tracing to the right.

"There you are. Right this way, dearies!" She slammed the book shut, dust flying yet again. She hopped off the stool, her body disappearing behind the desk. When she rounded the corner, she looked about three feet tall and waddled past us. She motioned with her finger for us to follow, and I held my hand out for Phoebe to go first.

Iris led us down a hallway with several doors. One room housed a couple who were enjoying some private time together. In another, two men argued with slurred speech, and one had the TV turned up so loud I could tell they were watching *The Godfather*.

"'ere we are," Iris said, pulling out a set of large keys on an even larger ring from the front of her apron.

As we entered the room, I couldn't see my hand in front of me and bumped into Phoebe's back with a grunt. Shuffling feet scraped against the wooden floor before the room brightened. Iris stood on her tiptoes, adjusting the turn-dial-styled light switch. A lump formed in my throat as I took in our living conditions. College dorm rooms were larger. The three of us had just enough room to shuffle around each other.

"A quick tour then," Iris began. "Here be the bed." She pointed at the child-sized bed with bedspreads that looked like they'd been around since the eighteenth century.

"Here be the closet." She opened a small wooden closet,

moths flying toward the ceiling light.

"The toilet be in the hall, shared amongst the rooms, and here be your view." She whisked open the curtains to reveal a stone alleyway. We risked a peek outside, where a drunken man peed on the wall. I blinked a few times before Iris let the curtains fall back. The sight of the man peeing, seemingly old news, unfazed her. She waddled back, slipping the large key into my palm.

"Breakfast is downstairs at half six. A pleasure to have you at The Lucky Cove.'" She smiled with her one tooth and slammed the door shut behind her.

We both jumped.

Phoebe cleared her throat and shuffled around the room, attempting to find somewhere to rest her suitcase. "Well, it's not so bad, right?"

I could tell she felt awful and hadn't the heart to make her feel bad. It'd be an adventure.

"It's perfect, Phoebe."

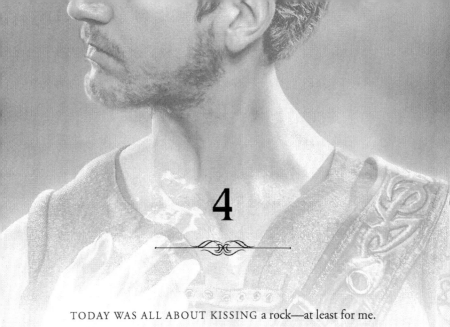

4

TODAY WAS ALL ABOUT KISSING a rock—at least for me.

Phoebe would've been okay skipping the entire day and getting to the part where we went to some dive pub with Patrick. I wrung my hands in my lap, watching the green hills roll by as the taxi drove us to Cork. For the first time since the airport, Phoebe looked unenthused, staring out the window, her head resting on her hand.

"I can't believe you're dragging me three hours so you can go smack your lips on some rock," Phoebe mumbled.

"Usually when people go on vacation together, they compromise with the activities? Besides, how are you, a full-blooded Irish woman, not interested in seeing the Blarney Stone?"

"Do you have any idea the amount of lip fungus that's probably on that thing? Centuries worth."

"Let me get this straight. You're all for caravanning about with a stranger you met in an airport, but when it comes to the possibility of a little lip fungus, you bow out?"

Phoebe pursed her lips and stared at me, silent. "Fine. You can kiss the stupid stone, gain your illustriousness, and I'll stay in the car."

"It's eloquence, and no, you won't. At least take a tour of the castle, princess."

Her head whipped around. "Wait, the stone is in a castle?"

"Uh, yeah. Did you look at *any* of the websites I sent you?"

Again, she stared at me, silent.

"I swear you're like the little sister I never had." I snickered and perked as the Blarney Castle came into view. I made a quick mental check-list of everything I wanted to see while at the castle. Unlike Phoebe, I'd done my research on some of Ireland's historical spots. Who knew when I would be back?

As the taxi came to a halt, I swiped my card for payment. As I gazed up at the gorgeous stone castle that'd been around since the fifteenth century, my chest swelled. We were about to set foot on ancient grounds. Such rich history here. Phoebe gazed at the castle, slack-jawed.

"I told you." With a warm smile, I led us toward a small line of people waiting their turn.

"I've changed my mind. I want to give the stone a smooch," Phoebe said, trotting to catch up.

"I knew you'd come around." We held on to the railings, slowly progressing our way up the stone steps.

Once there were only several people in front of us, an older man with delicate features and a calming demeanor crouched by two handrails.

A woman with pepper-colored hair and a yellow raincoat lay on her back. He held onto each of her sides as she used the rails to lower her head toward the stone. Mrs.Raincoat screamed and screeched, "Lift me, lift me up!"

The man, undoubtedly used to this behavior, calmly lifted her and patted her arm. "Do you want to try again?"

She shook her head with such persistence it threw her hood off. "Eloquence be damned." She scrambled to her feet.

I bit back a smile as she stomped past us. Once it was my turn, I lay on my back like all others before me and scooted back, reaching my hands for the railings. The assisting man's bright green eyes brightened as he went for my sides.

"What's your name?" I asked.

He looked taken aback as if no one else had bothered to ask.

"Charlie." He offered a calm smile.

"Pleasure to meet you, Charlie."

"You ready, miss?" He pressed his hands against each side of my ribs.

I nodded and slid back further, dipping my head back toward the stone. As I looked down, adrenaline coursed through me, staring at the straight plummet to my death. Ignoring the absurd possibility, I planted my lips on the cold stone while closing my eyes. A wave passed over me like the backdraft from an explosion. Gasping, I lost my grip on the railings, and Charlie gripped me tighter.

"Woah, you alright there?" He asked, a tremor in his tone.

I opened my eyes, pulling myself up. The waiting tourists looked concerned.

Was I the only one who'd felt it?

I nodded, wrinkling my brow. He helped me stand, and I scampered off to the side, running my hands through my hair.

I waited for Phoebe as she went through the same motions, but she removed a small bottle of antibacterial from her pocket before she bent backward.

"Could I—?" She asked Charlie.

"Be my guest, dearie," he replied.

She slathered the stone with a colorless glob, and her eyes sparkled as she kissed the stone.

As we descended the stairs, the mysterious draft I'd felt plagued my thoughts. "Phoebe, did you...feel anything when you kissed the stone?"

"What do you mean? Aside from the tingling on my lips from the antibacterial, I felt a stone on my mouth." She eyed me curiously.

"Maybe it was the blood rushing to my head or something." I tightened my jacket around me like a security blanket.

I knew I wasn't crazy. I *felt* something.

As we approached an area called Rock Close, I led Phoebe through an archway of limestone with steps leading down. A small, rickety sign displayed the words *Wishing Steps*.

"Ooo, what are these?" Phoebe moved for the first step.

I grabbed her elbow. "Let me explain this first. Legend says if you can walk down these steps and then back up backward, whatever you wish for while making the walk will come true within one year."

"Well, that sounds pretty easy." She stepped forward.

Again, I held her fast. "With your eyes closed."

"Oh. Okay, then." She closed her eyes and kept one hand on the wall, making it down without issue. It was when she started her way up, backward, that she tripped and nearly fell.

I caught her. "Careful, Phoebs, we don't want to have to go to the ER on our vacation."

She dusted off her jeans. "Well, I guess that wish isn't coming true. Your turn."

My limbs slightly numbed, and I closed my eyes. Like Phoebe, I descended without any problems. As I worked my way back up in reverse, I counted the steps—slow and steady. Once I reached the top, trip-free, that same wave crashed over me. I had to grip the wall for balance as this time, it almost brought me to my knees.

"Are you okay?" Phoebe grabbed my arm.

The feeling left as quickly as it came. "I'm fine. Maybe we should leave. I feel a bit lightheaded."

"Wow. Must have been some wish." She curled her arm through mine, and we made our way out of the castle.

I studied myself in the mirror, gazing into hazel eyes I'd inherited but didn't know from whom. After applying some lip gloss, I gave one final tussle to my hair before I stood and smoothed my white ribbed tank top, leaving the three buttons over my cleavage undone. I beamed at Phoebe, whose red locks bounced around in tight curls. She spun a few times, making her flowy green dress swirl in cascades around her.

"Combat boots? Really, Abs?" Phoebe raised a brow.

"We're only going to some pub."

"Patrick said it's amazing. What if you meet someone? Maybe a leprechaun since you seem to have a thing for short guys." She elbowed me.

"I'm going to pretend you didn't say that. Besides, Owen wasn't *that* short."

She stuck her lips out like a duck before turning for the door. I followed her, locking it behind us and giving the handle a jiggle for reassurance. We entered the pub below our room where Patrick stood outside, leaning against his Fiat.

I ignored the steady gazes we received from the scattered pub-goers. Phoebe's focus remained on Patrick, oblivious to all else.

He stood straight, his eyes widening at us.

"I'll be, aren't you two a couple'ah stunners." Removing a toothpick from his mouth, he gave a dimpled grin.

He wore faded washed jeans, a white polo with the collar popped, and bright white sneakers—Phoebe's dream guy if I ever I saw one. Phoebe sauntered to him, slipping a bit of her hair behind her ear.

"And you're dashing." Phoebe swayed her hips.

"Dashin'? Can't say I've ever been called that before." He blushed as he opened the car doors.

We arrived at the pub, a massive white building with crisscrossed wooden planks making X designs down either side. It looked like an ancient cottage, with the words "Hole in The Wall," displayed out front in scrolling calligraphy. Phoebe pounced in her seat. She tackled Patrick as soon as he opened the door. And I took it upon myself to let *myself* out.

Once inside, it was like being transported back in time.

Though it looked large from the outside, the interior felt cozy. Small, worn wooden tables were everywhere, heaps of collected candle wax spread over them. Electricity lit only the bar area, and even there, the lighting dimmed. My favorite part was the large dance floor, complete with a full band in the corner. Dozens of couples danced Irish jigs to the lively music, while others sat at tables nursing mugs of beer or tumblers of whiskey. Aside from the castles and rolling green meadows—Ireland in its truest form.

I felt a bit of a third wheel as the three of us walked up to the bar, Phoebe's arm clutching Patrick's as she continued to jump around. He ordered us pints of a beer I hadn't heard of but was too distracted taking in my surroundings to care. Phoebe clutched my bicep, a pint of beer landing in my hands a moment later, and the three of us held our glasses up.

"To Ireland," Phoebe cheered.

I faced away from the entrance while Phoebe's back pressed against the bar top. Her pint glass slowly lowered from her mouth, a mustache of foam settled on her upper lip. Her eyes froze, and her mouth fell open.

"Phoebe?" I waved my hand in front of her face.

"Who...is...that?" She asked, her gaze focused behind me.

"Never seen 'im before." Patrick shrugged.

Phoebe leaned over to whisper in my ear, "I'm pretty sure my panties just became one with my body."

It didn't take long to spot the reason for Phoebe's staring. Short, messy, dark blonde locks, blue eyes, perfectly squared jaw with a light beard, high cheekbones, and tall. *Really* tall. As he made his way through the sea of tables, every woman's gaze followed him, but his eyes were fixed on me. He masked the expression on his face, giving only a hint of curiosity from the way his brow bounced and the skin between his eyes creased.

His tight white T-shirt seemed a second skin over the muscular curves of his arms—arms with full Celtic sleeve tattoos going down to his wrists. Over the T-shirt was a plain black leather vest. He wore a pair of torn jeans that clung to all the right places with a chain hanging from his hips, drawing my attention to his…boots, likely once black but were now dark grey from scuff marks and excessive use.

He sauntered to the bar like he owned the place. Maybe he did? Phoebe nonchalantly wiped the back of her hand across her mouth, ridding it of foam. She leaned in to whisper again, "He's a hottie, Abs. You should talk to him."

"He's…okay," I responded, flicking my wrist in the air.

Phoebe stared at me. "How do you sleep at night being such a liar to yourself?" She didn't bother whispering that time.

The mystery man flagged the bartender, and a tumbler of whiskey appeared next to my pint. Mystery Man seized my gaze with the bluest pair of eyes I'd ever seen. He reached for the tumbler, letting his forearm graze my knuckle. I ignored the twinge that sprung in my belly and moved my hand to my hip.

He squinted at me over the rim of his glass, bringing it to his lips. Our gazes locked, and I couldn't look away.

Glaonna Cinniúint.

The words fluttered through my skull like a fairy wisp.

"Do you need some ice water, Abs?" Phoebe asked, snapping me from my trance.

My heart raced, and I looked at her. "What?"

"You look a little flushed." She gave a toothy grin.

I masked the heat pooling in my cheeks by covering my face with my pint.

"What's your name?" Mystery Man asked with a thick Irish accent—a variant that sounded aged somehow. His body inched closer, heat radiating from his arm like a furnace.

"Beth," I lied.

"Uh-huh." The deep baritone of his voice dropped an octave, his eyes panning to the floor.

I tapped my nail against the glass. "You come here often?"

"Isn't that supposed to be my line?" A snarky grin tugged at his lips.

I took a quick sip of my stout. My eyes wouldn't budge from his, despite my best efforts. "That's the best line you could come up with?"

"Call it a hunch, but you don't seem the type to fall for corny pick-up lines." His gaze lowered to my cleavage, traveling up my collar bone, my neck, and back to my face. Slow. Deliberate.

"I'm not going to say a guy got me into bed with one, but I can appreciate well-thought-out corn."

"Mm. What does get you into bed then?" He slid an inch closer, leaning on the bar.

My gaze dropped to his ass for a fraction of a second. "Not you."

He loosed a slow, rumbling chuckle and took a swig of his whiskey.

Red flags sprouted from him with each passing moment, but my stomach tried to wave the white flag of surrender with each flip it made.

His breath wafted down my arm as he moved closer. "Do you…have some Irish in you?" He canted his head to the side, scanning my eyes, my features.

"I have no idea."

He leaned in, hovering his lips near my ear, and whispered, "Would ye like to?"

I held my breath to keep it from escaping my throat haggardly.

He sat back with a knowing grin. "See? No foolin' you."

"Nope." A nervous laugh escaped my belly. "Cold as ice over here." I chugged half of my pint.

He reached for a napkin, the sleeve of his T-shirt pulling up to reveal more of the tattoo and muscle. I traced the swirls of intricate Celtic knots with my eyes, quickly looking away once he sat back down. He scribbled something on the napkin and slid it toward me.

One word: *Erimon.*

A chill flashed down my spine. "What's this?"

"A name you won't forget," he said while walking backward, his arms out at his sides.

Arrogant, much?

A part of me wanted to throw the napkin in a crumple at his boots, but another part of me, one I couldn't ignore, compelled me to slip it in my pocket.

Mischief spread over Erimon's lips as he kept eye contact with me. A woman with platinum blonde hair and breasts bigger than my head stood from a table of young, giggly girls, her hips immediately pressing into Erimon's side.

Erimon shifted his attention briefly to the woman, smiling

before he looked back at me. I turned away from the entire ordeal, draining more of the beer from my glass, landing my attention on Patrick and Phoebe's conversation, Phoebe perched on Patrick's lap.

That escalated quickly.

"Opening doors, using words like 'courting,' you're so old-fashioned," Phoebe slipped a finger into his belt loop.

Patrick glanced at her hand, blushing. "You have no idea. I'll be back. I've got to go drain the snake." He cleared his throat before delicately moving her from his lap.

"So, how'd it go?" Phoebe asked in a loud whisper.

"How'd what go?"

She jutted her head at Erimon. He had one woman draped across his lap while another stood behind him, massaging his shoulders. My neck grew hot and clammy.

"No, Phoebe. That man has bad news written all over him. That's the kind of guy you make a mistake with when you're nineteen, not thirty." I took a long swig of my beer.

"Who says you have to marry the guy? He's clearly interested in you." She bumped our hips.

"We came here to spend time together. Not hunt for guys." I pinched my eyes shut.

"So, you want me to ignore Patrick?"

Resting a hand on my best friend's arm, I lowered my voice. "No. Of course, not. I'm sorry. I—"

Risking a glance at Erimon, he'd already been looking at me, piercing me with his gaze as a woman continued to massage his shoulders. The woman tried to kiss him, but he turned his head away and flicked his wrist for her to walk away. His eyes never left mine.

Snapping away, I called the bartender. "Three shots of Jameson, please."

Alcohol wouldn't cause Erimon to disappear, but it'd most certainly make his steely gazes easier to ignore.

5

I SIPPED ON MY FOURTH pint of beer for the night, still attempting to avoid Erimon's continued glances in my direction.

Any time I risked a peek at him, he'd be looking at me with the same curious expression despite woman after woman hanging over him, running their fingers through his hair, and begging for his attention. As soon as one would try anything further, he'd send them away.

I bit the inside of my cheek and swiveled on my stool. A light breeze fluttered over my thigh, the intensity enough to feel it through my jeans. Furrowing my brow, I rested my hand on my knee, and crossed my legs. A moment later, another breath flitted over my nape, giving me goosebumps.

"Is there a vent or something somewhere?" I asked anyone who would answer, looking above and below me, frowning when I saw no vents.

"No," Patrick said, eyeing me quizzically.

No fans. No open windows. Was I losing my mind? Was I

that tipsy?

My gaze landed on Erimon. His lips took a devilish curl.

"So, what is the deal with the Wishing Steps, anywho?" Phoebe asked Patrick through slurred words. She sat in Patrick's lap, and he kept a hand around her waist but made no attempts to explore further. I'm sure she would've let him.

"Ah, you two went to the Wishin' Steps, did you?" Patrick looked at me.

"Yup. Abby made it down and up flawlessly. She still won't tell me what she wished for." Phoebe pouted, giving me her puppy dog eyes.

I kept my hands plastered on my thighs to avoid any other rogue wind gusts.

"She can't. Or else it won't come true." Patrick bounced his knee, jostling a giggling Phoebe.

"What makes stone steps so special?" Phoebe asked.

"Well, for starters, with the Wishin' Steps being in Rock Close makes it mythical. You see, the entirety of Rock Close is built atop ancient Druidic grounds."

A tingle sizzled down my legs.

"Druids? Old men with long beards and bathrobes?" Phoebe rested her head on his shoulder.

"They're a bit more than that, but yeah. So, the whole story of Blarney Castle revolves around a witch. She was drownin', and the MacCarthys saved her. To show her utmost gratitude, she told them of the stone's power and how to use it."

I listened to Patrick's story, hoping something he said would explain the bizarre events I encountered. "That explains the stone, but what about the steps?"

"I was gettin' to that part," he continued. "So, the witch lived around the castle. Every few nights or so, she would steal firewood from the estate, usin' those steps. They let her get away with it, under the condition that anyone who successfully made the journey blind on those steps, she'd have to grant their wish within one year."

Phoebe straightened. "You tell stories like a medieval bard."

"That might be the nicest thing anyone ever said to me." He gave me a toothy grin.

"That story is ridiculous," I said, more annoyed the story hadn't helped me at all.

"*You're* ridiculous," Phoebe snorted.

"It might be silly, but I don't make them up. Tis legend." He shrugged and drained the rest of his beer.

The band in the corner started to play a new song, making nearly every person leap from their seats. They all moved to the dance floor, drinks still in hand. Patrick slammed his pint glass down and scooted Phoebe off his lap.

"O'right ladies, you be in Ireland. It's customary to dance to this song." He grabbed both our hands. I barely had time to set my glass down before being involuntarily dragged to the dance floor.

"What makes this song so special?" I pinned my hands at my sides.

"It's the *Belle of Belfast City*," he guffawed.

"Oh, I love this song." Phoebe beamed, and we took our places in a large circle, facing all other participants.

"Follow everyone's leads, and you'll be fine," Patrick said.

We started to move in a circle before everyone broke off in

pairs. Patrick ended up with Phoebe first, while I ended up in the hands of an older fellow. He smiled with yellow-stained teeth and placed one hand on my hip while the other grabbed my hand. He twirled me in a circle, a jig I could only compare to a polka. He nodded once before passing me onto the next man, this one younger with a bright red, bushy beard.

He moved quite a bit faster, and I laughed as I fought to keep up with him. His hand roamed further down my hips, and I cocked an eyebrow. He offered an innocent smirk, spun me, and passed me to the next person. I turned to greet Phoebe, and we both giggled. We hadn't a clue what we were doing, so we laced our fingers and danced a circle, imitating the most cliché Irish jig one could imagine. As we watched the rest of the couples depart, we let go and turned to face the next partner. I collided straight into the broad chest of…Erimon.

My eyes panned up until our gazes met, and a snarky grin slid over his lips. He took my right hand into his left, pressing the other against the small of my back and pulling my hips flush to him.

"You don't give up, do you?"

The blue of his eyes danced with the devilry of a riptide—a roaring force pulling the loose buoy in with no surrender.

"I do love a challenge." He twirled me. His moves were effortless and smooth. Using his hand on my back to push my hip, he spun me. Once both our arms fully extended, he yanked me back to his chest. "And something tells me you liked to be chased."

My chest pumped up and down as I peered up at him. "I'm the vulnerable doe in your crosshair?"

"Nah." He pressed our cheeks together. "You're the prized lioness."

I closed my eyes, breathing him in. He smelled like he'd been in the woods all day. Soil. Sun. Salt.

I snapped my eyes open when he peeled back, peering down at me with a hooded gaze before brushing his lips against my ear. "Do you remember my name?"

I fought every firework going off in my brain, my chest, my stomach. "Let me think. Eric? Erin? Irritatin'?"

It was time to pass me to the next partner, but Erimon gripped tighter, twirling me for another round. "I get the sense you don't like me much." His upper lip curled.

"Whatever gave you that impression?"

He drummed his fingers on my back. "I promise I'm not as bad as people make me out to be." His breath skirted over my cheek as he whispered in my ear, "Once you get to know me."

My shoulders tensed. "You're everything I shouldn't want."

"Such assumptions against someone you just met." He made a *tsk tsk* sound. "And what *should* you want, I imagine?"

The question left me mute.

I spotted Patrick and Phoebe laughing as they waltzed the dance floor. "I don't know. Someone like him."

Erimon snapped his chin toward Patrick and smirked. "A wuss?"

"What do you *want*?" I'd almost made the mistake of saying his name.

He gave a broad smile, making the skin at the corner of his eyes crinkle. "I'll be seein' you again, Abby." His arm fell from my back, and he turned, disappearing into the crowd of dancing people. It happened so quickly it was as if he vanished into thin air.

I stood there dumbfounded amidst the dozens of spinning bodies. How did he know my name? Phoebe. It had to be. There was no other explanation. I glared and pushed through the bouncing forms of people, making my way to the window. He mounted a black and silver motorcycle, slamming his foot down to bring the iron beast to life. He rode a *motorcycle*. Of course, he did.

My brain and groin had a momentary battle, my brain winning...for now.

"Oh man, he rides a motorcycle too?" Phoebe asked, making me jump.

She stared out the window, lifting a newly filled pint to her lips.

"Did you tell him my name, Phoebe?" I folded my arms.

"What? No. Why would I do that?" She burped.

I narrowed my eyes.

"Abs, I swear, I didn't. Why? Did he guess your name? Maybe you *did* find a leprechaun, you know, a really, really tall one." She attempted to drink more of her beer, stumbling forward.

I grimaced, some of the cool beer splashing over my chest.

"Alright, you. I think you're done for the night." I took one of her arms and draped it over my shoulders, prying the beer away from her Kung Fu-like death grip.

"Told you. You're a party pooper," she whined as I led her to Patrick.

"Uh-huh, how's that tolerance treating you?"

The way her cheeks puffed and her eyes glazed told me she was thirty seconds away from vomiting her guts out. I eyed Patrick chatting it up with a few men at the bar.

Resting Phoebe on a stool, I turned my back for the one moment it took to get Patrick's attention. I tapped his shoulder, and he turned around in time to watch Phoebe slide off the stool, hit the ground, and puke.

"Holy shite." Patrick dove to the floor. The white knight on an epic quest to save the damsel in distress.

I left her alone for a second—*one* second. Dropping to my knees, I performed my best friend's obligatory act, pulling her hair away from her face. Too late. I winced, trying to ignore the goo lacing my finger, and fought the compulsion not to vomit also.

She looked up at me with her big green eyes. "Is it bad, Abs?"

The smell hit my nostrils like a tidal wave, and I forced myself to breathe from of my mouth. "No, Phoebe, not bad at all, but I'm going to need you to stand up so we can get out of here."

Phoebe pushed to her feet with Patrick's help.

"You must think I look so hideous right now." She sobbed, looking at Patrick.

"Are you kiddin'? It wouldn't be a true Irish vacation if you didn't puke at least once."

My heart fluttered. He *was* rather sweet—a stark contrast to the psycho serial killer I initially labeled him. Together, we carried Phoebe out of the pub. She spread herself across the backseat of his car and passed out as soon as her head hit the seat cushion.

"Guess I'm taking shotgun this time," I said, moving to the right side.

Patrick tossed the fob in his hand, peering at me over the roof of the car. "You drivin'?"

Through the window, I eyed the steering wheel. "Sorry, I don't think I'd ever get used to the concept of driving on the opposite side of the road." I moved to the other door, slipping into the passenger seat.

Patrick and I remained silent for several awkward minutes as I watched the dark-lit sky outside pass by. The moon cast grey shadows through the dispersed clouds, creating hints of blue.

"He said his name was Erimon." My gaze stayed locked on the stars.

"Who?"

"That guy at the bar. What kind of name is Erimon?"

"You sure he didn't say Erin or somethin'?"

"I'm positive it's Erimon. He wrote it down." My fingers trailed my pocket, feeling the outline of folded paper.

"Strange. His folks must be old-fashioned."

"What do you mean?" I finally looked at him.

"That name is ancient. Not so common to hear nowadays. You get names more like Jack, Danny, Michael, Joseph."

"Patrick?" I grinned.

"Exactly."

Silence fell over us again. Erimon's gaze haunted my thoughts. The way he looked at me felt like he'd known me but had forgotten my existence. We'd never met before. A face like his was admittedly hard to forget.

"Tis a neem you woont ferget," I blurted in the most cliché, horrible version of an Irish accent I could muster, mocking Erimon. "So sure of himself."

Patrick's lip twitched. "But you didn't forget, did you?"

Heat coiled in my chest. "You know nothing, Irishman."

He tapped his finger on the steering wheel with a shrug. We were silent for the rest of the ride. If I said that Erimon hadn't come up in my thoughts again, I'd be a big, fat liar.

6

I WOKE UP THE NEXT morning with Sleeping Beauty at my side.

Phoebe's mouth laid open with a puddle of drool caked on her pillowcase. She looked like an angel if ever I saw one. I slid from the bed, praying it wouldn't creak. Not that it mattered. Phoebe was so out of it, I could've jumped on her, and she would've kept right on snoring.

After I showered and dressed, I shook her. "I'm going downstairs for breakfast. Do you want anything?"

Phoebe groaned and rolled over, turning her back to me.

"Bacon? Sure thing."

She groaned louder, and I snickered to myself. Downstairs, a man with white hair, a green shirt, and suspenders played soft tunes with his fiddle, filling the otherwise quiet space. The rays of the early morning sun flooded the room, causing random streaks of light. All eyes turned on me as I descended the stairs, and I wrapped my arms around myself, wondering if I should wave or salute or something.

I smoothed my hair and found an empty table. Sitting down, I looked around at other customer's plates of food.

What did one order for breakfast in Ireland?

No sooner had my eyes returned to the table, Iris, the woman from the front desk, placed a plate in front of me. I blinked as she pointed to each food.

"Bacon, black puddin', white puddin', potato bread, eggs, and o'course...tea." She placed a mug of the steaming beverage on the table, her face beaming.

"Thank you very much." I politely waited for her to leave before tearing into the plate as if I'd been stuck on an island.

While in the middle of a rather large bite of bacon, a woman sat across from me. She clutched a mug of tea to her chest, eyeing my hamster cheeks filled with food.

"Um, hello?" I said, which sounded more like "Urm, hahro."

She sipped from her mug, saying nothing. Peppered colored hair, a bit unruly, pulled into a bun at the nape of her neck. Her large brown eyes didn't blink, and her pointy nose wiggled as the steam coated it.

I gulped down my food. This wasn't awkward at all. "Can I...help you?"

The woman extended her thin hand littered with liver spots. "I wanted to introduce myself."

I hesitated but obliged. Her hand gripped me tightly, holding it longer than an average handshake. She eyed me as if she were dissecting me with her gaze.

"My name is Aibell. What be yours?" Her paper-thin lips slid into a grin.

"Abby."

She let go. "Abby," she repeated. "Enjoyin' Ireland so far?" She took another sip of her tea, not moving her gaze.

"What's not to enjoy?" I busied my mouth with more food.

"I run one of the local tour groups around town. You and your friends should stop by. Past reviews state it's one of the more unique tours this side of Ireland. I take you to all the most mystical spots." Her lips took a sinister curl.

"I'll uh, see what they think of the idea." I had zero plans to take her offer. Was this her typical marketing scheme?

"Grand." She slid a business card across the table.

Without picking it up, I read "Mystical Ireland Tours. Voted 'Best This Side of Ireland.'" Well, at least she was consistent.

"Enjoy your breakfast, Abby." She rose, still clutching the mug to her chest.

I eyed her warily as she walked away, her steps so fluid it looked as if she floated. That had to have been one of the strangest encounters I've had since arriving in the Emerald Isle. I watched her until she left, stuffing my cheeks with the rest of my eggs. I nearly choked on said eggs when I saw Patrick rush in and head straight for the stairs leading to our room.

I shot up and dashed to stop him. "You aren't near as smart as you look if you think she's up yet."

Patrick looked to the stairs and back to me. "You think I look smart?" He ran a hand over his short locks.

"You want some breakfast, Dimples?"

Patrick's eyes brightened. "I'm Henry Marvin," he exclaimed, walking past me towards the table.

I squinted. "You're *what*?"

"Means I'm hungry. Very, in fact." He sat in *my* seat and started eating *my* leftovers. I wasn't sure if I'd been done yet, but his comment so threw me off, I barely noticed.

"Why didn't you say that?" I sat in the seat across from him.

"You know you be in Ireland, right? We live for our sayin's." He stuffed the remainder of *my* bacon into his mouth.

"Hey, have you ever heard of this woman?" I tapped the business card resting on the table.

Patrick picked it up with his ring finger and pinky, the only two fingers not covered with bacon grease, and canted his head. "Yeah, seen her around. Always thought she was a bit mental if you ask me."

"Yeah, I got that vibe too." I swiped the card, turning it left to right, letting the light play over it. "I guess that means no to the tour." I ripped the card in half and let it plop onto my now empty plate in front of Patrick.

"No one's takin' my job, anyhow. I have quite the tour planned for you ladies today. That is if Sleepin' Red graces us with her presence."

As if speaking of the devil herself, Phoebe trudged down the stairs. Her red hair remained an absolute mess, and her face was paler than usual.

"Phoebe? How are you feeling?" It was a rhetorical question, really.

"I feel like a steamroller ran over me, backed up, and then ran over me again, but slower," she said with a groan, flopping down into a chair. She was so out of it she didn't see Patrick.

"I got just the thing for you." Patrick rubbed his hands together.

Phoebe's eyes bulged at me. She smoothed her unruly hair in a panic as Patrick snickered and walked off. "How bad do I look, Abby?" She looked at me with those adorable bloodshot eyes.

I flashed what I hoped was a convincing enough smile. "On a scale of one to ten?"

She whimpered and dragged her hands down her face. Somehow, her make-up did not morph into that of a clown's overnight.

Patrick returned with two glasses. One had a dark brown liquid, with foam at the top. Was that a Guinness? The other had two eggs. Raw eggs.

"Is this your attempt to make her vomit again?" I asked.

Phoebe's cheeks puffed.

"Nah, it's an Irish cure. Hair a Dog followed by two raw eggs. Works every time."

Phoebe clamped her hand over her mouth like she was about to throw up.

"I'm serious. The iron in the Guinness helps wonders." He held the glasses out to Phoebe.

She looked like a frightened doe.

I shrugged. "What have you got to lose?"

Phoebe took a deep breath and took one glass in each hand. She winced before tilting her head back to guzzle the Guinness down first. Once she finished, she picked up the glass of eggs and started to gag. After taking a deep breath, in they went.

"I can't believe that worked. I feel as good as new." Phoebe spun circles like Maria in *The Sound of Music* as we walked down the streets of Dublin.

Patrick looked rather proud of himself. Yet again, he had saved his darling damsel.

"Now ladies, what we're approachin' here is King's Hill Garden. Albeit beautiful in her own right, there's something specific I wish to show you." We passed a greyed-out brick building with several pillars lining the front and a teal dome on top. And we walked right past it.

Hm. Okay?

A beautiful sculpture of three women caught my eye. "Oh, is this it? This is amazing."

"That's nice too, but nah, right this way." He motioned with his hand.

Perplexed, I took a moment to appreciate the statue before he led us to a tree with a bench in its trunk.

"A bench. Stuck inside a tree." I raised a brow.

"The locals call it, 'The Hungry Tree.'"

"Oh, I see it. The tree *does* look like it's eating the bench. See Abs?"

"Yes, it does." To say I was unimpressed was putting it mildly. But Patrick could do no wrong in Phoebe's eyes.

"This tree is famous. It's been in a bunch of flicks." Patrick sat on the bench and leaned forward to avoid the tree's trunk protruding through most of the seated area.

Phoebe giggled, sitting on the bench in the same pose.

"Onwards." Patrick bellowed and leaped from the bench.

We walked for several minutes before we approached

another building with the word "Library."

"Here we have Monkeys Playin' Billiard." He pointed to the columns.

Phoebe squinted and then laughed.

It took some staring, but sure enough, small monkeys were indeed playing pool.

Okay. This was kind of cute.

"How does this make any sense outside of a library, though?" I asked.

"Funny you should ask," Patrick started.

"Storytime." Phoebe clapped.

"You see, this buildin' used to be owned by the Kildare Street Club, which was a club only attended by Dublin's finest and richest. They loved billiard. So, the O'Shea Brothers commissioned to design the buildin' added it in as a bit of a joke."

"I'm shocked they allowed it to stay." Phoebe chimed.

"They were probably so consumed with themselves they didn't notice." I crossed my arms.

Like an irritatingly handsome Irishman I met last night.

Patrick tapped his nose and pointed to me. "Right you are, Abby. Onto the Silicon Docks." He pointed in the opposite direction.

"Silicon Docks?" Phoebe caught up with him brushing against his side.

"I think I read about this. Some high-end technology district, right?"

"Right-o, but it's the treasury buildin' we seek."

"That sounds enthralling." Sarcasm. An ill-used artform.

"She's completely and utterly stark naked." I stared up at the marble statue of a nude woman climbing up the side of the treasury building.

"I'm jealous of her butt. Do you think someone modeled for it?" Phoebe cocked her head back and forth.

I pinched the bridge of my nose. "Alright, Patrick, I'll bite. What's the story behind this one?"

Patrick snapped his fingers. "Glad you asked. So, the statue is called Aspirations, and they built it to commemorate our country's struggle for freedom. She *be* Ireland."

"Why a woman, though? And why is she naked?" Phoebe asked.

"Well, funny enough, at first it was a man, but the commissioner of the buildin' said absolutely not. Reason bein' is that his office was right there by the lady's bosom, and he didn't want a naked man climbin' up his window. So, they made it a lady."

I slowly narrowed my eyes.

Patrick steepled his fingers with a pout. "I personally would've been fine seein' a man's willy out my window."

Silence.

Patrick interlaced his fingers behind his back. "That be the end of the tour. Fancy a pint?" He added, heading for a nearby pub.

I let Patrick take the lead, following a few steps behind him as Phoebe's arm interlaced with mine.

"Wouldn't it be nice to have a big, burly, tattooed arm to wrap your delicate limb around right about now?"

"I honestly can't believe you. You couldn't make it twenty-four hours?"

"Why, whoever did you think I was talking about?" She used her innocent Disney Princess tone, placing a hand atop her chest.

"I'm going to stab you. I'll use a toothpick from the bar if I have to."

"No, you wouldn't. I'm too much fun." She rested her chin on my shoulder as she batted her eyelashes.

"I'm beginning to question that."

"What do you think he's doing right now? Oh, I bet he's at the gym doing a bunch of…oh what are those things called?" She dipped herself backward, making fists at her chest, and raised them up and down.

"Bench press?"

"Yes. I bet he's doing that."

"No, he's probably tracing his face on the wall using a projector or something." I scrunched my nose.

"That's oddly specific."

We walked into the pub. Dozens of televisions lined the wall, all playing the same boxing match.

"What gives?" I asked Patrick. "They're fighting with gloves. Shouldn't they be bare-knuckled, no rules, bloodied and broken and all that?"

"They don't televise those fights."

"Are you saying underground bare-knuckle boxing exists?" Phoebe's lips parted.

"O'course it does. You simply need to know where to find 'em."

I slipped my hands over my hips. "I don't believe you."

"Alright, fine then. Not exactly my scene, but tomorrow night, I'll take you. Hope you don't mind a bit of blood in your eye."

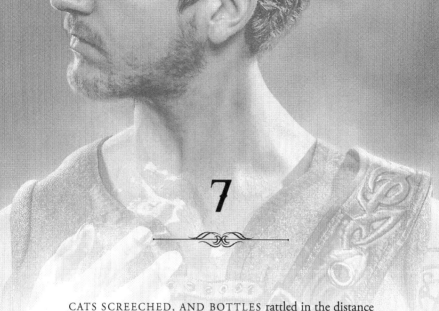

7

CATS SCREECHED, AND BOTTLES rattled in the distance as we walked the darkened alley. My heart thumped against my chest.

Phoebe clutched to my side, her nails digging into my arm, almost enough to draw blood.

"Phoebs, remember that time at the haunted house?" I gritted my teeth.

"Huh?" She turned her attention back to me, glancing down at her hands, and immediately released them with a nervous bout of laughter. "Sorry. This place gives me the creeps. Patrick, are you sure we're going the right way?"

"I told you gals this be an underground boxin' match, yeah? Where'd you think it'd be?" He stopped in front of a large, rusted metal door.

"I don't know, but I certainly didn't imagine it being in a place where I was afraid of stepping on a used needle." I squinted at the ground.

Phoebe looked at her partially exposed feet, her toes poking out from a pair of red heels.

"I told you. Should've worn sneakers."

She stuck out her tongue.

"That's so adult of you."

"Ladies," Patrick interrupted, raising a single finger to his lips in a hush.

Patrick knocked on the door, the sound of bone hitting metal bouncing off the alley walls. A small slit slid open at the top of the door, and a pair of dark eyes appeared.

Patrick cleared his throat. "May the cat eat you, and may the devil eat the cat."

The slit slammed shut, and the sounds of metallic locks turning followed. The door creaked open, and Patrick held his hand out, beckoning us to enter.

I tugged on my leather bomber jacket. The sounds hit my ears like a sonic boom. As if the metal door had been the only barrier between us and the chaos within. Men held pints of beer, shoving fistfuls of money into the air, whooping and hollering at a man standing in front of a giant chalkboard as another jotted numbers next to a list of names.

"They're makin' bets," Patrick said.

"This is something straight out of—" I started to say.

"Fight Club." Phoebe finished.

"It's like we're one person, Phoebs."

The man in front of the chalkboard swiped his arms in front of him like a referee. "No more bets, lads."

All men groaned in protest, turning their attention to the center—a simple rope held by poles served as markers for the makeshift ring.

"Shouldn't there be a cage or something?" Phoebe asked.

"Different type 'o fightin', Red." Patrick rubbed the light stubble on his chin.

A man wearing only boots, pants, and suspenders crawled into the ring. His eyes went wide and menacing before he ran a hand over the red spikes of his Mohawk and plucked the suspenders with his thumbs. An Irish punk song blared through the large speakers hung at each corner.

This was exhilarating.

"In this corner, Whanker," a man with a megaphone announced.

"Why's he calling him that?" I asked.

"It's his fightin' name." Patrick tapped his lips.

I quirked a brow. "Did you make a bet?"

"What? Me? Pssh." His cheeks turned pink.

Biting back a smile, I turned back to the ring.

"And in this corner, Cap'n Pain!"

"Oh, that's creative," Phoebe scoffed.

Cap'n Pain stood two feet shorter than Whanker, wore plaid trouser pants, and a stained tank that pulled tight over his portly belly. The Irish punk music faded to a classic Irish folk song as Cap'n Pain threw his hands up. All of the men surrounding us hoisted their fists in the air.

"*That* guy is the one pegged to win?" I pointed at the shorter, fatter man.

"You'd be surprised." Patrick slipped his hands in his pockets, jingling his keys.

"Remember the rules, lads. There be none," the announcer said before hurrying over the rope.

Whanker immediately threw a right hook. Cap'n Pain crouched, his height allowing him to dodge the move smoothly. Pain launched his fist into Whanker's gut, causing him to stagger backward. Pain slammed his foot down on Whanker's.

"This is insane, but a really good insane." Phoebe clapped her hands.

"It's something alright," I mumbled.

"You 'lil—." Whanker brought his elbow down on Pain's head.

My hands flew to my mouth in a gasp.

It hadn't seemed to faze Pain in the slightest as he threw an uppercut, planting into Whanker's chin. I never thought I'd see a man of Pain's stature launch a man twice his size halfway across a room. Whanker landed with a loud thud, blood spewing from his mouth.

"How do you know when it's over?" Phoebe asked.

Whanker lay there motionless, several seconds passing by.

"Oh, it's done," Patrick responded.

Cap'n Pain threw his fists up while a couple of other men dragged Whanker away.

I froze.

Why would any grown man do this to win a few bucks?

"And now the moment you all have been waitin' for. Here he is, The Wild Rover," the announcer yelled, elongating the "o" in "Rover." The Irish rap song *Top 'o The Mornin' To You* by House of Pain blared.

The Wild Rover slipped into the ring, clad in a long, black duster jacket. He removed the coat, keeping his head down. I eyed the full sleeve Celtic tattoos on his arms peeking from beneath a white tank top stretched over his muscular chest. *Wait a minute.* He removed the shirt, revealing the tattoo that continued across the entirety of his rippling back. My breath caught in my throat when the man lifted his chin.

"Abby," Phoebe said, staring at the face we all recognized.

"I know, Phoebe."

"Abby, that's Erimon." She tapped my shoulder.

"Yes, I know that, Phoebe." I swatted her finger away like an annoying gnat.

"Bleedin' stars. That man is a walkin' Irish cliché." Patrick shook his head.

Erimon surveyed the crowd, turning his gaze in my direction. I immediately crouched behind the first person I could find. Peering through the varying gaps amidst the sea of people, I stared at a shirtless Erimon. Abs. For. Days. It came as no surprise that he was chiseled to perfection over every nook and cranny. I bit my lip hard enough to draw blood as I panned to those hipbone grooves that always drove me crazy.

"What you lookin' at?" Phoebe's cheek pressed against mine.

I stood and pulled at the hem of my jacket.

"His opponent, see there." I pointed. A man in a kilt as tall as Erimon but not near as muscular entered the ring.

Muscular.

"His challenger, Scottie."

"Do they name themselves?" Phoebe asked.

"No. You never fight with a name you give yourself," Patrick said as if he knew all the ins-and-outs of underground fighting.

"Oh? Fought in these before, have you?" I asked.

"Hell no. I've far too pretty a face for that. My brother did it awhile." He winked at Phoebe.

Erimon raised his fists and circled Scottie, who threw a right hook, followed by a left jab. Erimon dodged both attacks.

The man knew how to fight.

My stomach flipped.

Scottie jabbed at Erimon's face. With each swing, I felt my nose scrunch into a grimace. Erimon leaned back, dodged to the right, and planted the palm of his hand into the man's nose. Scottie's head flew back, blood oozing down his cheeks.

A fire lit in Scottie's eyes, and he let out a monstrous growl. Erimon grinned and made "come at me gestures." Scottie threw a barrage of desperate punches, not landing a single one, and Erimon dodged with little effort. Scottie threw a sudden left hook, aimed for Erimon's cheek.

I involuntarily gasped.

Erimon's gaze shifted to me. Somehow, through all the noise, he zeroed in on *my* voice. Erimon snapped his attention back to the fight just as Scottie's fist clipped the corner of his brow, cutting it.

The room fell silent.

Erimon dragged his fingers over the wound on his forehead. Glancing at his hand, he rubbed his blood-stained fingers together. Scottie's eyes widened as he backed away. Erimon threw a right hook, smashing into Scottie's face and sending teeth flying. Blood and spit followed.

Phoebe shrieked. "Is that—please tell me that's not."

Blood speckled the top of her feet.

Phoebe shook her hands, whimpering. Patrick produced a random tissue from his inside jacket pocket. He crouched and wiped the blood from her feet, unflinching. When he stood, she gave him a quick peck on the lips.

"What was that for?" He rubbed the back of his neck with a sheepish grin.

"You're sweet."

"I'll take it."

"Alright, lovebirds, let's scoot before he spots us." I turned, forcing my way through the crowd, not bothering to check if Patrick and Phoebe were in tow.

"Before who spots you?" His voice boomed like the purr of a tiger.

Erimon folded his burly arms over his still *very* bare chest.

Eyes up. Eyes up, up, up.

I finally managed to focus on his face.

"I thought you'd be reveling in your victory by now."

"I don't revel." He licked his lips.

"Oh? Well, I think all this fighting is barbaric." I eyed the cut on his brow.

He wiped the blood away. "Is that so?"

There was no cut. Not even a little scratch.

"Yes?" I blinked several times in case my eyes played tricks on me.

He stepped closer. "Is that why you couldn't stop staring? Why the sight gave you goosebumps?" His gaze turned predatory.

"Are you always so sure of yourself?" My throat dried, but I let him get closer.

"I know what I am." His eyes scanned my body before snapping back to my face. "Do you?"

A tingle sizzled through my mind. I didn't answer.

"Face it, Abby. You liked what you saw."

"Are you admitting you put on a show for my sake?"

He rubbed the light beard on his chin. "I may have taken it up a notch."

"Did you—did you know I'd be here?" What compelled me to ask such a stupid question?

His bottom lip rolled past his teeth. "When I spotted ye, my reason to fight, to win, changed. Was I doing it to impress you, though? Doing it to prove something? Or maybe I just wanted to see the look on your face when you saw me half-naked for the first time."

As if on cue, my eyes fell to the swell of his pecs before snapping back to look at his wicked, filthy grin.

"The fact I can defend and protect entices you." His arm muscles tensed, the overlights creating the perfect contouring shadows.

I played with the seam of my jeans. "What makes you think I need protecting?"

Another step closer. So close I could smell dirt and pine on his skin. "You have a sense of danger about you. And it never hurts havin' someone to watch your back."

"I wouldn't even trust you with my front." My jaw tightened as my breasts felt heavier.

A raspy chuckle escaped his lungs.

"You better go to your friends. They're waitin' on you." He waved, grabbing their attention.

Phoebe and Patrick gave me thumbs up. Though, Phoebe's was far more enthusiastic. When I turned back to Erimon, he'd vanished.

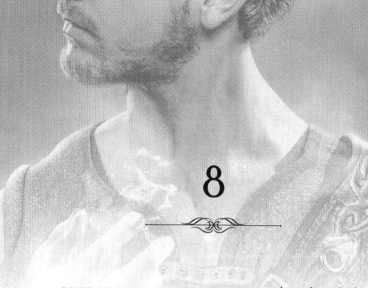

8

DUST LIFTED FROM THE ROADS, sneaking through the cracked windows. Soon, the small, rusted van sputtered away after dropping us off where I'd requested—the crossing streets of Bohereengloss and Palmer's Hill. I shaded my eyes with my hand and looked left to right.

"Remind me again why we didn't wait for Patrick to go on this little outing?" Phoebe tapped her foot.

"Because Patrick was busy today and we don't need him for absolutely everything. That's why," I snapped.

"And what are we looking for?"

Deciding between two paths, I opted to head further down Palmer's Hill. According to the directions I received from a kind fellow back at the inn, the castle I sought was "a hop, skip, and a jump" down this street—his words exactly.

"The Rock of Cashel." I guided Phoebe down the dirt road that seemingly led to nothing. It stood to reason that the castle would be in the middle of nowhere, right?

"Are you taking me to see another rock?"

"It's called that, but it's not actual rock. I'm taking you to a castle. No kissing this time, I promise. Unless you feel so inclined, that is." I gave her a sardonic grin over my shoulder.

We continued down the road, my faith in the man from the inn dwindling the further we walked.

"Are you sure we're going in the right direction? I'd think I'd be able to see a castle in the distance at this point," Phoebe said most sensibly.

I stopped, and Phoebe ran into me with a grumble.

"The guy said it was a little way down this road."

"Did he happen to mention in what direction?"

I narrowed my eyes, brushing past her, and walked the other way.

"See, if Patrick were with us—"

"Patrick, this. Patrick, that. The world does not revolve around the illustrious Patrick O'*Cool*ahan." My tone came out a tad more venomous than intended.

"Callahan," Phoebe replied coolly.

I turned to face her. "What?"

"Callahan. His name is Patrick Callahan. You know, you can't be all that jealous. I've tried on numerous occasions to get you to jump back in the saddle. We could always go back to that leprechaun museum we spotted back in Dublin, you know? Find yourself a lucky little charm?"

At least she had the decency to leave Erimon out of the conversation.

Silence fell between us. Various small shops and cottages lined the roads on each side. Eventually, off in the distance, the castle appeared on the horizon. "See, it's right there. We'll be gazing at its exquisite architecture in no time."

"Why didn't you have the van drop us off in front of the castle?"

I looked at the road, watching it continue toward the castle, and frowned.

"The man said there wasn't a drivable road leading to it."

"This 'man' seemed to be wrong." She walked past me backward. "You know what I want to say right now, right?"

I glared.

"Good. Then I don't have to say it." She did a one-shouldered shrug and grinned.

We walked for another hour before we reached the castle. Seeing your desired destination in the distance always seemed so much closer than it actually was. I took a deep breath, slightly winded, before taking in the gorgeous architecture perched upon a limestone rock formation. The Rock of Cashel wasn't only a castle—it also had Medieval buildings, including a tower, cathedral, and chapel.

"Well, I'll admit it. This is pretty impressive." Phoebe gazed up in awe.

"There are several centuries represented here. From the twelfth to fifteenth centuries." I made my way closer.

"Okay, Dr. Doolittle, since when did you gain an interest in buildings over animals?"

"Oh, that would never happen. I told you, I researched."

"You know what I want to research? How much money it would cost to get two full Celtic sleeves and a full back tattoo." She froze, pointing to her back, her expression similar to the kid with their hand in the cookie jar.

"You can't help it, can you?"

"Can you blame me after what we witnessed yesterday? It's all for you, Abs."

I shook my head, taking a step back, oblivious to my surroundings. My ankle rolled, catching the edge of a hole. I reached for Phoebe. She lurched forward, but not in time. Our fingertips grazed, and I fell backward, plummeting into darkness.

My rear end, followed by the back of my head, collided harshly with the dirt ground. My entire body groaned in protest, and I sat up, rubbing my skull. *What just happened?* The only light poured from the top of the hole.

Phoebe's head appeared at the surface with frantic eyes. "Abby! Oh my God, are you okay?"

I groaned again, feeling my limbs. Nothing broken. That was a good start. I crawled to my feet.

"Yes. Wait, no. No, I'm not." Bits of rock and dirt broke off in my hand as I felt around me. Panic seeped in. "Phoebe, I have no idea how to get out of here."

"Are you concussed?"

I blinked with the speed of a hummingbird. "I have no idea."

"I'm going to see if I can find a rope." She disappeared.

I pressed my back against one of the dirt walls. It was just my luck to fall into a random hole in the middle nowhere. It was too deep and wide to be a burial hole, thank goodness. Phoebe's absence felt like an hour as I waited helplessly for her return. I'd tried to climb up twice, but both times ended up right where I'd started. On my ass.

"Abby, I can't find anything," Phoebe said as her head reappeared.

My throat tightened, and I concentrated in front of me. I knew what Phoebe needed to do, but I didn't want to fathom it.

"Phoebe, you're going to have to go back to town. Find help. Find Patrick if you have to."

Phoebe stared down at me. "Are you sure, Abs? It's going to get dark soon."

"What could possibly happen to me in a hole, right?" I shrugged, trying to ignore the dreading thought of rain and drowning in a hole in Ireland.

Phoebe frowned. "I'll be back as soon as I can. I promise."

All I could give was a nod, fearing spoken words would come out shaky and weak. Once Phoebe's head disappeared, I slid down the dirt wall until I sat on the cold ground. I rubbed my hands over my face, trying to prepare myself for the long wait…alone…in a dark hole.

The wind picked up outside as dusk overtook the sky. Trees groaned, welcoming the crisp air.

"What a predicament you've gotten yourself into." A deep voice, smooth like velvet, spoke from the darkness.

I jumped to my feet with a gasp, pushing myself against the furthest wall.

"Who—who are you?" I tried to focus, see through the dark, and attempt to make out the face in the shadows.

"You tryin' to tell me you don't recognize my voice by now?" He whispered in my ear.

I slowly turned my head. Erimon.

I backed away, still clutching my chest. "How did you—"

Heat splashed over my face as an orange glow illuminated the hole. Erimon held a lit torch.

"How did you get down here?" I looked up to the surface. No rope. No ladder.

He leaned against one of the surrounding walls, folding his arms, wearing the same black duster jacket he wore at the boxing match.

"Magic," he replied.

I stared at him blankly. "Magic?"

"The same magic that played at your thighs the other night." He lazily pointed at my legs. "Your neck." He bit his lower lip.

My breaths quickened, and I pushed hard against the wall as if I could move it.

"Fine. Then if you have 'magic' like you say, why can't you get us out of here?"

He shrugged. "Who says I can't?" The flame from the torch cast a villainous shadow over his face.

I pushed off the wall with clenched fists. "Then do it."

The wind howled outside, sounding like a growl as it whipped through the branches.

"What are you?" I tried to keep my lip from trembling.

"Ah. Now you ask the right question. I, my dear Abby, am a Druid."

A gust sent an entire tree limb plummeting into the hole, landing between us.

His answer should've made me think he was crazy. So why did I find it hard not to believe him?

"What exactly is a Druid?"

His eyes sparkled. "Many have claimed themselves of the

Druid race. Priests, magicians, soothsayers. The true Druids, like myself, can be considered deities. We control nature, lore. We keep a balance and have done so for thousands of years."

I pressed my fingers against the wall behind me, the feel of the dirt against my skin calming me.

"I'll get you out of here, Abigail."

I seethed. "Don't call me that."

He made a *tsk tsk* sound with his teeth. "Never reveal a weakness so easily."

"It's not a weakness, I—"

"Then why are you so flustered?" The fire played in his eyes, orange flickers of mischief.

I dug my fingernails into the wall, splitting one against a rock.

"Why did you come to Ireland?" He canted his head.

I ground my teeth together to keep them from chattering. "You said you'd get me out of here."

"I did." He moved forward. The torch became the only shield between him and me. "But you've got a lot more to worry about than bein' stuck in a hole."

"What are you talking about?"

He pointed up. "You don't hear it? Don't sense it?"

The wind howled, and I masked my expression with a sneer.

"You've been marked by The Dullahan. And he's come to collect."

A chill settled in my bones like a snake slithering over my grave. "What's The Dullahan?" It took every ounce of strength not to stutter.

"Someone you don't stand a chance against alone." His eyes

penetrated me like shrapnel, carving through my body and claiming any point of impact.

I tried to gulp through the dryness settling in my mouth. "How would you know if I were 'marked'?"

He leaned in, taking a deep inhale at my nape. "I could smell it on you at the pub."

"And you're just telling me now? Stranded in a hole?"

His eyes, with the quiet confidence of a prowling jaguar, dropped to my lips. "I like to capitalize on my services."

My jaw chattered—both from the cold, his news, and how freaking close his nose was to my cheek.

He pushed a hand against the wall near my head, staring down at me with devious intent. "I will get you out of here and will help you fight it if you make a deal with me."

"You can't be serious," I said through a husky breath, feeling the warmth from his chest over mine.

His eyelids grew heavy. "Deadly."

The wind roared outside like a stirring hurricane.

"Tick tock, Abigail. What'll it be?" His gaze dropped to my lips.

He left me with no choice. The worst part was…he knew it. "What's the deal?"

He leaned in, nearing his lips to mine. "At a moment of my choosing, I get to kiss you."

I loosed a shuddered breath. "A kiss? That's all?"

A sly grin floated over his lips. "That's all."

He could've been lying about The Dullahan to get me to agree—to scare me. But what if he told the truth?

"Fine."

His smile turned into pure male satisfaction. "Fine indeed."

He splayed his hand at the ground. Bits of iron seeped from the dirt, flowing in a swirl into his palm. He wiggled his fingers and clenched his hand into a fist. When he opened his hand, a ring rested on his palm—two hands holding a heart with a crown. He dropped the torch, blanketing the hole with darkness. His callused hand snatched my right wrist.

"What are you—"

Cool iron slipped over my ring finger, and a jolt of electricity like an intense static shock pulsed down my arm.

His lips pressed to my ear, his beard tickling my chin. "So you don't forget."

He wrapped his arms around me in a bear hug. I blinked, and in a flash, we were out of the hole, outside, surrounded by forest.

Erimon dropped to one knee and grabbed my arm, dragging me down with him behind a fallen tree. He glared into the clearing as red smoke swirled.

A creature similar to the Headless Horseman from *The Legend of Sleepy Hollow*, but far more demonic, sat on a large black horse with glowing red eyes, its snout billowing smoke. The rider bore dark, spiky armor with a shield that resembled a large devil's face, a long tongue, and pointed teeth. It swung a whip—an elongated spiky human spine, the handle a human skull—around its headless form. A glowing yellow head hung from the horses' saddlebag like a lantern. I gasped, falling back on my heels.

The Dullahan.

9

"STAY HERE." ERIMON'S STARE WAS glued on The Dullahan.

Gusts flapped the tattered cape draping from The Dullahan's shoulders.

"Abby?"

The head hanging from the horse's saddle glowed brighter, and I stared wide-eyed.

"Abigail." Erimon raised his voice.

I snapped my attention to him. "Yes. Alright. I'll stay here."

He walked to the clearing with his hands in his pockets, crossing one booted foot over the other. The Dullahan bristled, and the horse snorted.

"Dullahan. Been a while."

The Dullahan laughed—a thousand lost souls wailed in unison. "You know why I have come, Druid." The demonic horse hoofed the ground.

"Mmhmm. Then you know why I need to stop you."

An eerie chuckle floated from the demon's throat. "Nothing

and no one will keep me from her."

Erimon splayed one hand out to his side, making the rocks on the ground vibrate. He reached his other hand to the opposite side, and splinters from a nearby tree peeled away. Iron ore seeped from the ground beneath Erimon's feet, the blade of a sword forming in his hand. The wood fragments from nearby trees swirled in his palm, creating a hilt, and a vine wound itself around one flat side of the sword.

A Druid appeared out of thin air, rescued me, and now stood toe-to-toe with a headless horseman wielding a human spine as a whip.

Maybe I really was concussed.

"Tell me." Erimon twirled the sword. "You run out of warriors to recruit? Had to settle for a zoologist?"

I never told him that.

"Her essence," The Dullahan growled.

Erimon's head snapped to attention.

My heart raced, soon catapulting to an all-out gallop.

This was *happening.*

Dullahan swung his whip, snapping it at Erimon, who dodged, raising his sword to block the spine from nipping him.

Dullahan growled and charged his horse, its snout releasing sparks as it picked up speed. He galloped past Erimon, making another attempt to strike him with his whip. Erimon slid under the horse and jumped up, swinging the sword around in his palm as he snarled into the wind.

Dullahan roared, and small holes formed in the ground. Smoke and orange light billowed from the openings as tiny creatures emerged. Some were black, some were green or brown, and they were no more than a foot tall. Their long noses and pointy ears twitched as they hunched forward. The creatures let out high-pitched squeals before running at Erimon. He threw his hand out, sending a gust of wind and making the creatures fly into the trees.

"Sendin' your goblins, eh? Losin' your touch in your old age?"

"You will die this day, Druid," Dullahan spat as he charged.

Erimon scooped a pile of dead leaves into his palm and held it at his side, making smoke swirl over them before igniting into flame. He hurled the fireball at The Dullahan, and the demon raised his shield, the fire eating straight through it.

Bits of bark broke off in my hand as I clutched the log.

Dullahan sneered at the damaged shield, tossing it to the ground. He hopped off the horse, removing a sword from the innards of his armor as a dozen goblins charged at Erimon. He stomped his boot on the ground, causing the earth to crack. The goblins shrieked, most of them falling into the newly formed splits in the dirt. Erimon scooped a pile of dirt into his palm, eyeing the approaching Dullahan. He dropped to one knee, tossing the soil across the rift like throwing dice. The crack sealed, trapping the goblins within.

Dullahan brought his sword down, and Erimon raised his blade, blocking the attack. Erimon matched every move The Dullahan swung at him, his long jacket swirling around him like paint in water. Every time the goblins returned, Erimon would whisk them away with a gust of wind or thwart them with surrounding rocks.

I felt a pinprick on my ankle. "Ouch!"

A goblin bit me with its sharp, pointy teeth, and I kicked it in the head. It held on to my feet with its grotesquely long fingers. The pain shot up my leg, and I beat the goblin against the ground, swinging my leg, but it still latched on.

The wind blew through my hair, guiding my gaze to a large rock. I scooted across the dirt on my butt, wincing, and grabbed the stone with two hands. Bringing it down in one swift motion, I slammed it over the creature. Green goo oozed from beneath the rock, and the creature's flattened limbs stuck out from every corner. Blood tendrils dripped down my ankle. With a grimace, I clapped my hand over the wound.

Peering back over the log, I saw The Dullahan's horse galloping at a full charge toward Erimon, who had his back turned, preoccupied with goblins.

"Erimon!"

Erimon turned toward me, gaining sight of the horse approaching. He splayed his fingers before raising his hand in a sweeping motion. Rocks from the nearby dirt shot into the air, and he balled his hand into a fist. All stones molded together, creating one large rock wall. The horse ran into it headfirst, staggering back. The horse snorted and shook its head. Erimon tossed his gaze to me long enough to point down, and I ducked behind the log.

Dullahan roared and caught Erimon by the ankles with his whip. Erimon fell onto his back with a grunt. He twirled his sword, stabbing the whip with a loud *crack*, splitting it in half. Erimon yanked away the half still wrapped around his ankles and leaped to his feet.

Dullahan growled, tossing the remains of his shattered whip

to the ground.

"Tough break. I'd offer my own spine as a replacement, but it's currently occupied." Erimon rolled his shoulders.

"Typical, Erimon. Jesting in battle." Dullahan tapped his bony fingers together, making them clack.

One-by-one the goblins faded away, some groaning in protest.

Where did they go when they weren't terrorizing?

"Mark my words, Druid. She *will* be mine." Dullahan pointed his sword.

"We'll see what fate has to say, Dully."

Dullahan snarled before galloping away on his horse, dematerializing himself into the air.

I remained behind the log, my chest heaving, trying to make sense of everything. Pain surged up my leg, reminding me how real it all was. Leaves rustled nearby, and I grabbed a rock, holding it above my head.

"It's me." Erimon held his palms up. He squatted, eyeing my flattened handiwork. He lifted the rock, grimaced, and let it drop with a gurgle. "Nice work."

"What the hell is going on, Erimon?" I put pressure on my ankle and winced.

Erimon furrowed his brow and coaxd my hand away, tsking once he saw the wound.

He waved his hand at the ground between us, making two small plants grow. "I told you, Abby. The Dullahan marked you. You're not the first mortal, and you won't be the last." He tore the plants from the ground and smashed them into his palm.

"That tells me nothing."

A light growl vibrated in the back of his throat. He pressed the plant mixture to my ankle and caught my gaze. "I think you've had more than enough of an introduction to our world for the day. Wouldn't you say?"

I hissed, the plants burning at first but soon soothing. "What if it comes back?"

Erimon kept his hand on my leg, his fingertips brushing my skin. "He will. And he won't stop until you're dead."

My stomach gurgled. "That's not making me feel better."

"I'm not tryin' to. I'm simply offerin' the truth."

"What am I supposed to do?"

He peeled the plants away and tossed the remnants aside. "Stay alive."

I slow-blinked.

He brought our faces closer as his hand massaged above my wound. "You made the deal. I'll do all I can to keep him away from ye." His gaze dropped to my mouth. "I'm a man of my word."

My lips parted, and I held my breath.

He patted my calf and stood, brushing off his jacket. He grabbed the sword he'd made, and it began to unravel itself. The iron used for the blade flowed back into the ground while the wood circled back to the tree, leaving the trunk unharmed.

I hobbled to my feet. "So, I'm to go about my vacation like none of this happened?"

He dragged a hand over his beard. "It happened. And it's happening. There's no sense in you gettin' mixed up in it all if I can keep it away from you. Don't be alone. Ever. You hear me, Abby?"

My chest tightening, I eyed the fierceness in his steely gaze. "Why are you doing this?"

His lip twitched, and he looked away. "Do you want my help or not, hm?"

Staring at the iron ring on my finger, I rubbed a thumb over it. "I'm not ready to die."

He gave a curt nod. "Remember. Never be alone." He swirled his hand into the air and disappeared in a gust of leaves.

A car door slammed behind me. Phoebe ran over, her red waves bouncing over her shoulders.

"Oh my God, Abby! Are you okay?" She hugged me.

I numbly wrapped an arm around her, staring at the vacant space where Erimon had been.

She pulled away, gripping my shoulders. "Abby? How the hell did you get out of there?"

I pursed my lips, contemplating my answer. If I didn't tell the truth, how *would* I explain it?

Patrick trotted up next to Phoebe, looking around. "I thought you said she was stuck in a hole?"

"She was." Both of them stared at me with raised eyebrows.

I felt the cold metal on my finger and curled it against my palm. "I got tired of waiting, so I managed some footholds and crawled out."

Phoebe's eyes panned over my dirt-ridden clothes.

Patrick pointed at my ankle. "And how the hell did you do that?"

"I cut it on some jagged rocks on the way out." I managed a weak smile.

It stung lying to Phoebe. We told each other everything. Sometimes, too much. But I still tried to wrap my brain around everything that happened, so how could I explain it to anyone else?

Phoebe opened her arms. "Come on, Abs. We'll get you cleaned up. I wish you would've waited, though, you impatient thing." She chuckled and led me to the car.

I sat in the backseat silent for the entire ride back to The Lucky Cove.

Sneaking a peek at the ring, I glared at it and tried to pull it off—stuck. Nausea boiled in my core. Bound to a Druid in exchange for my life—a life The Dullahan would stop at nothing to claim. It wasn't the vacation I had in mind.

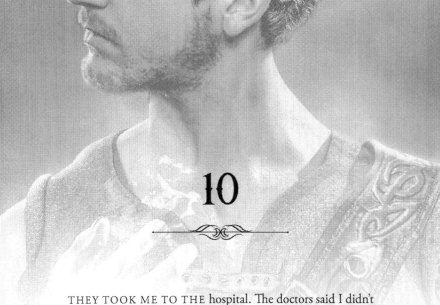

10

THEY TOOK ME TO THE hospital. The doctors said I didn't have a concussion and may have experienced a mild shock. Erimon and The Dullahan were a shock indeed.

Patrick took us on another tour the next day, a slightly less weird one over the previous. I can't say I'd listened to anything he said, considering I was far too distracted remembering everything I'd seen the day before. Aside from witnessing demonic beings, I kept replaying Erimon's words—his actions. Not to mention the ring I couldn't seem to pry off my finger. The kiss I owed him and had no idea when it'd happen.

"Abby." Phoebe snapped her fingers in my face.

"Hm, what?"

"I've called your name three times. You've been staring off into space. What are you thinking about?"

"Nothing. Just thinking about yesterday. The hole."

She wrapped her arm around my shoulders. "You took quite a fall."

"Yeah, it's impressive you only bruised your arse over hittin' your head," Patrick added.

I had bruised my tailbone, which made walking unpleasant, but I wasn't about to spend any part of my vacation cooped up in my "fancy" hotel room.

"Where we headed next, Patrick?" Phoebe asked.

I rubbed my arms, feeling chilly as we climbed over the hill.

"Ever heard of the Hellfire Club?"

An old, run-down structure made of stone blocks came into view.

"Wasn't it a hunting lodge?" I gripped my biceps, watching several birds squawk and fly away from a tree hanging over the building.

The Dullahan. I wasn't alone, but what would stop him from attacking at any moment? And how would Erimon know?

"Far more than that, my dear," Patrick said as we walked toward the building. "It started as such by a man named Conolly. After he died, a lad named Parsons, who practiced the dark arts, used it as the meetin' place for the club."

Phoebe frowned. "And we're going to this place, why?"

"It's said that it's haunted." He wriggled his fingers, making a ghostly 'ooo' sound.

"Do either of you feel a chill?" I asked, goosebumps littering my skin the closer we got inside.

"That's all in your head." Patrick waved me off.

I shivered, standing in front of the building. It smelled of sulfur, and the wind that blew through its open passages made an eerie sound echo.

"Why does this place look like it's been burned a time or two?" I didn't dare touch the walls.

"Supposedly, the club did it on purpose. Made the buildin' look more akin to its hellish counterpart."

Phoebe and I hesitated near the threshold, clutching each other's arms.

"Are you ladies chicken?" Patrick taunted as he clucked in a circle.

I urged Phoebe onward, my heart racing as another chill crept up my spine. Something tugged one of my earrings.

"Phoebe, stop it. That's not funny."

Phoebe scrunched her nose. "I'm not doing anything."

I rubbed my ear lobe. No spider, no loose hair. Another tug at my ear, but this time far harsher. Remembering the goblin gnawing on my ankle, I grabbed a jagged rock from the ground, holding it up like a dagger.

"Uh, Abby. You okay?" Phoebe cocked a brow.

"Wait, be quiet. Do you hear that?" Patrick froze.

We all stood still, listening. Several people murmured right outside the building. We ducked behind a half-destroyed stone slab as a group of people scuffled in, led by a familiar-looking woman.

"That's the crazy woman, Aibell, from the hotel," I whispered.

"Here we are in the infamous Hellfire Club," Aibell spoke. She led one of her mystical tours.

"Can you feel their presence? It's said that several of them haunt this buildin' to this very day," she said, all the tourists nodding emphatically.

Phoebe slipped her hand over mine, her finger brushing the ring. Her gaze dropped, and she narrowed her eyes at me. I snatched my hand away and slid it under my leg, not looking at her.

Aibell moved over to an open area. "About here is where they had their meetin' table. They always made sure to leave an empty chair for the Devil himself, should he have chosen to grace them with his presence."

Phoebe pinched Patrick on the arm. "Where did you bring us?"

"I thought you'd get a kick out of it bein' haunted," Patrick whispered back.

"It's also said that durin' a card game one evenin', one of the men dropped a card." Aibell reached for the ground. "When he went to retrieve it, he noticed one of the men had hooves instead of feet. It was then they realized the Devil sat amongst them."

All tourists reacted with "ooos" and "aahs" as if they were watching fireworks. I couldn't believe these people paid for this load of hogwash.

"It was that night that an unknowin' woman came upon their buildin' lookin' for shelter. Little did she know, Lucifer himself greeted her. The men wished to make a sacrifice, so they put the young woman in a barrel, lit it on fire, and sent it rollin' down the hill." As Aibell finished her story, her eyes turned, landing straight on me.

I ducked to the ground, a sharp pain vibrating in the back of my skull. Grabbing my head, wincing, I curled into the fetal position.

A hand touched my shoulder. My eyes flew open, and I batted it away.

Phoebe held her palms up. "They left, Abs. They didn't see us."

Patrick and Phoebe looked at me as if I were in a straight jacket.

"Are you okay, Abby? You're awfully jumpy today."

My throat tightened as I imagined myself in the barrel in place of the woman. "This place gives me the creeps."

"You and me both," Phoebe said with a snort.

"I need a drink." I poked Patrick in the chest. "And you're buying."

"Fair enough." Patrick stuck his bottom lip out.

Patrick drove us to Hole in the Wall, and a pit in my gut hoped Erimon would be there. I'd spent the entire day spooked by an off-putting sound and fearing for my life with every corner I turned. As questionable as Erimon's intentions were, I knew he was my only chance of surviving this mystical marking. Bile threatened to work its way up my throat, and I dug my nails into the upholstery of Patrick's Fiat.

"When did you get the Claddagh ring?" Phoebe asked with a fluttery voice.

My eyes snapped to meet hers. "The what?"

"The Claddagh ring?" She pointed at the circle of iron on my finger.

"I grabbed it from a gift shop. Thought it was pretty."

Phoebe's emerald eyes searched my face. "When did you have time to do that?"

"You were busy with Patrick." I dragged a hand through my hair, growing increasingly uncomfortable with lying to her.

"Do you know what it means?" She tapped her finger against the heart.

I simply shook my head, staring at it.

"It's a relationship ring."

My neck tensed.

"The hands represent friendship, the crown for loyalty, and the heart is fairly obvious." She offered a small smile. "With the heart facing toward you like it is, it means your heart is open."

I curled my hand into a fist, hiding the ring away. "Good thing I put the ring on the correct way then, huh?"

"True. We wouldn't want all eligible bachelors thinking you're already tied up." A wide grin tugged at her lips.

I glared at her as we rolled into the pub parking lot, where a familiar black and silver motorcycle rested in a nearby spot.

Erimon.

My heart did a curious flutter.

As we walked in, Patrick threw his arm over Phoebe's shoulder, leaving me to trail behind in their wake. The usual lively hustle and bustle of patrons drinking, singing, and dancing hit me like a slap to the face.

"I never got a chance to introduce myself," Phoebe said, tugging on Patrick's shirt sleeve as she flittered to the bar.

Erimon sat at one end, nursing a tumbler of whiskey.

Phoebe stuck her hand out, her usual cheery demeanor making her fiery red hair bounce. "I'm Phoebe. A friend of Abby's."

As I did, Patrick walked with the same sloth-like speed, clearly not as enthusiastic about making Erimon's acquaintance.

The ring on my finger tingled against my skin the closer I got to him. As Erimon shook Phoebe's hand, his eyes peered over his shoulder at me, like he could sense my presence. He one-eye squinted at Patrick.

Phoebe's grin hadn't left as she caught Patrick by the crook of the arm and dragged him to her side. "Erimon, this is Patrick."

Patrick looked anywhere else as the two shook hands so quickly, blink, and you would've missed it.

"Hi," I said, slipping one hand into my jeans pocket and rubbing the back of my neck with the other.

Erimon lifted his glass, casually leaning against the bar with one elbow. "Hi."

"On that note, Patrick, let's go dance." Phoebe grabbed Patrick by the shirt, jutting her head toward the dancefloor.

"Gladly," Patrick mumbled.

Erimon flagged the bartender, and a twin glass of whiskey appeared in front of me. Erimon motioned only with his eyes at the offered drink.

I wrapped both hands around it, tapping my fingernails to the rhythm of the fiddle playing in the corner. "I'm surprised you're here."

"Oh? Where else should I be?"

"I don't know, hunting The Dullahan maybe?" I took a long sip of the drink, licking the excess from the corner of my mouth.

He chuckled—deep and breathy. "Contrary to what you might think, you're *not* my only priority."

"And pub-crawling is?"

A wicked smile pulled at his lips, and he let the glass dangle from two fingers. "What exactly do you think I do all day, hm? Commune with the forest, dance around a bonfire, make special appearances at weddin's?"

My grip tightened around my glass, and I slid closer to keep my voice low. "Don't patronize me. Up until yesterday, I didn't even know any of this existed, that Druids existed."

He leaned on his elbow, bringing our faces closer. "But when you found out, it wasn't as hard to wrap your brain around it as you imagined. Was it?"

I searched his eyes. Those cerulean pools that undoubtedly countless women drowned in.

He lifted my hand, tightening his grip when I tried to pull it away. "Celtic looks good on you." He smiled, those lips dripping with a deviousness that both infuriated me and made my stomach clench.

"I can't take it off."

"Of course, you can't. What kind of a reminder would it be if you let it collect dust in a drawer somewhere?" He let go with a flick of his wrist.

I sulked onto my stool, hugging the glass to my chest. "I'm glad to see my death is a joke to you." My heart seemed to stop as I said the word aloud, and I let my eyes fall shut.

Erimon's hand slid over my shoulder, coaxing me to look at him. "If it were a joke, I wouldn't have offered to help. Don't take my assistance for granted, though. The Dullahan would never show up in public and isn't exactly a fan of witnesses." The corners of his jaw tightened. "I've been alive for over a thousand years, battling creatures, humans, all forms of magic, and chaos. You'll have to excuse me if now and again, I like to sit down in my favorite pub and have a whiskey or two."

I'd thought him an arrogant prick the first moment I met him, and now he blurred the lines between which one of us was more selfish.

We stared at each other for what seemed an eternity before Phoebe and Patrick returned. His hand fell away from my shoulder, and the tranquil beat of discovery disappeared with it.

"Abby, Abby, Abby. Patrick just told me the funniest joke." She tugged on Patrick's sleeve. "Tell them, Patty."

Erimon smacked his lips together, not bothering to face them as he continued to sip from his glass.

Patrick tugged on his collar. "'Young man,' said the judge, lookin' sternly at the defendant. 'It's alcohol and alcohol alone that's responsible for your present sorry state.'" Patrick clapped his hand over his chest. "'I'm glad to hear you say that,' replied Murphy, with a sigh of relief. "'Everyone else says it's all my fault!"

Phoebe burst into a fit of laughter, and I forced a mild chuckle. Erimon shook his head, still not turning in his stool. The band played a Dropkick Murphy's song, and Phoebe's face brightened as she dragged Patrick back to the dance floor.

I shifted closer, letting our sleeves brush. "How did you know I was a zoologist?"

His eyes focused on our arms touching before lifting his gaze. "I *am* a Druid."

"Does that mean you can read minds?"

"Something like that." He rested his empty glass on the bar and tapped a ringed finger against it, asking for another. "Why animals?"

"I've always had a connection with them." I clutched my glass, remembering back to that first pivotal moment.

"Do tell." He grabbed the seat of my stool and pulled me closer, resting his foot on the wrung of my chair with his knee pressing against mine.

I traced the rim of my glass, trying not to concentrate on the way my stomach bubbled at how close he was—how close his knee was between my legs.

"The first time I felt it was when I'd run away from a foster home—the fourth one. I'd gone to the only refuge that never disappointed me. The woods." I paused to sip some whiskey and caught Erimon's gaze falling to my lips as I drank before immediately darting back to my eyes when I set the tumbler down.

"Out of nowhere, this doe and her fawn emerged from a thicket. They weren't afraid of me, and all I wanted to do was run my fingers over their soft chestnut-colored fur."

He didn't speak nor interrupt. Simply watched me talk as if every word interested him more than the last.

I closed my eyes, remembering the day so vividly I could still smell the pine of the forest and feel the sun rays on my cheeks. "The doe let me touch her for a fraction of a second before they darted back into the woods. I couldn't blame her—protecting her young and all, but that singular moment told me I had a connection most didn't have."

"And this connection you think you possess, where does it come from, do you imagine?" His knee coaxd mine apart with natural grace and simply rested there.

"I honestly have no idea."

He ran a finger over the hair surrounding his mouth as a playful smile crept his lips.

"Hey, you two," Phoebe said, trotting up beside us. "We, uh, we're getting out of here." Her cheeks turned crimson.

Erimon and I shared a glance.

"Yes, just…the two of us," Patrick coughed into his fist.

"I'm sure Erimon would be willing to give you a ride back to the hotel. Right?" Phoebe asked, smiling.

"I think I can manage." Erimon leaned against the bar, propping his elbow on it.

"Great. See you tomorrow, Abby," Phoebe said as Patrick snaked his arm around her waist.

I could feel Erimon's sultry gaze.

"I'll get a taxi." I hopped off my stool.

"Already forgetting what I said?"

Don't ever be alone.

"They're going to be gone all night, I couldn't possibly—"

He slid from his stool, slipping several colorful bills onto the bar. "Then I guess we better find ways to busy ourselves, hm?"

My insides folded over themselves at the implication.

He headed for the door, ignoring the table of women fawning over him, begging for his attention as he passed. I hitch-stepped to catch up with him. Erimon's hand slammed into the swinging door, the cool night air splashing over my face. I rubbed at my bare arms. He whisked off his jacket and held it out to me. When I stood there motionless, he jiggled it. I moved closer and turned my back to him, and he slid the jacket onto my arms, his knuckles grazing my skin.

"What about you?"

"I'll be fine." He walked around to face me. I tried not to eye his now bared, muscular arms, a singular vein snaking down one of them. He secured the buttons, eyes focused on my face, and I felt a lump form in my throat.

He climbed on the bike, swinging a booted foot over one side. As the steel beast roared to life, I froze. He revved the engine, glancing at the empty seat behind him.

"Come on, Abby," he urged, motioning with his hand. He patted the space behind him.

With a gulp, I swung my leg over, mimicking his movement. Adjusting on the seat, I leaned my hips away from him.

"What about helmets?" I asked.

"Never needed 'em. Immortal, remember?"

"Um, *not* immortal." I pointed to myself.

Erimon turned in his seat. "If I said I wouldn't let The Dullahan kill you, what makes you think I'd let a motorcycle do it?"

I believed him—despite his ego and bravado. Despite a Celtic death god hot on my trail, I believed him.

"Mind scootin' a little closer? Throws off the balance of the bike otherwise." He motioned to the foot of space between him and me before gripping the handles and waiting.

I moved forward until my waist was flush with his back and wrapped my arms around him. We took off, and I held on so tight I worried about suffocating him. My face pushed into his back as the wind picked up. His hand patted my thigh, seemingly not bothered by my death grip around his ribs.

As we rode, my bravery grew, becoming used to the feeling

of the intense winds. I lifted my head, catching sight of the world flying by. I didn't recognize any of the street signs.

"Are you taking a different way to the hotel?"

"We're not goin' to the hotel. Not yet," he yelled over the wind.

If it weren't for our bargain, I may have worried this would be the part where he drags me in the middle of the woods to kill me.

He took us to a clearing in the forest. He held his hand out to me after he dismounted, helping me slip off and avoiding my leg brushing against the hot tailpipe.

"This way," he beckoned, leading me deeper into the thick canopy.

The trees were numerous, with leaves so green, the moonlight caused an emerald tint to flood over everything surrounding them. A breath caught in my throat, and I dragged my fingertips across the bushes on the ground, tiny drops of dew making them sparkle.

Small blue swirls formed in Erimon's palm, and he held it out. A rustle sounded from a nearby bush, and I stiffened, stepping near Erimon. Out of the bushes, a family of deer walked out. They moved toward us without a care in the world, chewing on grass. My mouth fell open as a small fawn wobbled forward, approaching me. Its brown, round eyes peered up at me with such vulnerability I wanted to cry.

"She likes you," Erimon said with a smile that rivaled the brightness of the moon.

Tears threatened my eyes, and I knelt to the ground, cautiously moving my hand until it landed on the fawn's head.

She nuzzled against my touch. The other two deer moved forward, surrounding Erimon, and rubbing their muzzles against his legs.

"Is this all your doing?"

"Mostly. I'm one with nature, and they know they have no reason to fear me." He scratched one behind its ears. "The fawn...is all you."

The fawn wobbled forward, nuzzling its head against my neck. A single tear rolled down my cheek. "But, how? I don't understand."

He stroked his fingers down one deer's back, keeping watch on my interaction with the fawn. "I have my suspicions, but answers will reveal themselves in due time."

"And you're not going to tell me?"

He crouched to rub his beard against a deer's cheek. "Not until I'm certain, no."

His bluntness shouldn't have surprised me. He'd been that way since we first met, and something told me deep in my soul every word he spoke, every action he took all had their underlying reasons. You didn't live as long as he had and not learn ways to weave the world as you saw fit. But what unsettled me was, if that were true, where did I fit into all of this?

Somehow, we shared a tranquil silence for hours in the woods. We stroked the deer's fur, letting the wind serve as the only form of communication between us. Thoughts carried as a whisper with each passing breeze, fleeting gazes shadowed by moonbeams. The night grew chillier as it wore on, but I didn't notice until my breath curled in the air like fog.

I sat on the back of his bike, curling my arms around him,

my knees hugging his sides. The rift built between us lowered an inch in those woods, and I'd forgotten the supernatural threat on my life—forgot I was mortal. The bike stopped in front of The Lucky Cove, and I pressed my forehead against his back.

"We're here, Abby," he whispered, borderline purring it.

I slid off the bike, still hugging his jacket around me. "Is it crazy to say I could've spent all night in those woods?"

"No tent?" His eyes held a bemused glow.

I curled my lip under my teeth. "Nope. Just the tree branches and a mossy knoll."

He playfully nudged my hip with his knuckle.

I started to slip the jacket from my shoulders to hand back to him with a deep sigh.

He grabbed my bicep. "Keep it. You can give it back to me the next time I see you."

"So confident we'll see each other again?"

His eyes dropped to the ring on my finger with a curl of his lip.

"Right." I held back an eye roll.

"I'll wait out here until Phoebe gets back." He swung a leg over his bike, leaning against it with his arms folded.

"What if she doesn't come back until morning?"

He traced his fingers over the unruly spikes of his hair. "Then I guess it's goin' to be a long night."

Hugging the jacket around my neck, I moved for the door. "Goodnight."

"Oíche mhaith." A glint flashed in his gaze, and I couldn't tell if it was from the moon or...something else.

I walked to my room in a daze, the scents of pine and earth

engulfing my senses, wafting from Erimon's jacket. That night I fell asleep dreaming of white silk around a blazing fire and wet dirt between my toes. It was dusk when Phoebe crawled into bed with me, and a smile pulled at my lips when I heard the roar of a motorcycle shortly after.

11

THE BED DIPPED AS PHOEBE flopped onto it.

Yawning, I parted unruly strands of dark hair from my face and turned on my side, squinting into the darkness. "Had a good night, I take it?"

Phoebe stared at the wall across the room. "Abs, I think I'm in love."

I sat up on one elbow. "Really? That seems kind of fast."

Phoebe curled her hair over her ears, her gaze dropping to her folded hands in her lap. "I know. I mean, I'm crazy, right? How could I possibly fall for someone that quickly?" She bit her thumbnail.

"It could be infatuation, Phoebs. You were all googly-eyed over him since the airport, remember?"

"I've never met anyone like him. He gets me. He's so nice, so intuitive, so…oh my God. He's going to dump me. He's way too good to be true." Phoebe slapped her hands over her face.

Sitting up, I calmly peeled her fingers away from her cheeks. "Stop talking like that. He's not going to dump you. Why would he?"

"There has to be something wrong with him. I need to figure it out." Her bright green eyes widened at me.

"Phoebs, I love you, but Patrick is the lucky one here. If you don't say you agree with that, I will punch you in the boob."

"You wouldn't."

I glared at her. "Try me."

She blew pieces of red hair from her eyes. "I'm sorry. I like this guy. Plus. Holy. Cow. He's phenomenal in bed."

"And that's where this conversation ends. I'm very happy for you. Stop acting like a crazy person. Let it play it out, and it'll all be fine. If you two were meant to be together, it'd happen. If not, there are still plenty of Irishmen in the Irish Sea. Hm?"

"True."

"What time is it anyway?"

She stared at the floor. "Three in the morning."

"Think you can lay down and let me sleep for another few hours, or is that too much to ask?"

"Yes." She nodded. "Absolutely." She lay on her back and smoothed her hair, interlacing her fingers on her stomach.

"So, he sort of wants to go on a picnic this afternoon. Would you come with us? Please?" She propped herself on an elbow, facing me with her puppy dog eyes.

"A picnic? No. That's for couples."

"Abby, you're my best friend. I *need* you there. In case he turns out to be a devil worshipper or something."

"You're letting that Hellfire Club thing get to you, huh?"

Don't. Ever. Be. Alone.

I folded the pillow over my head and let out a muffled, "Fine."

She jounced on the bed, causing a mild earthquake.

"Okay, okay, stop. I don't think this old thing can handle that." I chuckled.

She hugged me, smooshing the side of her face against mine, and managed to fall asleep after an hour of Patrick O'*Cool*ahan talk.

Patrick peered at Phoebe sidelong, snapping the red and white checkered blanket out to lay it on the grass.

I knew right then—this was a horrible idea. Here I was, honing in on a moment that should've been for the two of them. I was a complete tool. Phoebe smiled at Patrick and then looked at me. I tried to make my expression one that resembled someone who wanted to be there.

"It was nice of you to come with us, Abby. You get to enjoy the emerald countryside, hm?" Patrick forced a grin.

Translation: Your presence is not wanted here. Why are you cock-blocking me?

I plucked a blade of grass and twirled it around my finger. "It is an amazing view. Isn't it, Phoebe?"

"Oh, definitely." Phoebe flipped open the wicker basket. "Ooo cheese!"

I plopped onto the blanket, leaned back on my elbows, and turned my attention away from the two lovebirds, concentrating instead on the gorgeous view—rolling emerald hills, with a sunset similar to an oil painting, pinks melting into oranges and reds.

"I, uh, brought wine if you wanted some, Abby." Patrick held a bottle of red wine by its neck.

I felt bad for the guy. "I'm good, thank you. You two enjoy it. I'll munch on this." Absently grabbing some cheese, I turned my back on them.

I closed my eyes, feeling the calm winds from the surrounding hills wash over me, taking in the scents. Irish Spring soap didn't, in actuality, smell anything like Ireland. That wasn't to say Ireland didn't have its pleasant aroma—barley, dew, and salty sea spray.

Lips smacking together sounded behind me, and my eyes flew open.

Patrick lay on Phoebe, fully-clothed, thank God, but they made out like a pair of horny teenagers.

I scrambled to my feet, dusting off my hands. "I'll leave you two alone."

They didn't respond. No surprise there.

The woods weren't far off. If I only went out far enough to be out of view of them, that wouldn't count as alone. As I passed the threshold leading from open land to tree-covered forest, the wind picked up, tossing my hair over my shoulder. I froze, squatting to pick up a rock. The sun rays lit various parts of the forest ablaze, marking each step I took with a brightened patch.

A bubbling brook sparkled in the distance, the water sliding over the flat-worn river rocks like a lover's caress. I crouched, and dipping my hand, let the cool water trickle between my fingers. The surface bubbled and frothed like a simmering boil. I sat back on my haunches, clutching the rock above my head.

A white horse emerged—its long, snowy mane dripping water beads. The horse walked to the bank, shaking its head and spraying water in shimmering tendrils.

So beautiful. So angelic.

All I could do was stare, and the rock fell to the ground, dropping from my palm with a *thud*.

A wild horse swimming in a river in the middle of Ireland. The thought seemed crazy, yet I still couldn't help reaching for it with cautious steps. The horse snapped its attention to me with a snort.

"Hey there, pretty girl," I cooed, edging my way closer.

The horse neighed and scraped her hooves against the ground. I stretched my fingers near its neck, inches away.

A masculine hand slapped the top of mine, and I snatched it back with a yelp.

"No," Erimon said, holding up a chastising finger.

I frowned. "It's a horse." I ignored him and reached again.

Erimon growled and curled an arm around my waist, forcing me backward. He stood in front of me, blocking my path.

"What the hell are you doing?" I asked.

"That isn't a horse. It's a kelpie."

I leaned around him. The same shiny horse remained. "A what?"

"A kelpie. That thing is as much of a horse as I'm fae."

I didn't blink, my eyes fixed on the gorgeous creature beckoning me. I pushed past Erimon.

"It will drag you underwater and spit your entrails on the

bank when it's through with ye."

I paused, staring at the wavy locks of the horse's mane swirling in mid-air as if submerged in water.

The creature morphed into a naked woman. As her mouth formed to human, she laughed—sultry and villainous. The horse's once white mane transformed into black hair, clinging to the woman's hipbones. She stretched her arms above her head, peering at me with glowing white eyes.

"You can't blame a girl for trying," the creature hissed, her words trailing off as if caught by the wind.

I backpedaled, feeling for the rock I'd picked up that was no longer in my hand.

"It's been quite a long time, Erimon." The kelpie moved past me, leaving a liquid trail—dark and thick like blood.

Erimon's brow bounced. "Oh? Did you not get my letters?" Sarcasm laced his tone.

The woman circled him, dragging her hand over his chest, his shoulder, his back.

I dug my nails into my palms.

"I don't recall you stopping any of my meals before," she cooed, stopping in front of him, her forearms resting on his shoulders, staring up at him with bedroom eyes.

"That was a long time ago, Sgathan." He plucked her arms away, dropping them aside.

My shoulders relaxd, but my jaw stayed tight.

Sgathan frowned. "How one hundred years can change a man. We had some good times, didn't we, Erimon? The sea sprays. The grove." She dragged a finger across his face and trailed it down, reaching his abdomen. As it neared the front of his pants, Erimon snatched her wrist.

Sgathan glared at him.

"If you're runnin' short on victims, perhaps you should set up shop in a new river." He released her with a sneer. "Abby is off-limits."

Her lips curled like a serpent, her brow bouncing. "He put a name to the human woman. Interesting indeed." She turned away from him, slithering to me.

"You're quite the pretty little thing, aren't you?" She raised her hand to my face.

I couldn't move, my eyes transfixed on the glowing pools of her eyes.

Erimon stood between her and me, letting Sgathan's finger land on his chest. "Do. Not. Touch. Her. Go back to your hole, Sgathan," he growled.

Sgathan cackled, slinking back to the river. "A pity. You know how much I love the taste of a mortal touched by death." She licked her teeth with an exaggerated swirl of her tongue. "You're a fool if you think you can stop The Dullahan. And I'll laugh into the wind when you realize it."

"I'll be sure to wear earplugs." Erimon's knuckles whitened as he clenched his hands.

She stepped into the water, descending inch-by-inch with her crooked smile until the river consumed her.

"Do I want to ask who that was?" I absently played with the ring.

"An ex-conquest. One I admittedly regret." He kicked a pebble.

I stared at the water. What once had a kelpie emerge from it reduced to faded ripples.

"I can't do this," I whispered.

"What do you mean?"

"I came to Ireland for a vacation. And in the past few days, I've been marked by a headless horseman, rescued by a thousand-year-old Druid, and almost eaten by a kelpie." I lifted my gaze to him. "A kelpie, Erimon."

He squared his jaw, watching me, silent.

"I don't want anything to do with any of this."

His nostrils flared. "Tough."

"Excuse me?" Heat flushed my face.

"You don't have the luxury of bowing out, Abby. You're involved whether ye like or not. And quite frankly, you should start takin' this more seriously." His hand shot out, pulling iron from the earth. His other hand splayed, siphoning wood from the closest tree, never taking his gaze off me.

My jaw dropped. "How *dare* you."

"I get this is all a lot to take in. But you need to come to grips with it, and you need to do it *now*. Things are only goin' to get worse." He swirled his hands in a circle until a dagger formed in mid-air.

"You couldn't begin to understand what I'm going through." My jaw chattered, anger swirling in my belly like a looming storm.

"You're right. I can't. But I'm locked into this with you, aren't I?" He raised a thick brow, his gaze dropping to the ring on my finger.

I ground my teeth together and yanked on it with every ounce of strength I had, shrieking when it didn't budge. "I need space. I need room to breathe."

"Abby—" He gripped the newly formed weapon in his hand, his face turning stone-cold.

"How did you know I was in trouble with the kelpie?"

He opened his mouth.

"Magic," I interrupted. "Of course, right?"

He thinned his lips.

"Just go away." I turned my back on him.

"Go and ask me arse."

I scrunched my nose at him over my shoulder.

He lowered his face to mine. "Means 'no.'"

"Is your plan to *force* your way into my life?"

He removed a leather holster from within his jacket. "If that's what it takes." He twirled his finger. "Turn around."

My brows pinched together as I slowly turned my back to him. His hand slipped past my hips, undoing my belt.

"Hey!" I tried to move, but he gripped my waist.

"Calm down. If I were tryin' to make a pass at ye, you would know, trust me." He pulled the belt free from my jeans.

My stomach tightened, and I pinched my thighs together.

He slipped the belt back through the loops, a heaviness resting at my lower back. "There. You should at least be armed with more than bleedin' rocks."

"What is it?"

"A seax."

I gazed over my shoulder at the knife's hilt—light wood with a Celtic knot on the pommel. "I don't know how to use that."

"Sure, you do. Stab them with it."

A lump formed in my throat. "I need a break from it. From

magic. From you. From—"

"Fine." Erimon's expression fell stoic. "But when The Dullahan returns...and he will. Know that I'm showin' up because of that—" He pointed to the ring. "And nothin' else. We Druids hold our words above all else." The corner of his lip curled in a snarl as he cut his hand through the air and disappeared.

His sudden vanish took the breath from my lungs, and I raised my hand to the space in front of me.

"Abby, there you are. We were about ready to send out a search party," Phoebe joked as she walked up behind me.

I couldn't hide this anymore. Not from Phoebe.

"Where did you get the knife?" She said with a light snicker, poking at the holster.

Whirling around, I slipped my hands on her shoulders. "I need to tell you something, and it's going to sound crazy."

Her eyes shifted, and her full smile slipped into half of one. "Okay? You're scaring me."

Where to start...

I showed her the ring. "I lied about this."

"Did Erimon give it to you?" Her eyes brightened.

I blanched. "Yes, but—"

She clapped and let out a high-pitched squeal.

I pushed down on her shoulders to ground her. "Not in the way you think."

She pouted.

"When I was in that hole, Erimon showed up out of nowhere."

She cocked her head to the side like a curious puppy. "How

did he know?"

"He *appeared* in the hole, Phoebe. No ladder. No rope. Appeared."

Her eyes formed slits. "…how?"

"He's a Druid."

Her cinnamon eyebrows shot up. "A Druid."

"Yes. This ring? I made a deal with him to get out of the hole and fight The Dullahan."

"The Dullahan. The mythical creature my dad used to tell me stories about to scare me into eating my vegetables?"

I was losing her at a rapid pace.

"Yes. That's the one. He marked me, Phoebe. Erimon's the only reason I'm alive right now."

And I told him to go away…

"Maybe we should go see a different doctor. Get a second opinion? You might have a concussion after all." She grabbed my hand and yanked me, but I pulled her back.

"I don't have a concussion. I'm serious. Try to pull the ring off my finger."

She squinted at me with one eye and grabbed the ring. After grunting and trying to use both her arms and legs to pry it from my finger, she gave up.

"This knife?" I pulled it from its sheath with a *shtnk*. "Erimon made it from pulling iron out of the ground."

Her lips parted as she dragged a fingertip over the hilt.

"My ankle wound?" I pull up my pant leg. "It's from a goblin biting me."

She slow-blinked and crouched, shoving her face so close to my foot, her nose brushed my skin. "Those do look like teeth marks…"

"I know it sounds insane, Phoebe."

"If this is real…if The Dullahan is real…you're in some serious shit." Her eyes widened like two big limes.

Nausea coiled in my gut. "I know."

"And this—" She grabbed my hand and shoved the ring in my face. "Guarantees Erimon's protection?"

I leaned back. "Apparently."

"I—" She let my hand drop. "Wow."

"Phoebe, you can't say a *word*. Not to anyone. Not even Patrick."

She chewed on her lip.

"Phoebe—"

She threw up her hands. "Fine. Alright."

"You two ready to go?" Patrick asked, knocking on a tree trunk as if it were a door.

Phoebe yelped and whirled around to face him.

"Yeah, sorry we were talking about—girl…things." I nudged Phoebe.

"Mmhmm. Yup."

Patrick gave a lopsided grin. "Alright? The car's all warmed up for ye."

Making our way through the woods to Patrick's Fiat, I dragged my fingernails down my throat, recalling how close I was to being kelpie food. Whatever reason The Dullahan marked me, it awoke the attention of other mythical creatures. And the only person who knew a thing about them I'd stupidly pissed off.

12

I HADN'T WAITED FOR PHOEBE as I sprinted for The Lucky Cove's door. A migraine had started pulsing in my temple, and all I wanted was sleep. Peace. Nothingness.

As my hands pushed against the door, a brightness flashed, causing me momentary blindness. I blinked several times, trying to regain focus, and blocked it with my forearm. Once the light disappeared, I lowered my arm. The pub was empty. Strange. There'd always been a musician, the bartender, and at least one customer at any given moment.

"Miss Weber, won't you please take a seat," a voice sounded from a darkened corner.

My breathing quickened, and I turned for the door, slamming my hands into it. Locked. I plowed my shoulder into it several times to no avail and slapped my hand against it, calling for Phoebe.

"No one can hear you, Abigail. We're in a mirrored dimension. Harder for your Druid to find you here," the mystery voice said.

My Druid.

My chest heaved, and I turned to look at the eerie shadow.

"There is nothing left for you to do but sit down and listen," he continued.

"I'll stay right here if it's all the same to you." I pressed my back against the door.

The man snapped his fingers, and I appeared in the chair across from him. I gripped the table, waiting for my stomach to stop churning. When I tried to stand up, I couldn't. My butt stuck to the chair, and I couldn't move anything from the waist down. From the shadow, a figure leaned forward. The moonlight from a nearby window shone over his face. He was pencil thin—Jack Skellington thin with long and grotesque facial features. Wads of hair sprouted from his nose and ears, and his eyebrows were bushy like furry caterpillars.

"Who are you?"

He steepled his gnarled fingers. "Some know me as Crom. Others…The Dullahan."

Terror shot down my spine.

"Fortunately for you, I can't kill you here."

"Then why bring me here at all?"

He tapped his fingers together. "As I said, to chat."

"You're not making much sense.

"Have you not wondered why he's so drawn to you?" His lips curled back, revealing blackened crooked teeth.

"Who?"

He let out a raspy chuckle. "You have a mystical essence about you. And I need it. My time on this earth dwindles, and I need warriors to follow me into the afterlife."

My nails dug into the table. "I'm no warrior."

"I have no interest in sparring with you for eternity, Abigail. I'm after what's in here." He tapped his chest. "The essence— the spirit. To spread throughout my horde."

I gulped, clenching my jaw to keep it from chattering.

"And the only way to suck it from you—" He leaned forward, his eyes flashing red. "Is your death."

The only thing keeping my hands from shaking was the hard surface beneath them. "Why not do it now? Why play games?"

"Mortal witnesses can cause...complications."

Never. Be. Alone.

"Consider this a warning. You will die, and your Druid will only be able to stop me for so long." He appeared beside me, looming, the smell of decay and sulfur overtaking the air. "With each mortal life, I grow stronger, and I'll keep taking them until I can crush Erimon like a roach under my boot heel."

I leaned away, gagging on his scent.

Within a blink, Crom disappeared. People filled the seats of tables around me, and they stared as if I'd appeared out of thin air.

I had.

Pressing my hands to the table, I pushed to my feet and ran my hands through my hair.

People were dying because of me. Because of The Dullahan's thirst for my essence. Whatever that hell *that* was.

I weaved through the tables, bumping into several along the way.

Phoebe. Where was Phoebe?

In a panic, I stormed outside, frantically searching for her.

"I'm—I'm so sorry, Abs," Phoebe said, her voice small and trembling.

I spotted her red hair in the shadows. She sat on the ground with her arms wrapped about herself.

"Phoebe? Why are you sorry?" I knelt in front of her.

Her emerald eyes blinked up at me. "That I didn't believe you."

"What are you talking about?" She looked like she'd seen a ghost. Maybe she had.

"I—I spent the past ten minutes in a black room. It had no floor, no walls. It was…endless." She stared off into space. "I was right behind you, and instead of going into the pub, I sort of…appeared there."

"The Dullahan. He pulled me into some…mirrored reality. Called himself Crom."

Phoebe stared into the distance, rocking back and forth. "Abs, is Erimon seriously a thousand-year-old Druid?"

"Yes."

She went quiet.

"Phoebe, are you going to be okay?" Gripping one of her shoulders, I tightened my jaw.

"Maybe. No. Yes, yes, I will. You seem to be handling this all pretty well."

"I've had a bit more time to adjust." I rose and held a hand out to help her.

"You mean a whole twenty-four hours?"

"I want to go to the library. Research The Dullahan. He has to have a weakness. Everything has one." I trailed off in thought, biting my cuticles.

"Why don't you ask Erimon for help?"

"We had a…tiff."

"He didn't give you his number? Wait, do Druids use cell phones?"

"I have no idea how to contact him. And there's only one place I've seen him frequent consistently."

"The pub," we both said at the same time.

Once the taxi dropped us off in front of Hole in the Wall, I rushed inside, fixing my gaze on Erimon's usual seat—empty. My shoulders slumped.

Phoebe trotted up behind me, glancing around. "He isn't here, is he?"

"No, he's not. Maybe he'll decide to grace us with his presence tomorrow." I forced my expression to remain neutral. "In the meantime, we're still going to the library. I can't stand by while a Celtic demon plans to kill me."

"Fine. Alright. First thing tomorrow, we'll go to a library and…*read*." She made a gagging sound.

Explaining to a taxi driver to take you to a library was like trying to explain why I wanted to watch grass grow. Those movies where the characters inexplicably find a dusty basement within an old library that has ancient texts? Absolute hogwash.

"Don't you have a section with, I don't know, older books?"

I asked the librarian, who peered at me over the rim of her glasses.

"What exactly are you lookin' for?" The librarian crossed her arms with a huff.

"Celtic...myths," I decided on.

"Right this way." She beckoned with her finger.

I searched for Phoebe, who stumbled out of the romance section, cheeks almost the same color as her hair.

"Abs, these books are so naughty. I never realized how many different names there were to describe a man's penis." She giggled while saying the word for male genitalia in a whisper.

"Have you never read a romance novel?" I bit back a grin.

"They always seemed so corny."

"Here we are. There be only two shelves, but pretty much any Celtic myth you wish to research should be here. Happy huntin'," the librarian said before leaving.

"You can fantasize about burly lumberjacks after you help me." I snapped the paperback book in Phoebe's grasp shut and tossed it onto a table behind us, despite her pout. I cocked my head to the side to read the names of the books.

"Can you please explain to me again why we aren't using a little thing called the internet?"

"I don't think what I'm looking for has been digitally transcribed. I couldn't even find information on Erimon." I grabbed a book from the shelf titled *Ancient Celtic Myths Defined*.

"You've been looking him up, huh?" She grabbed a bright yellow book from the shelf.

"Only so I can know what I'm dealing with." I took a seat at the nearby table and flipped through the pages.

"Like metaphorically dealing with or…sexually dealing with?"

I looked at the book she chose and smacked my lips together. "Celtic Myths for Dummies? Do you really think what we're looking for is going to be in that modernized crap?"

"Hey, you never know. These things used to be my jam back in high school." She flipped to a random page. "See, look here. Druids. Ancient religious soothsayers. There you go," she read, flipping the book around so that I could read it myself.

"Yes, I read all about that on several websites, but Erimon isn't a soothsayer he has…powers."

"What kind of powers?" She sat on the table.

"If I tell you, will you drop this and help me research?"

"Deal."

"Erimon has these nature-like powers. As far as I can tell, he can control everything in nature around him, the dirt, the trees, wind—," I started, gulping at the thought of the breeze over my neck at the pub.

"Oh my God…okay, continue, continue." She bounced.

"That's all I've seen so far. That and he's an animal whisperer or something." My voice trailed off, thinking back to that night with the deer.

"He's an immortal warrior Druid with nature powers. How are you not more excited about this?"

"He's an immortal warrior Druid with nature powers," I repeated. "It's all a tad overwhelming, wouldn't you say?"

"Yeah, but—," she started.

"Phoebe. You promised. I told you, now read."

"Fine," she said. She stood to put the Dummies book back, grabbing another one.

I dragged my finger down the page. "As he said, Crom *is* The Dullahan. They're the same entity."

Phoebe sat down with another book, this one lined with red leather and aged pages. "What does it say?"

"The Dullahan is a bringer of death but is often cross-referenced with the god, Crom Dubh. He's synonymous with dark magic."

"Think that's who showed up at the Hellfire Club, not the Devil?" She opened to a random page within her book.

I tapped my finger against my lips. "Maybe?"

Phoebe's eyes scanned the page, and then she excitedly pointed. "Look here. It says: That every full moon, Crom can morph into that of the creature, Dullahan to choose those to die and fight for his soul's departure from earth."

It all matched up to what Crom said.

"Fight? Why would he choose you then?"

"I can hold my own."

"Tell that to your ankle."

"That goblin is rotting under a rock right now." I slapped the book shut, kicking a dust plume into the air.

Phoebe stared at me. "Do you want to know how to try to ward him off?"

I stood, moving behind her. "It says that?"

"Yes, apparently, you can attempt to ward him off with precious metals. In particular, pure gold."

"That's it?"

Phoebe turned in her chair. "That's it? Do you happen to

have a piece of *pure* gold in your pocket?"

I frowned. "No." Clicking my fingernail against my teeth, I paced the room.

"I know you don't want to hear this, but maybe we should ask Patrick. He probably knows people."

I stopped. "Absolutely not."

"Abby. This is your life we're talking about. We can't do this ourselves."

"Okay, fine, but we're not telling him about Erimon or Crom or anything else that's happened."

"So, I'm supposed to ask him if he knows of any pure gold laying around, without any reasoning?"

I stared at her before nodding. "Yes."

"I can handle that." She shrugged.

"Let me get this straight. You need a piece of pure gold, but you can't tell me why?" Patrick sat at his kitchen table, eyes scanning Phoebe's face skeptically.

I remained in the background, absentmindedly perusing Patrick's quaint abode as the two of them talked. He had a bookshelf filled to the brim with editions so old the bindings were weathered. Given the dust and cobwebs over them all, I'd also guess it'd been nearly as long since he read any of them.

"Yes." Phoebe nodded once.

"Are you in trouble with the mob?"

Phoebe widened her eyes at me as if looking for permission to use that excuse as *our* excuse. I covertly shook my head and turned my attention to a hat rack with various styles of hats—all in shades of green.

"No, I'm not. Just know it's for a worthy cause, and we will return the gold."

"You don't need to spend it?"

"Um, nope."

"Well, why didn't you say so?"

"I uh, didn't know that was a deciding factor," Phoebe said, idly shrugging at me.

Patrick slapped the table, pushing to his feet. "You two hang out here for a wee bit. I'll be right back." Patrick grabbed a scarf from a peg near the entranceway, draping it around his neck and whisking out the door.

"Well, that was easy. I thought I'd at least have to agree to some kinky stuff in bed or something."

I flopped down in the chair near Phoebe. "Almost too easy."

"I trust him, Abby."

"Well, I certainly hope so if you love him like you say you do." I softened my expression.

Phoebe's cheeks blushed, and she broke eye contact.

"Have you given any more thought to our conversation from last night?"

Phoebe nodded. "A lot, actually. You're right. I mean, what are the odds we happened to meet each other in the same bar, in the same airport, going to the same destination?"

"Glad to hear it." I squeezed her shoulder.

"Besides, I know you'd help me trash his prized Fiat if he hurt me, so that helps too."

I fist-bumped her, and we made explosion gestures with our

fingers. "Damn right I would." A chuckle escaped my belly, and I stood from my chair as the door suddenly swung open. It had only been a matter of minutes, so I wasn't expecting Patrick back that quickly.

Patrick's teeth shone brightly as he removed the scarf. His dimples were the most prominent I'd ever seen them. He reached into his pocket and held out a single gold coin. "I believe you requested pure gold."

Phoebe's eyes lit up, and she snatched the coin from his palm. She brought it to her mouth, biting down on it with her molars.

Both Patrick and I cocked our brows.

"What? Isn't that what you're supposed to do to check if it's real?"

"Maybe in a cartoon," I said with a snicker.

"I assure you it's as real as you or meself," Patrick said.

I plucked the coin from Phoebe's grasp, gazing at the designs. On one side was an intricately designed tree. The other had a Celtic design. "How did you come about this, Patrick?"

"Over the rainbow," he said with a playful wink. He snatched the coin from my fingers and flipped it over the tops of his knuckles.

I watched as the coin effortlessly rolled over one knuckle to the next.

"Now, you can borrow this on one condition. I need it back. If you were to happen to lose it, it would be dire straits for me, you understand?" His smile faded.

We nodded.

"Of course, we'll give it back, Patrick," I said, masking my unease.

He flipped the coin to me using his thumb. "Then you have yourself a gold coin to use for whatever mysterious thing you be usin' it for, though I must say I'm a bit disappointed you can't tell me."

"It's nothing personal. Trust me. It's for your own good." I frowned and slipped the coin into my back pocket.

He nodded. "May the luck 'o the Irish be with you then."

13

THE NEXT DAY, I SAT at the pub, having nursed two Guinness, waiting for Erimon to show. If the bartender gave me one more pitiful glance, I'd scream. I thumbed the gold coin in my pocket, still wondering how it had the power to weaken The Dullahan. Either Erimon was busy performing Druidic duties, or he was pissed at me. Maybe both.

He wasn't going to show. Who was I kidding?

I needed a different method to get his attention.

The taxi dropped me at Patrick's hovel, and I pounded furiously on the door. Phoebe had followed me to the pub so I wouldn't be alone, but after an hour, I'd sent her away, given there were plenty of customers.

"Alright, alright, houl yer horses!" Patrick's voice boomed from the other side of the door.

As the door swung open, Patrick stood there squinty-eyed

like he just rolled out of bed. He combed his tousled hair with a swipe of his hand, tightening the sheet around his waist with the other. I stared at his bare chest and the light scattering of auburn hair before snapping my eyes to his face.

"Oh my God, I'm so, so sorry." I moved my gaze to the doorframe, suddenly interested in its construction. "Is, uh, Phoebe here?"

Phoebe's red hair popped out from behind Patrick's shoulder. She leaned to one side with a sleepy grin, clutching a matching sheet to her chest.

"I didn't mean to interrupt."

"You didn't interrupt. We were just snuggling." Phoebe looked up at Patrick with a satiated smile.

I scratched the back of my head, becoming increasingly uncomfortable. "Can I borrow you for an hour or two?"

"Sure. Give me a minute to get dressed." She rose to her tippy toes, kissed Patrick on the cheek, and walked away.

"Did you want to wait inside?" Patrick stepped aside.

"Oh, no. I'm good. I'll wait out here on this…" I spotted a suitable seating area otherwise known as a horizontal log. "On this bench."

He peered outside. "That's a log."

"A log is nature's bench."

"Suit yourself." He gave a dimpled grin and shut the door.

I leaned back on the log, gazing at the sky. It was a dreary day, dark clouds rolled in, and the air smelled as if it were close to raining. Considering the unpredictable weather forecast I'd read about Ireland, we'd been lucky so far.

Phoebe walked out, smoothing her shirt. "So, what do you

need?"

"I need to stage myself in distress as a means to lure Erimon out from whatever celestial plane he's in."

Phoebe tapped her finger against her lips. "I like it. How very Lucy and Ethel of you. I'm Lucy, right?" She gave her red hair a toss.

"Sure." After patting my hands on my thighs, I added, "I need to strand myself in the hole again."

"Perfect."

"I sure hope he hurries up. I think I felt a raindrop." Phoebe said, grunting as she held onto the rope.

I lowered myself into the hole, jumping the remaining two feet. "If it starts raining, I really *will* be in distress. You can take the rope."

"Alright, I'm pulling it away, and then I'll go hide."

I pushed my back against the wall and tapped my nails against the pebbles and dirt.

Phoebe's head poked from the surface of the hole. "Maybe you should, I don't know, sound distressed?"

"Right." I plopped down and draped my hand across my forehead.

"Oh, woe is me. How could I have fallen again? How will I ever get out of this hole?"

Phoebe pointed at her open mouth, making gagging sounds. "And you wonder why you never got a speaking part in Hamlet in high school."

"Well, what would you suggest I do?"

"Have you tried calling out his name?"

I thinned my lips. "Erimon." Nothing. "Erimon, help." Still nothing. "Erimon, please?" Dead silence.

"Abs, this isn't working."

Rubbing my chin, I paced the hole and then froze. "Throw me the rope, Phoebs."

Dusting my hands off after crawling from the hole, I took extra care to rid my knees of dirt.

"The kelpie." I turned for the woods.

Phoebe fluttered behind me. "A kelpie? A shape-shifting water spirit that eats people?"

"That'd be the one. There's one in this river."

Phoebe grabbed my arm, turning me to face her. "How do you know that?"

"One attacked me."

Her hand dropped. "Both The Dullahan and a kelpie tried to kill you?"

"Yes." My eyes dropped to my feet.

"Why, Abby?"

"If I knew, all of this might be easier. They keep mentioning my 'essence,' whatever the hell that means. "

"Do you think this is a good idea? It seems risky. What if he doesn't show up?"

"He will."

"And if he doesn't?"

I undid the latches on the hilt resting at my back. "I'll run. And if all else fails—" I unsheathed the blade, holding it up. "I'll stab her until she stops."

Phoebe stared at the knife. "Who *are* you?"

"I don't know anymore." I slipped the seax back home with a furrowed brow.

Phoebe eyed the rope in her hands, her eyes brightening. "I have a better idea."

Phoebe plucked the taut rope with her finger after we secured it between two trees.

"Think this will work?" I noted the distance from the river to the rope.

"It better. Are you sure you want to do this?"

"I need his help. I don't have any other choice."

"Please be careful. I'm going to hide over here." She pointed at a boulder.

I wiped my clammy palms over my jeans and crouched at the river's edge, scooping water into my hand and letting my fingers caress the surface. It didn't take long at all.

"Well, well, either you are a complete idiot showing up here all alone, or today is my lucky day," Sgathan's voice hissed as she ascended from the water. Still naked.

I slowly stood, tracing my eyes on her.

"Neither. I'm using you." I took a step back for every step Sgathan slid forward.

"Using me?" She cackled. "I do not get used, human."

I scanned her naked body. "I find that hard to believe."

Sgathan's eyes glowed red, and she screamed, baring rows of tiny pointed teeth. Her hair flew in all directions, her fingers growing long and thin, the body growing larger.

My knees wobbled, and I stumbled before turning and running in a full sprint for the rope. Sgathan shifted into horse form. Its nostrils flared, billowing mist as it charged at me.

Where *was* he?

I leaped over the rope, clipping it with the toe of my boot, and fell to the ground. The horse followed, all four limbs tripping on the taut line.

I backpedaled across the dirt like a crab as the horse glowered at me, scarring the ground with a menacing hoof. I reached for the dagger, holding it in the air like a spear, my chest heaving as the horse galloped. The dirt and ground shifted around me as Erimon appeared with his fist planted on the ground. A stone wall rose in front of me, and the horse crashed into it, nearly coming out the other side.

I scrambled to my feet as Erimon grabbed the horse and hurled it toward the river. It morphed into the naked Sgathan in mid-air. She let out a blood-curdling scream before her body landed in the water with a splash.

Erimon turned around, glaring with a fire ignited in his gaze. As he passed the stone wall, he touched it, the rocks and dirt dematerializing back to the ground. He glowered at me, huffing and puffing as he made his way over.

"This is how you get my attention? By doin' the exact opposite of what I asked? To stay alive?"

"It got you here, didn't it?" I tightened my grip on the knife hilt.

He crossed his thick arms. "I should've made you stew a tad longer. Give you that sense of the moment before death."

"But you didn't." My jaw tightened.

He made a tsking sound and cracked his neck with a snarl of his lip. "Well, Abigail, you rang?"

"The Dullahan came to see me."

Erimon's eyes flickered. "What do you mean, he came to see you? Were you alone?"

I sheathed the blade, keeping his gaze. "He warped me into some parallel reality. He said he's going to become stronger to get you out of the way."

Erimon ran a hand over his beard.

"He called himself Crom. Looked like a decaying old man."

"Crom? He never appears as Crom. This is all makin' less sense." He clasped his hands behind his neck.

"Erimon, if what he says is true, that he could become stronger and—"

Erimon closed the distance between us and held a finger up. "No. That won't happen. I just can't bank on doin' this alone anymore."

My throat dried.

A twig snapped nearby, and Erimon raised a hand, fire blazing in his palm.

I grabbed his forearm and yanked it down as Phoebe yelped and held up her hands. "It's me."

Erimon tossed me a glare.

"She knows. I couldn't lie to her anymore. There's too much at stake."

"I didn't mean to interrupt. My legs were starting to cramp." She offered a meager smile.

Erimon growled and turned away, squelching the fire

roaring in his hand.

"We read that The Dullahan could be warded off with pure gold. Is that true?"

"I've never had to go to those lengths, but yes. I could conjure some for you, but it will take some time to locate—" he started before I took the gold coin from my pocket. "—it." He plucked it from my fingers, running his thumb over the designs. "Where did you get this?" His eyes formed slits.

"Patrick," Phoebe answered.

"I need to have a tad chat with *dear* Patrick." He balled his hand into a fist over the coin.

Erimon curled his arm with mine and dragged me over to Phoebe. He touched her shoulder, and, in a flash, we appeared outside of Patrick's place. Erimon's mouth twitched before he stormed for the door.

"Erimon." I scurried behind him, Phoebe on my heels.

Erimon's hand rose, the wooden door splitting in half, falling to the ground in slivers. My jaw dropped, and I paused at the threshold, staring at the wooden remains littered across the floor. Phoebe's mouth formed an oval shape as she stepped through the open doorway.

Patrick sat at his kitchen table, pushing his back into the chair when he saw Erimon stalking toward him. Erimon said nothing before he slammed the coin on the table. Patrick eyed the gold before looking over to us.

"I thought you said this was for you, Abby?" He asked, ignoring Erimon looming over him.

"It is. I—"

"She saw fit to share it with me." Erimon puffed his chest.

If he'd been a peacock, his tail would have saluted. "How long have you been on the surface, Leprechaun?"

"I'm sorry, what?" Phoebe asked.

"It's true what he says." Patrick's gaze fixed on Erimon.

"That you're a leprechaun?" Phoebe's hands raised.

"Yes."

"Well, I thought you would be—" She trailed off.

"Old and wrinkly?" Erimon interjected.

"I was going to say shorter."

"There hasn't been a rainbow in weeks. How'd ye find it?" Erimon pointed at the coin.

"Unlike some of my colleagues, Druid, I don't need a rainbow to find my gold." Patrick glared, reaching for the coin, and Erimon slapped his hand over it.

I stepped between the two mythical men. "Can we pause for a second? How did you know he was a Druid?"

Patrick sniffed the air. "I could smell his kind from a mile away."

"Lucky Charms's race here has been a thorn in the Druid's sides for centuries. They hoard everything and never give anything back."

"What do you call that?" Patrick pointed at my ring. "Plannin' on giving that back to the earth, Nature Lad?"

"That's different." Erimon fumed.

The two men glared at each other like bucks in rutting season.

"Do I need to remind you about The Dullahan? Do you think you two can put aside your differences for the moment?" I looked between them, leaving out the part that my neck was on the line.

"What are you talkin' about?" Patrick asked.

I grabbed the coin from the table, holding it in Patrick's face. "This is to help ward off The Dullahan. He's chosen me."

Patrick's gaze snapped to Erimon, who nodded in confirmation.

"But I—I only have one more day on the surface." Patrick scrubbed his face.

"Not unless…" Erimon started, trailing his voice, motioning at Phoebe with his chin.

"Absolutely not. It's too soon. I can't. Only you would be that selfish."

Erimon shoved his palm into Patrick's chest. "Selfish, Clover? I can't take on The Dullahan durin' his hunt alone. If you don't ask, Abby could die."

Patrick hung his head and moved toward Phoebe, wiping his palms on the sides of his pants.

"What's going on?" Phoebe wrapped her arms around herself.

Patrick knelt to one knee, interlacing his fingers, and looked up at Phoebe with downtrodden eyes. "Phoebe, will you marry me?"

14

PHOEBE STARED DOWN AT PATRICK, frozen. Gurgling noises escaped her throat, but no words followed at first. She pinched her eyes shut. "I've—I've only known you a week."

"I'm aware." Patrick stayed on his knee with his hands clasped together.

Her eyes flew open. "It's so soon." She blinked with the speed of a hummingbird in flight.

"It's crazy. I know. I've never met a mortal quite like ye Phoebe. This isn't how I saw a proposal goin'." His brows pinched together.

Phoebe sucked on her lip.

He had one thing right. This *was* crazy.

Patrick's shoulders slumped, and he dusted his knee as he stood. "I suppose an explanation is warranted."

Erimon snarled. "We don't have time for this." He stormed forward.

I blocked him with my arm as he passed. "Would you let him explain?"

Erimon's eyes dropped to my arm and slowly panned up to my face. His fingers grazed my skin as he slowly lowered my arm, keeping his eyes locked on me. "Make it quick, Chaun." Erimon turned away and leaned forward in a chair, spreading his legs wide.

"Yes, I'm a Leprechaun. Over time, the stories, the myths, they all got thrown completely out of context. To be honest, I'm not sure how the three feet tall, always wearin' green started."

"It's a downright mystery," Erimon mumbled.

I peeked at him over my shoulder, and his expression melted into a smolder.

"What is a leprechaun, then?" Phoebe asked.

"We're collectors."

Erimon coughed the word "thieves."

"We *do* steal from time to time, but only from those who don't need it. We create stockpiles. We're nature's bank in a manner of speakin'."

"Also called hoarders," Erimon added.

Phoebe walked from one end of the room to the other. "Do you have powers?"

"Not quite as exquisite as the Druid, but yes."

Erimon guffawed.

"What can you do?" Phoebe asked.

"I have a sense for precious metals. Every year I'm allowed to come to the surface, grant a human I see fit three wishes, add to my stockpile, and if there is a need, fight off mythical bad guys, if you will."

He could help fight The Dullahan. And needed to marry a mortal to stay on the surface...

"You can fight?" A glistening smile pulled at Phoebe's lips.

"What are you goin' to do, Patty? Throw gold coins at 'em?" Erimon narrowed his eyes.

Patrick glared at him. "You have no idea what I can do, Druid."

Erimon shot from his chair, coming toe-to-toe with the Leprechaun. "Ye wanna go? Right now. We'll see who the real warrior is here."

"Would you two stop?" I spat, shoving my shoulder between them.

"You're telling me you were going to have to go away in a day, and I wouldn't see you for a year?" Phoebe asked, her voice barely above a whisper.

Patrick turned to Phoebe with sunken eyes. "I was goin' to tell you. I didn't know what to say. I wasn't plannin' on meeting you, Phoebe. And I most certainly wasn't planning on fancyin' you the way I do."

Phoebe's lip trembled, and she bit it.

Erimon's breath wafted over my neck, my shoulder still near him.

My stomach fluttered, and I side-stepped away. "I still don't understand how marriage keeps you on the surface."

"It's not simply marryin'. It's a ritual that binds us together for eternity. With Leprechauns, if a human offers their heart to us, we're granted the right to come and go as we please. And more importantly, every year, those three wishes would eternally belong to them."

Phoebe stayed quiet, her fingers playing at each other, twisting and plucking.

"I think you've had my heart since the moment I saw Guinness foam on your lips at the airport." Pink flushed Patrick's cheeks.

"What were you doing in an American airport, anyway?" I asked.

"I sensed a stash of these gorgeous gold coins with little eagles on them in California."

Phoebe's eyes glistened with tears.

Patrick squeezed her hand. "What do you say, Phoebe? Marry me? Let me grant your wishes every year of your life?"

Erimon rolled his shoulders back, idly tapping his finger against his hip.

No. This was insane. All of this had been madness.

I jolted across the room and grabbed Phoebe's shoulders, moving her toward the door. "Let me talk to her first."

Erimon took one step forward. "Time is an enemy right now, Abby."

"Five minutes."

The corners of his jaw bulged as he tightened it, but he didn't make any further protests.

I stared at the door in pieces scattered across the floor and looked back to Erimon. "A little privacy?"

He raised his hand. "Five minutes," he said before the splinters of wood intertwined, creating a whole door.

I massaged Phoebe's shoulders. "Phoebe, if you're doing this because you think if you don't, I'll die, don't do it. I don't want you to sacrifice your life for mine."

"I wouldn't be sacrificing my life. I'd be making a new one. With Patrick."

Since when did she become so decisive? This was the same woman who could never make up her mind over a pizza place.

"You barely know him."

"Have you ever made a split-second decision and felt so confident that everything would turn out the way it should, based on this one singular decision? As if all the stones fell right into place?"

"I'm not the type for flying by the seat of my pants. You know me." I liked my pants with deep pockets. Very deep.

"That's how I feel right now. I know in my gut that marrying Patrick will cause all those stones to fall in all the right places. I've never felt so sure of anything in my entire life."

"Is he messing with your head? Does it feel fuzzy or hazy?" I turned her around, looking at her body as if there'd be evidence somewhere.

She batted my hands away. "I know it sounds crazy. You saw me. I panicked the moment he brought up the idea, but that look on his face when he told me I was the human he'd gladly be bound to for all of eternity? He thinks the world of me. If I could be with someone like that, and in turn, save my best friend's life, I think it's crazier not to go through with it." She started rubbing *my* shoulders.

"It's going to be okay, Abby." She butted her head against mine.

"I can't believe you're doing this."

The door flew open, and Erimon leaned out, his gaze focused on Phoebe. "What's your answer?"

She took a deep breath. "I'll do it." She grabbed my shoulders before turning for the door.

I followed behind her, narrowing my eyes as I passed Erimon. "Do you have to be so callous about it?"

He dropped his lips to my ear. "I'm as callous as I need to be." After squeezing my hip, he turned away.

Patrick's eyes lit up when he spotted Phoebe.

"I'll marry you, Patrick." She pressed her palms together.

Patrick flashed a broad smile and wrapped his arms around her, lifting her up and twirling them in circles.

My sinuses burned as I fought back tears, staring at how happy Phoebe looked.

Erimon leaned against the wall with his arms folded, glancing at an invisible watch on his wrist.

"How exactly does this work? Do we need a priest?" Phoebe asked as Patrick lowered her to the floor.

Erimon pushed from the wall with one of his booted feet. "You need me."

"You'd perform the ritual? For me?" Patrick asked.

"I'm not doin' it for you."

Patrick's eyes shifted to me and my throat dried.

"A Druid performin' a Chaun weddin' ceremony—I'd thought I'd seen it all," Patrick muttered.

Erimon motioned with his hands for the soon-to-be newlyweds to step in front of him. "Do you have rings?"

Patrick cleared his throat. "Would you mind doin' one more favor?"

Erimon held a palm out in front of me. "I'll need that coin if ye don't mind." He reached past my hip, his arm brushing my side, and dove into my back pocket. His fingertips grazed my butt through the fabric, making my stomach clench. He grazed his nose over my collarbone before turning away with the coin in his hand. "Patrick, will replace this for you as payment for my ceremonial duties, won't you, Patty?"

My skin tingled from the brief contact, and I traced a finger over my neck.

Patrick pulled at his collar. "Yes." His voice sounded like trying to push an apple through the opening of a bottle.

"That's a good lad." Blue swirls ascended from Erimon's palm with the coin clutched in his grasp. He opened his hand, revealing two gold rings, and held one up to Patrick. "This one is yours. The one with the four-leaf clover on it."

"How very kind," Patrick said through gritted teeth.

"Anything for you." Erimon patted Patrick's face, the last pat more like a slap.

I pinched the bridge of my nose.

"I'm goin' to forgo all the usual pleasantries as we are short on time." He took Phoebe's hand and placed Patrick's ring on her palm, coaxing her hand shut. He gripped her shoulder, and she gasped, staggering backward. "Do you, Phoebe, bind yourself to this...Leprechaun, in both mind and body, for all eternity, even if death fall upon either one of you?"

Phoebe nodded.

Erimon leaned forward. "You need to say it out loud."

"Yes."

Erimon dropped her ring in Patrick's hand and grabbed his shoulder, keeping hold of Phoebe. "Do you Patrick of the Chauns, bind yourself to this human, in both mind and body, for all eternity, forsaking wishes to all others even if death fall upon either one of you?"

"Yes," Patrick replied.

Erimon closed his eyes, and a beam of light spread from Patrick, waved over Erimon, and into Phoebe. She gasped, stumbling back. Erimon's grip tightened on her shoulder, keeping her upright. He grimaced but didn't let go of them. "Rings," he said through gritted teeth.

Patrick slipped Phoebe's ring onto her left ring finger, and Phoebe followed suit. The beam of light settled over Phoebe and Patrick, disappearing through their skin.

"By the power bestowed upon me by order of the Druids, I can vow that this bond be sound." He released his grip and sniffed as he took a step back.

Phoebe beamed at the ring on her finger.

Erimon's gaze dropped to the floor before he stormed past me and out the door.

"I feel...different," Phoebe said, staring at her arms.

"Different how?" Patrick mused.

"There's this swelling in my chest that travels to my toes. I feel...whole," she said, glowing, completely forgetting I was there.

"Perhaps us meetin' in that airport wasn't a coincidence." He kissed her softly.

I turned away from them, walking outside.

"Not interested in watchin' the happy couple?" Erimon sat on the ground, slumped against a tree. He curled one knee to his chest, resting his arm on it with a weak smile as I walked to him.

"You look exhausted."

"It takes a good deal of magic to perform a bonding. And it's been so bleedin' long since I've done one."

"You sure that's all it was?" I sat on the log near him and slid my hands underneath me.

"If I had somethin' to say, I'd say it." He kept his focus on the rings twirling on his fingers.

"What exactly happens during a bonding?"

"The light you saw was me bringin' their souls to the surface. And then combining them. Each will hold a crumb of the other for eternity."

His sky-blue eyes lifted to meet my gaze, and the ring hummed on my finger. He put on this façade of someone confident. But a heavy-weight settled in those eyes, disguised with swagger and bravado. It was as if his eyes revealed all to me and all I wanted to do was give him peace by helping him lift the weight.

"The light passed through you at one point. You had their souls *in* you?"

His eyes fell back to the rings. "Payin' that close of attention, were ye?"

I moved from the log to the ground next to him. "I'm serious. What's it feel like?"

He let out a slow breath, the tiredness in his eyes lifting. "Like bein' run through with a sword. There are only two species in the universe that can perform a bonding ritual. Not many can handle the transference."

"Druids and...?" I inched closer to him.

"Trolls."

"Trolls?" I pictured large, floppy ears and huge noses—grotesque, obese, mean creatures. "I didn't know trolls had powers. We are talking about the kind who like to dwell under bridges and make people pay tolls to pass, right?"

"Yes, but they can do far more. Convincin' one to perform the ritual is another matter entirely. Druids have always been preferred.

"You said it'd been a while. Why?"

Erimon picked up a pebble and bounced it in his palm. "I have turned down every couple who asked me through the centuries."

"How come?"

"I didn't care about their happiness. If I couldn't have it, why should anyone else?" He pierced me with his gaze before turning it away.

"That's…"

"Selfish?" He smirked. "Story of my mystical life, Abby."

"If you're so selfish, you wouldn't be going through all this trouble to help me." I pressed my knee against his thigh, willing him to look at me.

"I have my reasons." He peered at my lips. "I always have my reasons."

A blood-curdling shriek echoed the space around us. I clapped my hands over my ears as a spark of pain pulsed through my skull. Erimon leaped to his feet.

"What is that?" I yelled to Erimon over the unending scream.

Erimon's face tightened. "Stay behind me."

I stood, clamping my hands over my ears, pain shooting from my head to the base of my spine. Erimon turned, and I was no longer in his protective shadow, far too overwhelmed with the nauseating aches all over my body.

A ghostly woman surrounded by animated smoke appeared in front of me. Her long white hair floated around her, and she locked onto me with a pair of midnight eyes bulging from her skull-like face.

I lowered my hands from my ears, staring at the ghost before she let out another shriek, her skeletal hands reaching for me. The last thing I heard was Erimon yelling my name.

15

I JOLTED AWAKE, GREETED BY pure darkness. The cold stone beneath me made my bones ache. Frantically, I reached in front of me until my hands bumped against several rows of hardened steel—prison bars. My breaths quickened, and I wrapped my hands around the bars, pulling at them with all my might. The last thing I remembered was a ghostly woman grabbing me. I reached for my knife. Gone.

A light illuminated outside. Squinting, I waited for my eyes to adjust to the sudden brightness. Stone walls and steel bars surrounded me. The small beacon flickered like a lantern or torch, spilling more light as it got closer. An eerie hum floated past my ears to the tune of *Danny Boy*. A shadowy figure lifted the lantern once it stepped in front of my cell.

My shoulders tensed.

"Aibell?" I clutched the bars as if I could pry them apart with my bare hands.

Aibell shoved the lantern at my face, nearly blinding me. She narrowed her eyes, the hood of her cloak casting scattered shadows over her cheeks. "You're not one for subtle hints, are you?"

I concentrated on the dips and grooves of the bars within my grasp. "Clearly not."

Aibell tsked, turning away, taking the only light source with her.

I reached through the bars. "Wait."

Aibell whipped around, baring her pointy teeth.

I snapped my hand back into my cell. "Why am I here?"

Aibell chortled like a hyena, the bars framing her pale face.

"When The Dullahan shows such keen interest in a mortal, it tends to spark interest from others." She turned away.

"Others? What do you mean, others?"

Aibell peered at me over her shoulder. "Why don't you take a seat and practice the art of silence?"

Fear crept up my spine. My choices for death lately were not any more pleasant-sounding than the last.

She cackled, holding the lantern higher to witness my terror-stricken face as if she could sense it.

"My friends will come for me." I'd said it more for my benefit than any kind of threat toward her.

"No. They won't."

An itch formed in my throat.

"They have no idea where you are." Her laugher carried through the stone hallway, fading the further away she got.

My hands fell limp at my sides. Darkness blanketed the cell save for the ring on my finger which glowed like a stretched star. I sunk to the cold floor, staring at the white light. Closing my eyes, I thought of Erimon as if it'd make him appear in my cell and whisk me to safety.

I opened my eyes to the same emptiness. Alone.

Why was I surprised?

Pressing my skull against the stone behind me, I did the only thing I could...think.

Was I in a mirrored realm similar to where Crom had taken me? A place that's hidden by one form of magic from another?

A calm breeze fluttered through the cell from a crack in the shutter covering a small opening.

Whispers on the wind.

Scrambling to my feet, I raised to my toes, tilting my chin toward the window.

"Erimon," I whispered, letting the word float away in a phantom zephyr.

Now to wait—to hope by some warped twist of fate he heard me. Could tell where I was.

I backed up until my back hit the bars.

What a stupid notion. Whispering into the air? What was I thinking?

The cell door groaned. I whipped around, cocking a brow. Testing my theory, I pushed against the bars. *Creak.*

It'd make a hell of a lot of noise but...

I slammed my boot against the lock. *Groan.*

Gritting my teeth, I threw my shoulder and all my weight into it. The door flew open.

This had to be a setup.

I paused at the threshold, peering into darkness.

Screw it.

I reached in front of me, feeling through the hallway, my

fingertips brushing the walls' coarse texture.

"I'm curious as to what exactly you were plannin' on doin' in the pitch black of the halls once you were out of your cell?"

Aibell.

My blood froze. "I'd hoped to find you and club you over the head with a blunt object. You've saved me half the trouble."

Aibell snatched my hands with inhuman speed. I tried to pull away, but her grip tightened like a vice. Cold metal slid over my wrists, locking into place with a metallic *click*. Handcuffs.

"Did you call to him?" Her lips neared my ear, sending chills down my spine.

"Him?"

"Your Druid."

"Does it matter? You said no one could find me here." Whatever this thing had planned, I couldn't let her get the chance.

Aibell shoved me forward, raising the lit lantern between us. I flinched, squinting from the brightness, and she pointed a gnarled finger in front of me.

"Walk."

I shuffled forward. "Did you weaken the cell door?"

"The scent of hope melting into terror is quite appetizing."

I'd take that as a yes.

"Turn." She pointed at an ajar wooden door.

My knees wobbled, and I dug my heels into the ground, unmoving at the doorway before she pushed me into the room with one swift shove. Lit candles of different shapes, sizes, and colors rested atop stacks of books, pots, and jars. Some were mere piles of wax that burned themselves into the table. In the stone hearth in the back, a cauldron bubbled and smoked. A prickle shot down my neck.

Let's hope whatever brewed in that pot…wasn't meant for me.

My hands shook, making the cuffs clank together. They weren't modern cuffs. These were more like "irons"—something out of a pirate movie. If I tried hard enough, I might even be able to pull a hand free given the slack space.

Aibell dropped her face to mine, eyeing me staring at the smoke swirls floating from the cauldron. "Newt's eye and toad's tears, if you were curious."

Bile crept up my throat. I hadn't been. Not the least bit. "What are you?"

"A banshee. Sit." She motioned toward a chair near the boiling newt stew.

I sat, wrinkling my nose at the horrid stench wafting from the fireplace. *Did she say banshee?* The blood-curdling screams from earlier. Fear tugged at every beat of my heart, and I slid my hands between my knees, pinching them together to keep the irons quiet.

"Are you going to tell me why I'm here, or keep it a surprise?"

She dragged a hand over her red dress, not minding the dozens of black stains.

I tried to pry my hands free underneath the guise of the table but froze when the metal rattled.

"The Dullahan has marked you." She grabbed a large ladle, dipping it in the pot.

"I'm fully aware of that part by now. What I don't get is how *you* play into all this." I ran my finger over the obstacle stopping me from slipping my hand free—my thumb. I could dislocate it...no. There was no way I could keep from screaming.

"Your essence. I wish to consume it."

A breath burst from my lungs.

"The Dullahan doesn't seem like someone you want to piss off." Palms sweating, I pulled my wrist with all my strength as her back turned to me. Metal tore at my flesh, and I held back a wince.

"You think I care?" She snickered, stirring the liquid and dropping sprigs of something green into it.

She tossed a glance over her shoulder, and I pressed my hands together in my lap. "He won't be upset you stole his mark?"

"We are eternal enemies," she scoffed before turning back to her brew. "Besides, it won't matter."

My top lip beaded with sweat. "Why?"

"You'll be dead before the next full moon." She turned to face me, her lips curling with the devious tilt of a serpent.

My knee jerked, and I shifted my eyes to the fire roaring beneath the pot. "Is that what the brew is for?"

"Now you're catchin' on." She slapped the ladle on the table, spattering green liquid across the surface.

I ignored the drop landing on my cheek.

"I'll be eatin' your brain." She turned back to the pot, wafting it.

Once her back turned, I pulled furiously at the cuffs. "I must be worth more alive."

Except the small detail of everyone wanting to see me dead lately.

"I do not think so. I've never scented a magical essence like yours. I wonder where it came from." She leaned forward, sniffing my hair. "You're mortal after all."

"I'm a lucky, lucky girl."

"Tis a better fate for you over The Dullahan. I can promise ye that."

"You're so gracious." A fire poker rested near the cauldron.

Aibell dusted off her hands after stirring the pot one last time. "Now then, mustn't waste time." She moved toward me, blocking my path to the poker. I threw my knees up, knocking the table on its side, and kicked it at her. She grunted, curling forward, and I leaped to my feet.

Grabbing the poker, I pointed it at her. "My brain stays where it is."

Aibell cackled, resting her hands on her hips. "And what are you planning on doin' with that?"

I tightened my grip, focusing on the pointy end. Aibell had morphed into a floating figure of smoke. What would a poker do if she did it again?

She edged closer. A container of white dust rested on the counter near me. Hoping it was enough to impede her vision, I made a run for it. I grabbed it, popped the lid, and threw it all at her face.

Aibell cried out in agony, her hands trembling over her face. Was she…melting? As I ran for the door, the familiar scent of salt settled in the air, and I grabbed the lantern before stumbling into the hallway.

Left or right?

Relying on gut instincts, I sprinted to the right.

I ran as fast as my feet could carry me, glancing back on occasion to see if she followed. Guessing directions as I went, my chest heaved—searching, hoping to find a doorway to freedom. My heart fluttered with excitement, eyeing a sliver of light spilling into the hallway. A window. It'd be a tight squeeze, but it'd have to do.

I threw the lantern into the window, covering my eyes as glass shattered. The shackles clattered as I grabbed the window seal and climbed the wall. Shimmying myself through the opening, I grunted as my hips pushed against the sides and forced them through. I fell to the dirt outside with a groan, landing on my back. Dark clouds filled the sky from an approaching thunderstorm. A banshee's shrill scream pulsed through my ears, and I leaped up.

My lungs burned from the cold air as I ran into the woods, trying to ignore the scream getting closer. What possessed me to do what I did next, I couldn't say, but I dropped to the ground, pressing my fingers into the dirt. I thought his name over and over, willing it into the soil. The shrieks grew closer.

Just as the wailing loomed behind me, strong hands grasped my shoulders.

"Abby. I heard ye," Erimon said, pulling me to his chest.

Smoke from the banshee surrounded us, suffocating me. Erimon wrapped his arms around me, and we disappeared in a swirl of fog and embers.

I shoved my forehead against Erimon's chest, not daring to peek. My body trembled, both from the bitter cold and the surge of adrenaline.

"You're safe," Erimon said, his voice deep, rumbling through his chest.

I slowly lifted my head, clenching my jaw to keep it from shaking.

"Are ye alright?" With a single finger, he lifted my chin to look at him.

I nodded, forcing back threatening tears. "The dagger—I lost it. I—" I reached for the empty holster on my back, and he took my shackled hands into his.

"I'll make you another one." He traced his fingers over my knuckles, keeping our gazes locked. "Do you want these off?" He made the cuffs jangle. "Or is that something you're into?" He half-smiled, making me laugh despite my near brink of death.

He trailed his fingertips over the metal, making the shackles disintegrate, settling back to the earth from where they came. I rubbed the sores on my wrists—reminders of my failed attempts to free myself.

He turned my palms face up and swirled his hands, conjuring metal and wood, twisting it together until an identical seax rested in my hands. Curling a hand around the back of my neck, he brushed an escaped tear from my cheek with his thumb.

"How did you get away from a banshee?"

I winced, recalling the fear that'd consumed me almost to the point of paralysis—a terror that could've cost me my life. "A fire poker and salt." There'd been more to the story—her desire to consume my essence, to steal it from The Dullahan. But I couldn't manage the words. I pushed my finger against the sharp edge of the blade, wincing as it pricked me but didn't draw blood.

"Did you know salt was one of their weaknesses?"

I shook my head. "No. But that'd explain her face melting." My eyes fell to the wooden hilt, the Celtic pommel with more intricate designs than the last. "Did you hear me call your name?"

His face softened. "On the wind? Yes. I couldn't tell where you were, though."

I scraped my nail down the blade. "And the ground?"

"It pulled me straight to you."

I lifted my gaze to meet his, my insides folding, twisting, writhing.

"I think you're more warrior than you realize." He slipped a piece of hair over my ear.

"Staring death in the face can put a lot in perspective."

"You'd be surprised how many would still cower if they were in your position."

I looked behind me at Patrick's house. "Why are we here?"

"I need to get in touch with a few old friends. To ask their help in fightin' Dullahan. Even with the Chaun's help, it won't be enough. He grows stronger, and he's not the only one after ye now."

"And why are we in front of Patrick's house?"

Erimon squinted at the sky. "I'm going to ask him to take you underground with the Chauns."

My heart fell to my feet. "I don't understand. As long as Phoebe is with me, I'd be fine."

He chewed on his lip. "She's a part of our world now, Abby."

Dizziness washed over me.

"It'll be harder for anyone to track you there."

My eyes searched the ground, trying to piece it all together. "Why not leave me there then?"

"You can't stay for long as a mortal, but it'll be long enough for me to rally the troops. Understand?"

My heart pounded in my ears with an echoing ache. "You're leaving me?"

He scowled. "Never. I made you a promise, and I've every intention of keepin' it. Ye hear me?"

"What if something happens? What if we're attacked?" I flailed my arms, my breathing turning into gasping. "How will you know? How—"

He snatched my arms and held my right hand to my face. "The ring." He dragged a finger over it, making it shimmer. "It's not just a reminder of our deal."

"Then what is it?"

His nostril bounced. "It tracks you. I know where you are at all times. Except realms created by dark magic…which are rare."

I yanked my hands away, heat flooding my face. "You've been tracking me this entire time? You lied."

"Yeah. I lied. Would you have willingly put it on then? Hm?" He threw his arms out at his sides, raising his brow.

I slapped my hands over my face.

"My apologies I couldn't tell it only to track ye when you're in trouble." Bitterness laced his tone.

I hugged my elbows to my sides. "I overacted. I—"

He turned me to face him, running his hands up and down my arms. "You have every bleedin' right to be pissed.

You've been dealt a shitty hand. But know I'm not leavin' you. Alright?"

I nodded, sniffling.

"Now, I need to convince a Chaun to have a forced family reunion."

"Forced?"

He pressed his hand to the small of my back, leading me toward the front door. "Fortunately, there's the excuse of his new bride."

The ring. Patrick and Phoebe. The kelpie. He had every rock turned over before knowing it needed to be turned.

A light pressure pushed in my back pocket. I slipped a hand in, my fingertips grazing a coin. How did that get in there?

16

I TURNED FOR THE DOOR but Erimon caught my hand, pulling me back.

He squinted at the ground.

"What is it?" I tried to ignore how calming it was to have our skin touch.

"How did you do what you did?"

I gripped his hand tighter. "Do what?"

His eyes lifted, and he crouched, bringing me with him. "You know what I mean." He patted the dirt.

The smell of the soil seeped into my pores. It was as if I could sense every creature that'd stepped on it. "I don't know."

"Do it again." He took my hand in his and rested my palm on the ground.

My heart raced. "Erimon, I'm serious. I have no idea how or what I did."

His brow furrowed. "You did it once. You can do it again. Try." His voice was gruff as he pointed at my hand.

Gulping, I closed my eyes and thought his name, but the

same sensations didn't swirl inside me like before.

"I can't."

"Again. Try," Erimon barked.

I opened my eyes and balled my hands into fists. "I told you I couldn't," I yelled, rising to my feet.

Erimon stood, his nostrils flaring, opening his mouth to speak.

"Abby," Phoebe cried out from the woods with Patrick trailing behind her.

Phoebe threw her arms around me, hugging me tightly. I embraced her but eyed Erimon over her shoulder. He glared at the ground while rubbing his chin.

"I was so worried about you. Where have you been the past three days?"

"*Three* days? I've been gone that long?" It'd felt like hours.

Phoebe pressed her palm to my forehead and then my cheeks.

"Chaun, we need to talk," Erimon scoffed, his cheek twitching.

"Charmed to see you too, Druid. Care to go inside?" Patrick took Phoebe's hand and led us into the house.

Erimon kept his back to us as he rubbed his neck. After twirling his rings, he whirled around. "I need—" His lip curled in a snarl. "—a favor."

Patrick leaned back in a chair, clasping his hands behind his head. "Oh, do you now?"

"A *returned* favor," Erimon said through gritted teeth, motioning between Patrick and Phoebe.

"What be the favor?" Patrick wrapped an arm around

Phoebe's shoulder as she sat next to him.

"Abby." Erimon's lip bounced.

"The Dullahan, I know," Patrick said.

"She was kidnapped by a banshee. I'd been tryin' to contact her, find her, and wherever the banshee took her, blocked the signal."

Patrick's face fell, and he slipped his arm from behind Phoebe's chair, slowly rising to his feet. "A banshee? Bleedin' hell, Abby, are you alright?"

"I escaped." I offered a weak smile in Erimon's direction, but he wasn't looking at me.

"With The Dullahan's power growin' as it nears the hunt, and more than one interested party in Abby, we're going to need all the help we can get." Erimon scraped a hand through his hair.

"What's the favor, Erimon?" Patrick frowned at me.

Erimon stared at the ground before blowing out a harsh breath. "I want you to take Abby underground. It will be harder for The Dullahan or anythin' else to track her there."

"Underground? You mean with the Chauns?" Patrick asked.

"O'course, I mean with the Chauns. What else would I mean?"

"I've—I've never taken a human underground." Patrick rubbed his earlobe.

"You know as well as I do, I wouldn't be askin' you if it weren't important." Erimon gazed at Patrick with an intensity that could trigger a volcanic eruption.

"I know." Patrick played with the seam of his pants.

"It'll give me time to round up some old friends. And I need to know she's safe." Erimon rolled his shoulders, and a wicked grin pulled at his lips. "Besides, don't you want to introduce Papa Chaun to your new blushin' bride?"

"I could meet your father?" Phoebe jumped to her feet.

"The *entire* family is down there."

"That's great." Phoebe cocked her head to the side when Patrick kept silent. "Isn't it?"

"It's a whole other world," Patrick mumbled.

"I think you can manage, Patty. Or have you become even more of a wuss in your old age?" Erimon folded his arms.

"I'll take her, but consider my debt paid."

Erimon widened his stance. "Far from it. It's a *start*."

Patrick furiously rubbed the stubble on his chin. "Fine."

Erimon gently grabbed my elbow and pulled me aside. "While I'm gone, I want you to keep tryin' until you can do it again."

"Why is this so important to you?" I searched his face but it revealed nothing.

"Abby…" His eyes formed a harsh squint.

The ferocity in his stare had me reeling. "Alright."

"I'll be back as soon as I can." He took my hand and brushed his thumb over the ring. Turning away, he pointed at Patrick. "If anything happens to her, I'll beat your face green."

When Erimon vanished into thin air, it was like a piece of me disappeared with him—a hole in my chest. I stood staring numbly at the floor.

Phoebe's arms wrapped around me from behind, and her chin rested on my shoulder. "I'm glad you're okay. Not sure what I'd do without you."

I patted her arm.

Patrick moved in front of me. "May I have that coin back?"

"Were you the one who made another coin appear in my pocket?"

He cleared his throat. "Yes. If the other Chauns knew I'd lent out a piece of my treasure, they'd have my hide." He held his hand out.

Slipping the coin from my pocket, I tossed it to him.

He yelped and fumbled with it, curling it into his palm and making it disappear. "Right then. This way, ladies."

He led us outside to the woods. How did one enter the underground world of the leprechauns? Did a rainbow need to be present? Did you have to click your heels together three times? Patrick moved from tree to tree, pressing his ear against the trunks. Occasionally, he'd tap one with his knuckles, frown, and move onto the next.

He stepped to one, knocked on it, and grinned. "Found it."

"What are you looking for?" Phoebe asked, watching her new husband drop to his knees on the ground.

He parted a cluster of plants. "Ah-ha," he said, plucking something from the ground.

"Well, my dear wife, I was looking for the gateway, and this." He held a green plant.

I squinted at it. "A four-leaf clover? I don't think I've ever seen one in person."

"They're hard to find. If they were easy, humans would be that much closer to findin' us." He turned toward the tree, pressing the clover into it.

A door with a small handle formed in the trunk. The clover

disintegrated into shimmering flecks of gold dust, floating into the wind. The door creaked open, revealing nothing but darkness.

"Ladies first," Patrick said, holding his hand out to Phoebe.

Phoebe paused at the doorway with a sparkling grin. "I feel like I'm in a Disney movie."

As soon as she stepped in, she disappeared.

I lurched forward, grabbing the tree's bark. "What the hell just happened, Patrick?"

"It's a portal. She's underground perfectly fine, I promise."

Darkness. After my banshee experience, peering into it made me queasy. Every time I tried to step forward, my palms clammed up, and I froze.

Patrick touched my arm, making me jump. "I have to go last, Abby. I need to seal off the door behind us."

I nodded and tried to step forward again, fear tugging at my spine, pulling me back. Phoebe. She was alone down there. I pinched my eyes shut and hurled myself into the hole. The sound of water trickling over stone and dripping to the ground filled my ears. A cave.

"Phoebe?"

"Abby, come look."

A dim light glowed around the corner and grew brighter the closer I got, following Phoebe's voice.

She stood in front of a wooden door with swirling Celtic patterns.

"You found a door," I said, deadpan.

"Don't you hear it?"

Muffled sounds of fiddles and people chattering floated

through the wood.

"You ready to go inside?" Patrick's voice asked behind us. He held his arm out for Phoebe to wrap hers around, and she bounced on the balls of her feet.

As Patrick pushed open the door, the jovial sounds of Irish music—flutes, fiddles, and bagpipes boomed. The room looked like the base root of a tree—it was something out of a fairytale. A wide giant, gnarled root twisted from the floor to the ceiling in the center with a wooden bench circling it. Branches and over-sized leaves hung above like a woodland canopy. Lights peeked through the foliage casting cozy shadows and dim lighting. Emerald-colored grass skirted the floor, making every step soft and bouncy. I wanted to go barefoot and feel it against my skin.

Most patrons looked like usual, human Irishmen, like Patrick, but some looked far more like how I'd imagined a leprechaun. A man scuttled in front of me—four feet tall, bright red hair and beard, cradling a mug of ale as large as his head in each of his smallish hands. I tapped Patrick on the shoulder, pointing at the small man passing by.

"I didn't say *none* of us looked that way." Patrick shrugged.

As we neared the center, the music came to a screeching halt. All eyes turned to us, and I tensed.

"Patty?" a man's voice said from behind us.

A tall man with dark hair highlighted by gray stood slack-jawed. His silver beard hung to the middle of his chest. He wore brown, tweed trousers, a cream-colored, long-sleeve shirt, and red suspenders.

"Da," Patrick said.

"What—what are you doin' here, son? It's been," his father started, counting on his fingers, minus his thumb that clutched the mug in his palm. He ran out of fingers and frowned.

"A hundred years," Patrick finished for him with a heavy sigh.

Phoebe slapped Patrick on the shoulder. "You haven't seen your family in a hundred years? I thought my two years was bad."

"Who is this?" Patrick's father asked, eyeing Phoebe curiously.

"Da, this is my, ehm, well, she's my wife, Phoebe."

"Your what?" His father cupped a hand over his ear.

"My wife," Patrick shouted.

Whispers spread throughout the leprechauns, and I hid behind Phoebe, lowering myself to her level.

Phoebe thrust her hand at Patrick's dad. "It is a pleasure to meet you, sir."

His father's forehead wrinkled, eyeing her from head to toe before he took her hand into his, giving it a hearty shake. "Bah. Call me Da. Sir makes me sound old. That be quite the oath you took for my son. You're aware?"

"I'm aware. It was worth it," she said, her voice steady and confident.

Da smiled before turning to Patrick. "What troll did you convince to do the ritual?"

Patrick's gaze fell to his shoes, and Phoebe interlaced her arm within his. "It was a Druid."

Da slowly raised a brow, his eye twitching.

"He convinced the Druid, sir. You should've seen your son.

The Druid couldn't resist Patrick's charm." I could see Patrick smiling at me from the corner of my eye.

"And who are you?" Da asked.

"Abby. I'm a friend of Phoebe's. She wanted me to tag along for her first trip underground. I hope you don't mind." I pressed a hand over my chest.

Da's smile broadened as he shook my hand. "The more, the merrier. This be a time of celebration. Why are you all standin' around like dopes? Pour more ale, strike up that music. My son is married." He threw his hands into the air, the ale in his mug sloshing over the edges.

With his father's back turned, Patrick mouthed the words, thank you, to me, and I bowed my head. Several men and a shorter woman with red hair brighter than Phoebe's clamored up to the newlyweds. Within moments, they were both airborne atop the shoulders of several leprechauns. Phoebe shrieked as they were whisked away toward a table in the corner.

"Abby," Phoebe shouted through a giggle.

I dismissed it with a flick of my hand, smiling at her. "You two go have fun. I'll be at the bar." I waved at her. "Indefinitely," I muttered to myself, making my way to the most extensive bar I'd ever seen in my life. Nearly every type of whiskey known to man must've been bottled and on display. A smoothed flattened tree served as the bartop. There were so many beer taps I couldn't begin to count them. The stools were soft, squishy, and shaped like over-sized mushrooms—white with red polka dots, in the style of Alice in Wonderland.

The bartender, a stocky leprechaun with wire-rimmed glasses pushed to the tip of his nose, and thinning snowy white hair, wiped a glass mug with a rag. "What'll it be, miss?"

"Guinness, please." Patrick and Phoebe now sat on two wooden thrones, smiling and laughing. While I watched them, my Guinness slid across the bar top, perfectly poured.

The bartender winked at me and walked away, cleaning that same mug with a rag. I lifted the pint to my lips, taking a long, hard swallow. So. Fresh.

"You handlin' that pint like a champ," a voice near me said.

I looked to my left and then to my right. There was a light tug on my jacket sleeve, and I turned to look down at the source—two feet tall, wrinkled beyond compare, bald, save for a few random hairs atop his head, and a scraggly beard on his chin falling to his ankles. He grinned, revealing only one tooth with blackened edges. He wore dark green and yellow striped pants and a dirtied yellow shirt that looked like it had been white at some point.

I tapped the side of my pint glass and brought it to my lips, finishing it. With my cheeks full of Irish stout, I motioned the bartender for another. Before I could blink, another pint appeared in front of me. The bartender hadn't moved. Just kept cleaning that same mug, with the same smirk on his face. I eyed the glass, poking the brown liquid to make sure it was real.

Erimon couldn't get back fast enough.

17

"SO, LET ME GET THIS straight. Leprechauns *don't* hide a pot of gold at the end of a rainbow?" I asked Angus, the small leprechaun to my right. I'd been apprehensive about his company at first, but after a few exchanged pleasantries and several pints, he wasn't half bad.

"Nah. That'd be far too easy. We use rainbows to trace where we hide our stashes, but as a rule, you never put it at the end." Angus said, sliding the large mug between his small hands. He stood on his stool and plopped a green swirly straw into it.

"Huh. All I thought I knew, and I really knew nothing at all." My words began to slur, and I squinted over the rim of my mug at an elated Phoebe. They put a veil on her and threw flower petals as men twirled her in a chair. She held a mug of ale in her hand, laughing.

"What's the point of all this?" I asked Angus, waving my hand at the antics behind us.

"A wedding celebration only happens once every thousand years down here. They're pullin' out all the stops." He slurped through his straw.

"Thousand years? Why?"

"How many people do you know would be willin' to sacrifice themselves for an eternity? Even in the afterlife, those two will still be tied together." He stuck his bottom lip out. "No, sir. Even with the promise of remainin' on the surface forever, I'd never want to be tied to someone like that."

I looked down at the Claddagh ring resting on my finger. Thinning my lips, I balled my hand into a fist, shoving it out of sight. She barely knew Patrick and did it for the sake of a friend. For *my* sake. Would I have done the same?

"You would have," Angus said, puckering his lips on his straw.

My gaze dropped to the top of his head. "Excuse me?"

"You're wonderin', with the Druid, if you would have done the same for your friend, as she did for you. I'm tellin' you that you would have." The air whistled through his two teeth while he spoke.

"I never said—" I flattened my hands on the bar.

"Have you told him?"

"I'm not having this conversation with you, Angus." I shoved my nose in my mug, the conversation instantly sobering.

"I'll take that as a no."

I turned to face him. "How did you—" Pausing, I beat my fist against the edge of the bar. "Saying I feel *something* for him. How could you possibly know?"

"Providence." He fished for the straw with his mouth, keeping his eyes on me and missing the straw several times before claiming it.

I chuckled and shook my head. "No. Destinies aren't real."

"Says the woman surrounded by leprechauns wearing a magical ring given to her by a warrior Druid." He raised his bushy brows.

I sat upright as my cheeks flushed. "No. He just happened to be at the same pub."

"I know Ireland be an island, but it's not *that* small."

My breathing shallowed. "Angus, it's been grand chatting with you, but I think I'm going to stretch my legs."

Scooping my mug, I headed for the bench at the center tree.

"Ye can't outrun it, Abigail." Angus said to my back.

Maybe not, but I could sure as hell run away from this conversation.

Picking up the pace, I made it to the tree and plopped to the bench with a sigh.

Phoebe perched next to me, her veil resting crooked on her head. I rubbed the white lace between two fingers. "This is nice," I said with a soft voice.

"This celebration is insane. They had me play this game where they carted me around on a chair and gave me a full mug of ale. I had to keep it from spilling, or every one of them got to slap my butt." She sounded out of breath with a thin line of sweat beading over her brow.

"How sore is your ass?"

"What? You think I didn't do it?"

I raised a brow.

"My left cheek is pretty sore." She giggled and scooted closer, curling her arm through mine, and resting her head on my shoulder.

Patrick stood at a table with one hand tied behind his back and twelve mugs of ale lined up in front of him.

"Is the point of this game for Patrick to not pass out?" I asked.

"It takes a lot to get a Chaun drunk, apparently."

"That would explain the neverending, magical drink pours," I spoke into my half-empty mug.

Phoebe lifted her head and squinted one eye. "What's wrong, Abby?"

"Wrong? Nothing. I'm sitting here, drinking, and enjoying the festivities."

"Uh-huh. I've known you for twenty years. Do you really think I don't know when you're lying?" She scanned me like a detective interrogating a suspect in one of those old noir movies.

I blocked my face with my mug, taking a long swig. When I lowered the glass, her face was in front of mine.

"You miss him."

I groaned, letting my head flop against the tree root behind me. "Come on, Phoebe."

Phoebe gasped. "You do." She pointed at me, almost poking my eye.

"My life has been threatened several times. I somehow managed to escape a banshee, and Erimon has been there every time. It's not so much missing him as it is an uneasiness that he's not here."

"You don't want to talk about it. Got it." She patted her hands on her thighs as she looked around, whistling.

Whenever Phoebe did that, she hoped the silence would pry

the words from someone. I wasn't falling for it.

"To think all this time I'd been teasing you about setting you up with a leprechaun, and I end up marrying one, huh?"

Patrick downed the last mug in front of him, soaking his shirt as the ale drizzled down his chin. He threw his fists in the air, and the surrounding men gave him hearty slaps on the back, including his father.

"As crazy as I still think you are for marrying a guy you've only known for a week, I think he's one of the good ones, Phoebs."

"Why do you think my decision was so easy?"

Scanning the room of dancing drunken leprechauns, I rubbed my ring. "Do you believe in destiny?"

"Absolutely."

I snapped my head to her. "Why?"

"Everything happens for a reason. My mom used to say, 'A lesson or a blessing.'" She patted my knee. "And honestly? I find life steers us in the direction we most try to avoid."

I sucked on my bottom lip and shifted my gaze to Angus at the bar. He held his mug up with a toothy grin, and I looked away.

Patrick trotted over, running one of his arms over his mouth to mop up excess beer.

"Come on, ladies, stop bein' anti-social." He grabbed both of our hands, hoisting us from the bench.

Patrick pulled us over to a group of men who were chatting, laughing, and grabbing onto each other's shoulders.

"I want you to meet the rest of my family. This is uncle Bartley." He pointed to a man with black hair, a nose as wide as his face, and ears that stuck out like Dumbo.

"Cousin Danny." A portly miniature man with a handlebar mustache and hands larger than my head.

"Charmed," he said, his voice so high-pitched it sounded as if he inhaled helium before speaking. I tried to keep my eyes from visibly widening.

"And finally, my other uncle, Steve," Patrick finished, as a man the same age as Patrick stepped forward, bowing with a flourish. He had dusty blonde hair, bright green eyes, and a smile so intense it could shatter a lightbulb. Steve took my right hand, eyeing the Claddagh ring before placing a kiss on my knuckles.

I stiffened, yanking my hand away.

Patrick pulled Steve aside. "Um, Uncle, I think she's taken." He glanced over his shoulder at me, waving.

Steve pointed at my hand. "No, she's not." He puffed his chest as he made his way back to me, peering in my empty mug and yanking it from my fingers. "Let me freshen that up for ye."

I let him take the mug, and raised a brow at Patrick. "Care to explain why I'm supposedly taken?"

Patrick rubbed his cheek. "My uncle is a right fellow but not someone you want to get wrapped up with romantically. If you get my drift?"

Phoebe nudged me. "Pretend. Shouldn't be too hard."

I glared at her, and she flashed a bright smile.

Steve returned with a full mug, handing it to me while unabashedly taking a peek at my boobs.

"Thank you. Listen. I *am* taken. I'm new to the whole Ireland thing and must've put it on the wrong way this morning. Had no idea the heart's direction was so telling." I snort laughed.

"That's a downright shame, dearie. Haven't seen a beauty such as you in centuries." He let his eyes roam over my body.

Centuries?

I rubbed the back of my neck, discomfort prickling my skin. "You're too kind." And ducked my nose into my mug.

Phoebe wrapped her arm around mine, luring me away. "Come on, Abby. Patrick promised to show us some of his powers. Didn't you, Patrick?"

"I did?" he asked, raising an eyebrow.

Phoebe widened her eyes at him.

"Right. I did." He waved at his family before joining us across the room.

"What can you do, Patrick? Aside from finding four-leaf clovers and stealing gold?" I surveyed him as if his clothes had the answer.

Patrick showed me his empty hand, then reached forward, flicking his fingers behind my ear. When he pulled his hand back, he held a gold coin.

Phoebe clapped her hands excitedly. I, on the other hand, remained stoic, giving him an unimpressed stare. "That's not magic. It's a trick. You hide it in your sleeve."

Patrick frowned, palming the coin. He opened his fist to reveal the coin had disappeared, wriggling his fingers. Phoebe clapped again, gasping.

I didn't blink. "Back into your shirtsleeve."

Patrick puckered his lips. He peeled back his sleeve and shook his arm. Several gold coins fell to the floor, followed by hundreds more. My jaw dropped, watching Patrick make it rain treasure from his sleeve, the coins pooling at our feet.

"Where's all this coming from?" I asked.

"It's part of my stash. I can call on it whenever I please." He beamed, pinching his sleeve shut and stopping the coins.

Phoebe brushed the coins with her foot. "I wish we could see your entire treasure."

Patrick's mouth twitched, his body bending forward in a bow. "Your wish is my command, wife." He twisted his hand in the air, and we appeared in a cavern.

Phoebe threw her hands out at her sides. "What just happened?"

"You wished to see my treasure. I am duty-bound to oblige you three wishes a year, remember?"

"But I—I didn't mean it literally. I'd hate to think I wasted a wish," she said, pouting.

I walked further into the cavern and nearly dropped my mug when I rounded the corner. It expanded to the size of a football field, and there were so many coins one could swim in them.

"I don't know, Phoebe. This is pretty impressive," I called out to her, staring at the sea of gold in front of me.

Phoebe gasped behind me. "There must be millions of coins here!"

"More like billions, but I've honestly lost count. This is thousands of years worth of collecting." Patrick looked at his treasure like a doting father and sunk to his knees, running his fingers through the coins, clinking them together.

"Can I?" Phoebe asked, pointing at the treasure.

"Be my guest. You did wish to see it, didn't you?"

Her smile stretched, and she dove into the sea of coins, letting her arms drag through them. I sipped from my mug, watching her play like a kid in a ball pit.

"So, you teleport too, hm?" I asked.

"Not like Erimon. I can only port to my stash." His serene eyes never left Phoebe.

I watched his expression as he peered at my best friend. "You truly care about her, huh?"

Patrick smiled to himself, nodding. "I do. It was a brave thing she did. Made me fall for her even harder." Phoebe threw a pile of coins in the air and winced, blocking her head from getting hit by them.

"Good, because I'd hate to have to figure out a way to kill you." I drank from my mug with both hands.

"Is Erimon rubbing off on ye?" He chuckled.

The question made my stomach flutter, my mind dipping into treacherous territory.

Phoebe emerged from the coins, out of breath. "Patrick, I was thinking. I have two more wishes, right? Why don't I wish for Abby's safety? You know? Keep her alive?"

Patrick shook his head. "It doesn't work like that. There are rules to wishin'."

"What rules?" I tapped a nail against my mug.

"For starters, you can't wish someone falls in love with you—no messin' with free will. You can't wish someone back from the dead, and you can't play with fate. The Dullahan has chosen Abby. To wish her safety would be meddlin' with forces you shouldn't meddle with." His gaze fell to the ground.

"So, basically, I'm screwed," I snorted into my mug, holding back a burp.

Phoebe gave me a side hug.

Patrick tossed a coin in his palm. "We'll beat him. If you don't believe me, believe the Druid. We can't wish a change in fate but we can sure as hell fight to change it."

I stared into the daunting abyss that was my empty mug. "Can we go back? I'm feeling tired." I turned from them both, walking away from the glittering treasure.

I blinked, and we were back amidst the celebrating leprechauns. A hand touched my arm.

"You sure you don't want to stay up a little longer? Who knows when we'll be in an underground leprechaun lair again," Phoebe said.

"I'm exhausted, Phoebs. You have fun. Tell me all about it in the morning." I patted her hand, spotting Patrick waving me over to a wooden door.

It was a small room with a simple cot, fireplace, a nightstand with a kerosene lamp, and a bookshelf.

"This is a little hidey-hole I come to every once in a while. You're more than welcome to use it for sleepin'."

"Thank you. For everything."

He nodded before closing the door behind him.

I moved to the small rounded window and pushed it open enough to let a breeze flow through the room.

Laying down, I took a deep breath, and rested my hands on my stomach. The wind played through my hair, and I remembered Erimon's plea for me to try and contact him again. Letting my body relax, I concentrated on my toes melting into the sheets, followed by my knees, my hips, continuing my way up until I was a shimmering pool of calm. As another gust surged through the room, I whispered his name into it, letting it carry my voice away.

Ah. You did it. Good girl.

"Don't call me that."

Don't call you what? Good?

I could imagine his snarky grin.

"I still don't know how I'm doing this."

I have my theories.

"I can tell you where to shove those theories considering you won't tell me."

Nothin' good ever comes from impatience.

Erimon's voice soothed into my ear like warm velvet.

The wind wafted over my body, making my nipples pucker.

I'll be back soon.

My back arched as the breeze swirled over my stomach.

"Why rush?"

I wouldn't want to keep ye waiting too long considerin' your distaste with patience.

The wind fluttered over my thighs.

Admit it. You miss me.

As the breeze brushed lower between my legs, my eyes flew open, and I sat up with a gasp. His voice fluttered away, taking the draft with it. I dragged a finger between my breasts and shuddered.

Storming from the bed with a snarl, I slammed the window shut, and locked it.

18

KNOCK. KNOCK. KNOCK.

"Abby?" Patrick's calm voice spoke through the door.

My eyes flittered open, vision blurry. Sitting up, I rubbed my eyes with my palms, working through a brain fog. Still in Patrick's hidey-hole with the sun beaming through the small window. The wind. Erimon. I yanked the sheet over my chest like I was naked as the door creaked open, and Patrick's face appeared in the crack.

"Abby?" Patrick repeated.

The breeze last night had felt like silken fingertips. How'd he even do it? I trailed a hand over my collarbone, staring at the window.

"You alright? You looked like you seen a ghost." Patrick let himself in.

I dragged my hands down my face, one finger catching on my lip. "Something like that."

"How'd you sleep?"

"Like the dead." I winced. "Poor choice of words."

He slipped one hand in his pocket and rubbed his neck with the other. "Da made breakfast, and everyone's hangin' out in the dining room. Thought you'd like to join us?"

I smiled and crawled out of bed. "I'd love to. Let me just freshen up. Where's the uh—the dining room?"

"Oh, you can't miss it."

I blinked. "Why's that?"

"You'll see." He winked at me as he turned away and patted the doorframe.

"Oh, hey. Real quick."

He spun back around with raised brows.

"Can you read minds, Patrick?"

"No." He cocked his head to the side. "Why?"

Little meddling Angus had unique talents, it would seem.

"Nothing. Nevermind." I snickered and waved him off.

After scrunching his face at me, he left.

I washed up the best I could with hand soap and water from a sink, popped a mint in my mouth, and moved to the hallway.

Many of the leprechauns from the night before remained on the main floor, draped over chairs, and tables, while others lay sprawled on the floor, snoring. An area once bursting with life now as quiet and calm as the grave.

I really had to stop with the deathly analogies.

"If I were a dining room, where would I be?" I whispered to myself, taking a step over the grassy floor.

A patch of white peonies sprouted in front of my foot. Raising a brow, I took a step forward, and more flowers bloomed. With each step I took, another group would sprout, leading me to an open doorway with a long table.

Phoebe, Patrick, Da, Steve, Danny, and Bartley scattered the chairs with giant wooden mugs resting on the table in front of them. Plates filled the center piled high with various breakfast foods, and a huge bowl of porridge, leaking down the sides, was on one end.

"Abby, you're finally up," Phoebe chimed as she leaped from her seat to hug me.

I hugged her back but watched the leprechaun men over her shoulder.

"I have *never* passed out drunk," Bartley said.

Da slapped him in the chest. "O'course, that's a lie, you oaf. You were on the surface just last week passed out in that pig farm. Pissed your pants even."

"You were always horse shite at this game, Bart," Patrick said with a chuckle, scooping a pastry into his hand and taking a bite.

I tapped my fingers on my hips. "Are you all playing Two Truths and a Lie?"

"Heh?" Danny asked as all Chauns gave perplexed expressions to each other.

"It's Truth or Lie. Simple as Pie," Da said, clapping his hands together.

I quirked a brow and took an empty seat, sliding an empty plate in front of me and discreetly shoveling eggs and bacon on it.

"Mornin' grog?" Steve asked with a smile that bordered on mischievous and genuine, holding a clay pitcher in front of me, hovering it over an empty wooden mug.

I choked on some eggs.

Phoebe leaped up and smacked my back. "Do you require the Heimlich?"

Shaking my head, I motioned with my hand for whatever was in that pitcher.

Steve's grin widened as he poured the milky-orange liquid into my glass.

After he stopped, I snatched it with both hands and took a long swig. The drink was sweet and citrusy but laced heavily with alcohol. "Wow. You all start early, huh?"

"How else are you goin' to drink all day?" Danny wiggled his eyebrows and elbowed Bartley in the ribs, his high-pitched voice still inciting a giggle I held back.

"Phoebe, my dear new daughter, why don't you try next?" Da held his hand out to her.

She shoved some food to the side of her mouth and covered her lips with the back of her hand. "Oh, sure. Let me think." She squinted, swallowed, and slapped her hands on the table. "I have a lower back tattoo of Little Mermaid."

"Well, that's not fair." Bartley frowned. "Patty already knows that one." His large ears twitched.

"Oh, pipe down and play. I'm sure Abby knows all there is to know about her too." Da winked at me and rubbed his chin. "I'm goin' to say—"

Phoebe sat straighter, flashing a wide smile.

She did have a lower back tattoo, but it wasn't Little Mermaid. It was the word "dearg." Gaelic for "red."

"Truth," Da answered.

The rest shouted their guesses, with only Steve answering it as a lie.

Phoebe tapped her fingers on the table like a drumroll. "Steve's right. It's a lie."

"Wonderful deception, wife." Patrick kissed her cheek.

Danny stood on his chair to be the same height as the rest of us when we were seated. "I'll go next." He adjusted an imaginary tie. "I took ballet lessons last year to become more athletic."

He'd told the truth or lie as if reciting poetry, and I shoved bacon in my mouth to keep from laughing.

"Abby?" Da raised his brows.

After licking my lips, I tapped my lips with a finger. "I'll say, truth. You are rather spry, Danny."

He tugged on the hem of his jacket, standing straighter. "Here that gents? Me. Spry." He licked his pinky fingers and swiped them across his brows before dragging them down both sides of his long mustache.

"That's a damn lie if I ever heard of one." Bartley rubbed Danny's rounded belly.

Danny batted him away and cleared his throat. "I'll have ye all know, it's the truth. I took one lesson and then decided tights…are not ideal."

I thrust my fists into the air with a wide grin.

"Ah-ha. One point for Abby." Da clapped his hands.

"You're up, Steve." Patrick threw a pastry at him.

Steve let it hit him in the chest and shook his head. His eyes took a hooded gaze and he looked at me from across the table. "I've never had a brunette."

"Had one what?" Phoebe asked, looking around the table for an answer.

Quickly grabbing a roll, I started to break small pieces from it and popped them into my mouth one-by-one.

"That has to be a lie with how long you've been around, surely," Da said with a chuckle that faded when no one else laughed.

Steve traced his finger around a warp on the table, staring at me. "It's true. I haven't."

Patrick kicked Steve under the table, making it bounce. "There are plenty of them on the surface. I'll be sure to show ye next time your due for a visit."

"You do that," Steve said with a grimace, nonchalantly reaching under the table to rub his knee.

I kept my focus on the bread in my hand, the taste of it in my mouth—grainy with a slight hint of vanilla.

"Abby, care to go next?" Bartley asked, sticking his wide nose into his mug as he took a sip.

My throat dried, trying to think of something true as of late. The Claddagh ring glinted on my finger as it caught the overhead sconces.

"I uh…"

Erimon's voice as it carried through the wind last night played in my head as if it were happening again right here, right now.

Admit it. You miss me.

"I've never been in love," I said, my voice wispy and distant.

The room went silent.

I clenched my hand into a fist.

"True," Danny yelled. "True, true, I tell ye."

Pinching my eyes shut, I pushed my chair back and stormed

for the exit.

Someone's hand slapped Danny's chest. "Read the room, will ye?"

Feet fluttered after me. "Abby, wait," Phoebe said.

After I made it to the hallway, I leaned against the nearest wall and dropped my face in my hands.

Phoebe slowly curled them away to reveal her inviting smile and kind green eyes peering up at me. "What's going on?"

"I can't, Phoebe."

"Can't what?"

I folded my arms in a huff. "I don't get swept up in things like this. There's no way I could possibly be in love with someone this soon. It's *absurd*."

Phoebe slid back, her hands going stiff at her sides.

Shit.

"Phoebe, no I—" I reached out.

"No, no. The truth finally comes out, huh? I'm absurd."

Shit. Shit. Shitty shit.

"You're not. I am."

This wasn't getting any better.

"If you think you're crazy for falling for someone so fast, then what's the difference if it's you or someone else?" Her bottom lip trembled, and her eyes glossed over.

"Phoebe, no. You've always been more carefree than me, more spontaneous. I'm not wired this way. I have a hard time believing what I feel is real." I took a tentative step forward, testing the waters.

"You're not saying it because you know it'd hurt my feelings. Newsflash: It has." She turned her back on me with a sniffle.

"Hey, ladies." Patrick walked out, fumbling with a pager in his hand. "Our illustrious leader has summoned Team Druid to my house. Seems he's rounded up the rest of the crew."

Phoebe whipped back around, and I could feel her staring at me.

My knees buckled, making me stumble back a step, and a small smile tugged at the corner of my lips which I tried to hide by combing my hair with my fingers.

"Ah-ha." Phoebe snapped her fingers at me with a bright smile. "You're forgiven."

My mouth formed an "o," and I squinted at her, then I snapped my head to Patrick. "He gave you a pager?"

"Did he not give you one?" His brows shot up.

No. I guess we had…other means of communication.

Patrick's face lit up, peering into the main room at the center tree. "Oh, oh, oh. Before we leave, you both *have* to see this." He latched his arms around both of ours and hurled us to the tree.

The canopy over the main hall sparkled, and rays of yellow and white burst through, waking up the sleeping leprechauns. They smacked their mouths opened and closed, scratched their bellies, but once they looked up, they gasped and jumped to their feet.

"What's going on?" Phoebe asked.

Patrick crossed his arms. "Dance of the Sprites. Happens every time there's a rainbow. And underground…is the best seat in the house."

A wave of rainbow swirled around the canopy, stars appearing in flashes and bursts. Glowing orbs rotated around the rainbow, changing from white to pink to blue. Tiny female voices sang in unison—like wind chimes touched by a songbird. Shimmers of white glitter fell from the orbs, traveling the length of the rainbow. One orb floated away from the rest, moving around the hall as if searching for something.

It made a beeline for me and held itself in front of my face. It wasn't an orb at all. It was a tiny creature no bigger than my thumb with butterfly wings. Its ears were long and pointed, and its rounded face reminded me of a meerkat. It sneezed, sending white shimmers all through my hair and over my face before flying to join the others.

The light show faded away as the rainbow itself dimmed. Groans of disappointment echoed the halls from half-sleep Chauns.

I traced my hand through my hair, collecting some of the shimmers on my fingers, rubbing them together.

"Huh. They've never done *that* before." Patrick brushed off my shoulders like I had dandruff.

"That was incredible. Patrick, this place is magical. Can we come back here all the time?" Phoebe jumped up and down.

"Yes, yes. But whatever you do, please don't wish it."

She made the motion of zipping her mouth shut before pressing her side into mine. I still stared at my fingers rubbing together sprite dust.

"I've got so much to tell you about last night, Abby."

As Patrick drove us to his house, Phoebe regaled me with

tales from the night that I missed. Stories of the leprechauns arguing over the size of their stashes, especially as the night grew and they'd consumed more alcohol. Two got into a fistfight, resembling old-timey boxers, only they threw coins instead of punches. She spoke of the way Patrick and his father sang together, their arms draped over each other's shoulders as they swayed back and forth to the music, mugs raised. When she mentioned Patrick's father hugging her and kissing her forehead, welcoming her to the family, tears formed in her eyes.

When we arrived at Patrick's house, there sat Erimon's motorcycle. The sight made my skin tingle.

"Oh, lovely. I'm glad they welcomed themselves inside," Patrick mumbled, moving for the front door.

Erimon sat at the kitchen table with a tumbler of whiskey in hand. A giant man with pale blonde hair down to his hips sat next to him, hunched over to keep his head from hitting the ceiling. When Erimon's eyes shifted from their conversation to focus on me, my heart and stomach thrummed in euphoric harmony.

"Can you tell me again why my place got voted as our mythical headquarters?"

"Would you rather it be at Cu's place?" The large man at the table said, raising a thick brow.

"You mean under a rock?" A woman with flowing red hair and medieval armor said from the doorway. Her grey dress flowed as she breezed straight past us.

Phoebe hid behind Patrick as the woman made a beeline for the table, grabbing the open bottle of whiskey.

Erimon kept his attention on me, dipping his chin as he

rose and giving me that hooded sexy squint thing he did.

I backed up until my butt hit the doorframe.

He tapped one of his rings against his glass. "Hey."

My gaze dropped to his lips, panning over the stubble on his chin. "Hey."

"Nice weather we're havin'." He pointed to the gloomy dark clouds gathering outside.

"A bit windy for my taste."

He grinned, making his eyes squint more. "Funny. I've heard you're quite fond of a light breeze."

Wind from the open door tousled my hair, and I stifled a whimper.

"Monny, you can flirt with your 'not' girlfriend later, aye? Let's get these intros out of the way so we can plan." The burly blonde man at the table made a "hurry-up" gesture with his hand.

"Pour ye a whiskey?" Erimon motioned with his head for me to follow.

Phoebe sat in a chair with her back as stiff as a board. Patrick massaged her shoulders and frowned at the nearly empty bottle of scotch.

Erimon grabbed an empty glass and poured some before handing it to me without batting an eyelash. As if he'd performed the act of serving me a million times before today.

"Right then." He spun on his heel and sank into a seat, resting a booted foot on the edge of the table. "The hairy oaf to my right here is Finn MacCoul. Leader of the Fianna, slayer of giants *and* ladies' hearts." He winked at him with a sparkling grin.

Finn's long mustache bounced as he let out a hearty chuckle and slapped Erimon's back. "Pleasure to—" He rose from his chair, hitting his head on the ceiling with a growl. "Christ, Chaun. You'd think a dwarf lived here."

"Excuse me if you're *huge*," Patrick scoffed.

Phoebe's jaw dropped. "You're the biggest man I've ever seen."

"Oh, brother. Don't start, or it'll go straight to his head." The redheaded woman said, picking under her nails with a dagger.

Finn shook his head, making his golden hoop earrings sway.

"Abby," I said with a warm smile, offering my hand to Finn.

He stole a peek at Erimon before engulfing my hand with his to shake—a touch so gentle I'd barely felt it. "Oh, I've heard all about ye, Abby."

I shifted my eyes to Erimon, who pierced me with his stare. "Is that right?"

"For a woman facing death at every corner, you're rather optimistic. Have that much faith in the rebel Druid, do you?" The redhead said, popping a peanut from a wooden bowl into her mouth.

Rebel?

"The spitfire to my left is Queen Mave. Ruler of Connacht, warrior goddess, and talks too much most of the time," Erimon said, tossing her an exasperated glare.

Mave threw a peanut at him. "I only say what's on my mind."

"*Ruler* of Connacht? Hardly," a man said from the doorway.

"Look who decided to grace us with his presence." Dusting

off her hands, Mave shot to her feet.

The man's long red hair kicked up with the breeze gust through the doorway. His long stony features narrowed as he glared at Mave. A wide brown leather belt wrapped around his waist with silver studs and a Celtic tattoo traveled over his left shoulder. His tattered red kilt shifted as he stormed into the room.

"You said nothin' about *her* being here, Druid." The man pointed a gauntlet-covered arm at Mave.

"You're right. I didn't. You wouldn't have agreed otherwise." Running a finger around the rim of his glass, Erimon narrowed his eyes.

"Forget it." The man sliced his hands in front of him and turned for the door.

"You backin' out on your word, Cu?" Lightning flashed in Erimon's eyes just as a bolt streaked the sky.

Cu froze, his fists at his sides shaking before he turned back around. He grabbed a chair, dragged it away from the table, and flopped into it, sitting backward. "Not a word, Mave."

She tapped a finger against her teeth, a circular Celtic knot tattoo adorning the front of her hand. "No promises there, Hound."

Cu's lip bounced in a snarl.

Finn grinned, watching the two verbally jab each other like a tennis match.

Erimon pinched the bridge of his nose with a groan. "This is Cu Chulainn. Hound of Ulster, defender against Connacht, and a royal pain in me arse. But he fights as tough as he looks."

Phoebe and I waved at Cu rather than risking getting our

hands bitten off.

"You." Cu's death-glazed eyes landed on me. "You're the cursed one."

His tone made my blood curdle. "Excuse me?"

"The Dullahan's been slumberin' for nearly a century. You show up in Ireland and *poof.*" He made an explosion gesture. "Coincidence? I think not."

"That's enough, Cu," Erimon ordered.

Cu rose, and my hand shot to the dagger nestled against my back.

"Do you think all of us are riskin' our necks against The Dullahan because we *care* about your miserable mortal life?" He spat on the floor. "We're all here only because we owe the Druid favors. Don't think you're on any kind of a bleedin' pedestal."

"Shut. Your. Mouth, Cu," Erimon growled.

Cu chuckled and threw his arms out at each side. "You know you need me for this battle, Druid. You want to go up against my warp-spasm? Right here? Right now?"

Erimon scowled, and the hand clutching his glass caught fire. "We've been down this road before. Do not tempt me."

Patrick shot to his feet. "If you two are goin' to tear each other new arseholes until trumpets sound, could you do it *outside?*"

Erimon kept his glared fixed on Cu, the flame on his hand burning brighter.

"Shut up ye mouthpiece, and focus on what we're here to do," Finn added, kicking Cu's chair underneath his legs, forcing him to sit.

Cu's lip curled, and he leaned back, folding his arms.

Phoebe slipped her arm through the crook of mine, her skin chilling to the touch. I slid a hand over hers, offering some of my warmth.

Erimon's nostrils flared and the flame disappeared.

Mave cackled as she tossed several more peanuts in her mouth, the pearl hanging from her circlet tiara swaying. "You're such a buffoon," she said to Cu.

"Mave," Erimon snarled.

The smile faded away, and Mave sat back in her chair, holding her head low.

"Um. May I introduce myself?" Phoebe's small voice chimed—a voice so fluttery and innocent it changed room's entire demeanor.

Erimon rubbed his chin. "O'course."

"My name is Phoebe. I'm Abby's best friend and Patrick's wife. Despite your reasons for agreeing to help, just know she *is* a mortal worth fighting for." Her hands trembled underneath mine, and I pressed harder to hide it from the others, giving them another quick squeeze as a "thank you."

"Wife?" Finn raised a brow at Patrick.

Patrick nodded. "She agreed to it so I could stay on the surface to help."

"More than that." Phoebe grinned at Patrick with dovelike eyes.

Mave leaned forward and cocked her head at me. "Who *are* you?"

I parted my lips to stumble through an answer.

"Someone special. And that's all you need to know," Erimon

answered, not looking directly at me.

"Now, with *that* shitshow out of the way, care to talk about the plan?" Finn offered me a calming smile.

Erimon sat forward, concentration pinching his brow. "Let's talk strategy. Between all of us, we have plenty of firepower but we all know with Dullahan in full form, it won't be enough."

My chest tightened. Not enough? Between them *all*?

"Exploit his weaknesses." Mave shifted in her chair, causing the overhead light to darken the freckles on her cheek.

"Gold," Phoebe blurted, her cheeks blushing as she sunk into her chair.

Finn beamed at her. "Aye, gold. But where would we find enough? The Dullahan is bigger than I am."

Erimon's eyes shifted to Patrick, mischief in his gaze.

He didn't need Patrick to fight with us. He needed him for his gold. It was both ingenious and conniving all at once.

Patrick wrung his hands on the table. "Me."

"Your stash? What are we goin' to do? Throw coins at him?" Cu said with a smirk.

"Restraints," Mave said with a distant voice.

Erimon remained quiet, watching them piece it all together. And I, in turn, kept my gaze on him.

"So, we melt the gold down." Finn's massive shoulders shrugged, making the gold hoops tied in his mustache clink together.

"Melt?" Patrick gulped.

Phoebe slid her hand over Patrick's knee, patting it.

"Did any of you fail to mention you're a god of the forge? How are we supposed to make it into shackles? Let alone

195

magical ones?" Cu said.

Mave played with the serpent armband on her bicep. "I know someone."

Cu and Finn exchanged glances.

Erimon ran the tip of his thumb under his bottom lip, waiting.

"He won't be happy to see you, Erimon." Mave rested her hands flat on the table.

"You speakin' of Ilmarinen, I imagine?" Erimon sat back, hanging one arm over the back of his chair.

"The Finnish blacksmith?" Patrick raised a brow.

"Yes. He dwells in a cave no more than a day's travel from here." Mave's lips thinned.

"If he's still holdin' a grudge, I'll deal with him. He's our only option." Erimon stole a glance in my direction.

I kept quiet, tallying the never-ending questions building in my mind on the entire situation. On the crew. But most importantly—on Erimon.

"And you think Ilmarinen will just make these out of the goodness of his heart?" Cu bounced his knee.

"If I'm there, yes." Mave's hands curled into fists.

Finn nudged her shoulder. "Do I want to ask?"

"He has…a soft spot for me. Always has."

Erimon slapped the table. "It's settled then. Daybreak tomorrow, I can port everyone in twos to the cave."

"You can't port there," Mave said.

Erimon slow-blinked. "Why not?"

"He has a shield up. It stretches for miles. I'm not even sure where it stops."

"Good. Because I don't port." Finn shook his head.

"Aw. Does it upset your giant belly?" Cu poked Finn in the stomach.

Finn held a finger as thick as sub roll up to Cu. "Watch it."

"Come on, Finn. I could at least get us halfway. There's no way the shield extends *that* far." Erimon cocked an eyebrow at Mave.

"I. Don't. Port." Finn slammed his fist on the table, making all glasses bounce.

Erimon's eyes fell shut with a sigh. "Fine. Chaun, you're in charge of transportation."

"Me? Why me?"

Cu stood as he cracked his neck. "You're the most 'approachable.'"

Patrick scanned the room of mythical warriors. "Fair point."

"Everyone meets back here tomorrow mornin'." Erimon tapped his finger on the table like a gavel and rose to his feet.

Mave stared at her hands, not standing until the legs of Finn's chair squeaked as he pushed it back.

"You won't be alone, Mave." Finn bent forward, resting a hand that covered her entire shoulder and part of her back on her. "It'll be fine."

"I know, you big softy." She patted his hand, nodded to Erimon and me, and whisked out the door.

"Chaun, make sure ye find a vehicle with extra legroom," Finn said as he hobbled toward the door.

"In Ireland? Oh yeah, should be easy peasy," Patrick said before looking at me and shaking his head with wide eyes.

I covered my mouth with a hand to hide my smile.

Erimon's shoulders dropped, watching Finn leave, with a glaze in his eyes.

Shifting to his side of the table, I leaned against it with folded arms. "Are you always one step ahead of the game?"

He slid forward, hovering his thigh near my hip. "I don't play games. I plan for every possible outcome."

"And me? What am I in your list of outcomes?"

He pressed his lips to my ear. "You're the only thing I didn't plan for." His lips brushed my temple as he pulled away, walking to the door.

I stared at a stain in the floor boards, before turning around.

"I'll see you all in the mornin'. Be sure to come bright-eyed and bushy-tailed. And Patrick—" Erimon threw open the door, the wind howling from the approaching storm. "Don't forget that gold." Lightning sizzled over Erimon's fingers as thunder roared outside, and he slammed the door shut.

Like a lightning bolt striking an unknowing tree in the forest, Erimon had struck and split my mind into one confused burning mess.

19

I STARED AT THE BRIGHT green Toyota Corolla that the nineteen nineties should've taken back. A four-leaf clover was haphazardly spray-painted on the hood, and a half-worn Ireland flag sticker peeled off the passenger door.

"Our chariot awaits," Patrick said, displaying the vehicle to us like a Rolls Royce.

Finn stood with his arms folded, stroking his mustache with a raised brow. "You did hear me say something I could fit in, right? I'd barely get a leg in this heap."

"Beggars cannot be choosers. It's the best I could find on short notice." Patrick shrugged.

Erimon circled the car, dragging a finger over the molding. "Ah, see. There's a sunroof, Finn."

"You want me to ride with my head sticking from the sunroof? Is that what you're implyin'?"

Erimon leaned on the trunk with a grin. "Or we could port there. Your choice."

Finn's chest heaved, and he grumbled, storming toward the

car. "I'm gettin' in first."

The smile faded from Erimon's lips, and he held his head low.

"We're going on an epic quest…in a Corolla," Phoebe groaned but slipped a reassuring grin over her lips when Patrick frowned at her.

"I can't help but notice the lack of seats in this thing." Mave peered in the driver-side window with a sneer.

Finn's head poked from the sunroof with a grunt, and his mustache bristled. "I've been alive for centuries, and *this* is a new low."

"I'm sittin' upfront. The rest of you can figure it out." Mave slipped into the passenger seat, closing the door with a loud *thud*.

"I can sit on your lap, Patty." Phoebe tugged Patrick's sleeve.

Erimon's gaze snapped to mine, and I didn't need to be a soothsayer to know what he thought.

"I'm *not* drivin', and I'm *not* sittin' next to her." Cu pointed at Mave, who glared daggers into his soul from inside the car.

Erimon pushed off the car, slipping his hands in his jacket pockets. "Abby is *not* sittin' on your lap. You *will* drive, and you *will* tolerate Mave."

Cu stood in front of Erimon, glowering. "What's the matter, Druid? Afraid she'll get weak in the knees for me by the end of the ride?"

"No." Erimon rolled his shoulders back. "I'm afraid she'd be tempted to kill ye by the end of it."

My heart already raced at the thought of perching myself on Erimon's lap. With my ass so close to his…

"Come on, Abby," Phoebe said, nudging me toward the car.

Patrick slipped into the backseat yanking a squealing Phoebe on top of him. Scratching my ear, I paused by the car, and looked to the sky.

"You're pushin' it, Druid. Nothing's stopping me from beatin' your face into the ground after this is all over," Cu said as he took vast strides to the other side of the car.

"I've handled your warm-spasm before, even saved you from divin' straight off a cliff. Or did you forget?" Erimon raised his brow.

Cu ground his teeth together and shoved himself into the tight confinement of the driver's seat.

Erimon took in the sight of the lime-colored mess we all shoved ourselves into and sighed. "This is bleedin' embarrassing."

"I'm sure you've done worse," I said.

His gaze lifted. "I know you're certainly about to."

Sweat beaded at the base of my spine. He kept our eyes locked as he crawled into the car and beckoned me with his hands.

Sending a silent prayer into the wind, I slipped onto his lap, fighting with everything in me to not shiver as I nestled against him. He slipped an arm around my waist, making my insides writhe as he shut the door.

"Are you goin' to tell me where I'm going?" Cu said, not looking at Mave.

"I have an idea of *exactly* where you can go."

Erimon adjusted his hips, centering me, and I clasped my hands between my legs. "Mave. Please, my dear."

"Keep on this road for the next twenty-four kilometers. Then we'll take a turn at the end of the road, and keep goin' till you see a church, and—"

Phoebe interrupted her. "Oh my God, you're one of those people who give absolutely no street names. Just a bunch of, turn here at the gas station, and then the big yellow house."

Mave turned in her seat, narrowing her eyes at Phoebe. "I am an ancient warrior Queen who has been preoccupied with war for the last four centuries. Do you think at any given point I had the chance to memorize modern street titles?"

"No ma'am." Phoebe slunk against Patrick. "Sorry, ma'am."

"Can we get to it?" Finn's voice muffled from outside the car. "My arse is already gettin' sore."

"You'll have to excuse Mave. She's gotten rather finicky in her old age." Erimon rested his hand on my thigh.

Mave seethed at Erimon before facing forward. "Just drive, Hound."

We took off down the road—a Druid, a leprechaun and his wife, a giant, a goddess Queen, and a mortal claimed by a death god. An eclectic band of folks was we.

Erimon's finger casually stroked my leg before tapping in a rhythm that was hard to decipher.

"What song are you tapping?"

His eyes traveled up my body. "Kiss Me, I'm Irish."

My back stiffened.

He chuckled and jostled his knees. "Relax."

"You're certainly taking advantage of this situation." I eyed his other hand, curling fingers over my hip.

"I'd be a fool not to."

I bit back a smile. "You're lucky there are other people in the car."

"Oh? And what would you do if we were alone?" His eyes twinkled with wickedness.

I pressed my knees together tighter. "Not what you're thinking."

"Does it get any easier?" He dragged his finger under my elbow, cocking his head to one side.

"Does what?"

"Lying to yourself."

"Here. Turn here, Cu!" Mave threw her arm in front of Cu, pointing in the opposite direction.

Cu growled and yanked the steering wheel, making the turn at the last second.

"Buffoon," Mave growled.

My chest shoved into Erimon's, and I pressed my hands against the leather seat behind him to steady myself.

His minty breath moistened my nose, and he bit the air in front of me with a grin.

Snarling, I pushed back, retreating my palms back between my knees.

"You know, I'm glad my head is stuck outside," Finn mumbled.

"Why's that?" Patrick asked.

"I don't have to deal with any of ye." Finn let out a hearty laugh, shaking the entire car.

Cu glared at us from the rearview mirror. "Weren't you supposed to bring gold, Chaun?"

"I did. Don't you worry about where it be. You think I'd just throw it in a sack and toss it in the car?"

"I thought it'd be in a shiny black pot." Phoebe gave a brightened smile.

"Only for special occasions." Pressing his nose against Phoebe's cheeks, Patrick tickled her sides.

She cackled and shrieked, begging him to stop.

The car went silent for almost an hour. It was an amazing accomplishment with seven beings in one vehicle, two of whom didn't seem able to stop arguing.

Cu glared at the road ahead, twisting his hands on the steering wheel, making it creak and groan.

"Why are you grumpy virtually every minute of the day?" I asked.

Erimon coughed, slapping a hand over his mouth to hold back laughter.

"Grumpy?" Cu asked, deepening his scowl.

"Crotchety, testy, ill-tempered," Mave added.

Cu snapped his eyes to her. "I know what the word means."

"You still didn't answer the question.," Finn chimed in, tapping the roof above Cu's head.

"You try bein' me for a day and see if ye don't have a thing or two to be mad about."

Mave rolled her eyes. "Drama, drama, drama."

"Don't you even *start*," Cu snarled, his arm suddenly growing twice its average size.

Erimon shifted me to the side and leaned forward. "Do *not* warp-spasm in the car."

"Then you tell the redhead to my left to stop her yackin'."

Mave fumed and threw off her seatbelt.

The sun started to set, painting the sky in hues of purple, orange, and red.

"It'll be dark soon. Pull over, and we'll make camp for the night lest you wrap the car around a bleedin' tree and kill the one we're protecting before The Dullahan does."

I could feel Erimon's heart thudding against his chest through my shoulder.

"Do immortals need sleep?" I asked, keeping my tone calm and even.

"We live forever. We're not machines." A flash of a smile from Erimon, and then it disappeared.

"We don't have sleeping bags," Phoebe said.

"I'll be your sleeping bag," Patrick cooed.

Finn groaned from the sunroof.

When we parked, Cu stormed from the car with such force he almost bent the door's hinges. Mave trailed behind, letting ample space build between the two of them.

I paused on Erimon's lap, scraping my nail against the seam of his jacket.

"Comfortable?" He asked with extra gruff in his voice.

"It's another day and night gone." My throat seized.

His fingers kneaded my hip. "Another night closer to the full moon."

Nodding, I looked away from him, wrapping my arms around myself. "I feel like such a coward."

"Are you kiddin'? You're handling this whole situation like you do a pint."

I raised a brow.

"Kickin' it, showing it who's boss, and asking for more." His eyes sparkled.

"I don't know about more." I managed a small smile.

He patted my thigh. "Come on. Let's get over there so I can make a fire before these big babies all start whinin'."

After I slipped from his lap, we moved to a clearing where Cu had already gathered leaves, twigs, and logs, piling them up.

"I can handle this, Druid." Cu removed an ax from a sheath on his back.

Erimon arched a brow and lifted his palm, sparking a swirling flame. He canted his head to the side, tossed the fireball at the collected pile of kindling, and the fire blazed to life.

"Show off," Cu mumbled, resting the handle of the ax on his shoulder. "I'm chopping more wood."

"And here I thought we were going to make s'mores," Erimon said to Cu's back as he disappeared into the forest.

Rubbing my arms, I moved closer to the fire. "How do you conjure the fire?"

"I don't. I use the sun. Even at night, the sun is always there," he said, tossing a few more logs onto the fire. Orange embers floated in the wind, smoke billowing and spiraling toward the sky.

"Since when did Ireland get this cold every night?" Mave crouched by the fire, pulling the collar of her fur-trimmed coat around her neck.

"Since you were born, I'd imagine." Cu tossed an armful of chopped wood into a pile.

Mave shook her head.

"Why are you two *im*mortal enemies?" I glanced between

the two warriors.

Mave opened her mouth.

"I'll be tellin' this story. Otherwise, she'll embellish the bleedin' hell out of it," Cu interrupted, plopping on the ground across from her.

"I'll be sure to talk over you whenever you get something wrong," Mave countered.

Finn sat next to Mave, glancing between her and Cu. "This oughta be good." He held his palms to the flames, the gold rings hanging from his mustache catching glints of the fire's glow.

"Mave spoke of a bull. That refers to The Cattle Raid of Cooley," Cu began.

Patrick and Phoebe took the last empty spot near the fire, and Patrick wrapped himself around Phoebe, stroking her arms.

"Storytime?" Phoebe rubbed her hands together.

"I was a young lad but a fierce warrior and defended the land of Ulster from the army of Connacht. Mave was the Queen of Connacht, and she started an invasion as a means to steal the bull, Donn Cuailange." Cu paused.

"*Is* the Queen of Connacht." Mave glowered at Cu.

"Why did you want a bull?" I asked Mave.

"Because she is a greedy geebag." Cu glared at her.

Mave thinned her lips. "I wanted the bull to mate with my own cattle. Let me clarify—I'd tried to gain the bull honorably, even made a deal, but the town backed out at the last minute."

"She attacked the town in full force, and the bull went on a rampage. Dozens of Mave's men charged him, killing half the warriors before the battle even started," Cu continued.

"It was a handful, at most," Mave quipped.

"I was the only warrior left, and I agreed to meet Mave's army on the mount of Slieve Foy, where I engaged in single combat with all of her champions. I battled them for months." Cu's grip tightened on his knees.

"While he was busy fightin' I had my men steal the bull." Mave tugged the fur-lined collar of her cloak.

"But I found the man leadin' the charge, killed him, and the bull ran off." Cu guffawed. "Mave's army fought but eventually were forced to retreat."

"We *still* caught the bull and brought him back to Connacht," Mave said.

"He died three months later." Cu's scowl could scare snakes away.

"Did you at least get to mate him?" Phoebe asked.

"Only once. It was unfortunate." Mave narrowed her eyes at Cu from across the flames.

"Is anyone else the slightest bit bothered at how much of an arse this bull was? Seems to me you should be mad at him, not each other." Patrick scanned the group. When no one spoke, he coughed, dismissing the silence with a flick of his wrist.

"We'll be enemies for eternity, this is true, but Erimon himself has far more enemies. Isn't that right, Erimon?" Mave tossed a coy grin in his direction.

"Pullin' me into this to take the heat off yourself, Mave?" Erimon leaned on his elbow.

"He's lucky I don't hate his guts." Finn chuckled.

"Why?" I asked, catching Erimon's frown.

"It's not what he did per se, but one of his kinsmen." Fin's gaze dropped to his hands folded in his lap.

"I was huntin' one morn, and I came across the most beautiful deer I had ever seen," Finn began, his gruff voice cracking.

My mind sparked memories of that night under the stars with the deer and Erimon. When I shifted my gaze to look at him, he was staring at me with soft eyes.

"I had my hounds with me. They were once human but had been enchanted. They recognized her as human, and so instead of huntin' her as I normally would, I brought her home with me."

"Why was she transformed into a deer?" Patrick asked.

"A Druid named Fear Doirich turned her into one because she refused to marry him."

I snapped my eyes to Erimon.

"Don't look at me. I barely even knew him." Erimon rolled a twig between two fingers.

"The moment Sadhbh, that was her name, the moment she set foot on my land, she became a woman again. It was the one place she was able to regain her true form. Fate if I'd ever seen it. We married, she became with child, but when I had to go to war, the Druid returned and changed her back to a deer. I never saw her again." His chin dropped, fists clenching.

"And the child?" Phoebe asked, her eyes glistening with tears.

"Oisin, my son, that be the one happy part to this tale. My hounds found him as a fawn, I brought him back, and he became one of my fiercest warriors." He half-smiled, but it looked strained.

"That is an awful story, Finn. I'm so sorry." I frowned.

Finn punched Erimon in the shoulder. "I give Erimon here shite, but truth be told, he had no idea what the other Druid did. All Erimon's been guilty of is bein' an arrogant arse." He placed a hand on his stomach like Santa Claus and gave a hearty laugh.

"Don't believe a word of what any of these fools say. All lies." Erimon smirked as he ripped the twig, throwing piece-by-piece into the fire.

The five mythical beings went into conversations of life through the ages, and Phoebe and I listened intently to stories we couldn't begin to wrap our heads around. As the night grew heavier, each member fell asleep until only me, Erimon, and Finn remained awake.

"I want to make something clear to you, Abby," Finn said, dropping his face level with mine.

Erimon shifted next to me, rising to his feet. "I'm going to grab more kindling."

"I've no idea the reasons everyone else has agreed to fight The Dullahan. Favors owed. Glory. But I can say that I'm doing it to see you make it out alive."

My heart swelled. "But *why*, Finn? You don't know me. You owe me nothing."

He gently bumped my shoulder with his. "You have a hard time lettin' others help you, eh?"

Yes.

"I don't know how to begin thanking you—all of you."

He slipped a hand over my shoulder, lightly shaking me.

"You can start by lettin' us help ye, silly girl."

"Have you fought The Dullahan before, Finn?" I locked our gazes.

His hand slipped away from my arm and a deep sigh rippled from his gut. "Yes."

"That bad?"

"There's always far too much bloodshed. Far too many lives are lost when The Dullahan returns. At least when their casualties of war, there's usually an outcome. Lands obtained. Alliances formed. New governments established. But The Dullahan? All pointless squabbles."

The flames called to me, flicking to-and-fro, sending a surge of hope coiling in my stomach. "And how has he never been beaten?"

"It's not as easy as you'd think, Abby. But we've all taken him on separately. Never together." His thick brows rose when I looked at him.

"So, we have a chance?"

A warm smile spread over his lips, and he nudged my arm. "We have a chance."

My attention turned back to the fire, catching a flying ember on my fingertip. Its burn against my skin sizzled away within seconds, along with the glowing edges, leaving behind only a singular piece of ash.

"No mortal should have to endure this in their lifetime. But no mortal has ever been targeted quite like you either." He grunted as he stood. "If you need to hear a selfish reason from me to make it easier for you to accept my help...I want to know *why* that is." He gave a warm smile, patted my head, and moved into the woods.

I stared into the flames, their dancing colors putting me into a trance. Sleep pulled at my brain, and I curled into a ball. The scent of pine filled the air before warmth enveloped me from behind. A strong arm wrapped around me, hugging me to his chest.

I stiffened.

"Shh. Don't freak out. You were shivering like a loose leaf. Think of me only as a talking blanket." Erimon's breath floated over my cheek.

I let my body relax, nuzzling against him. His arms felt safe and calming—like home. "And you have zero desire to cop a feel?"

"I did *not* say that."

I peeked at him over my shoulder. "You better not."

A fox-like grin tugged at his lips. "I think you know by now I don't need to use my hands." His fingers drummed on my stomach, and it tightened under his touch.

My eyes dropped to his lips as I absently licked my own.

His nose brushed my cheek. "Not yet, Abby."

Heat flushed my neck, and I whipped my head away from him. "Do you have any idea how infuriating you can sometimes be?"

He smiled into my hair. "And do you know deep down you *like* it?"

I shuddered against him, fully prepared to blame it on the cold when leaves shifted in the thicket behind us.

Erimon sat up with one hand resting on my shoulder.

"Forgot my ax," Cu mumbled, raising a brow at us as he

grabbed the ax leaning against a log.

Phoebe lay across the way, coiled in her new husband's arms, smiling like an angel in her sleep. Her legs intertwined with his. They looked like they'd been together decades versus days.

Erimon scanned the surrounding forest, pulling the collar of his jacket around his face.

"Do you want me to leave you alone by the fire?" His voice rumbled in my ear.

I shook my head and closed my eyes as he slipped around me again. His warmth was enough to make me melt like spent candle wax.

"Are ye still cold?" He whispered, tickling his beard at my nape.

Again, I shook my head and pulled his arm tighter around my waist.

"Have I made you forget how to speak?" A light chuckle bounced through my hair.

I didn't want to talk. All I wanted to do was listen to his gruff Irish accent whispering in my ear, feel the rumble of his deep voice against my back, and drift to sleep.

"How is it that mythical beings and creatures exist, walk amongst us, but we have no idea?"

"No offense, but humans don't exactly have the best track record for acceptin' things they don't understand."

I chuckled. "I can take no offense to that because you're right."

"You're different, though."

I peeked at him over my shoulder. "What do you mean?"

"I'm usually not so quick to blurt me bein' a Druid." He

raised a brow.

"You were about to fight a headless horseman with a fire-breathing horse. I figured you came clean to prepare me for the worst."

He buried his face into my hair, muting his uproarious chuckle. "True. True. But regardless, you react with your gut. It's admirable."

My gut? Strange. If you were to tell Phoebe that about me, she'd laugh in your face.

"I've never been that way, Erimon."

"What are ye goin' on about?"

"Before I came here, I was an absolute worrywart. Always thinking of the worst possible outcomes."

His fingers tapped against my hipbone. "And here I thought I was the only one who felt different around ye."

I snapped my gaze to him with parted lips.

"Shh. The important thing is...don't fight it. It could be the very thing that helps defeat Dully."

My eyes turned back to the flames, curling my arms against my chest tighter as a chill snaked down my spine.

His hand splayed over my stomach, pulling me tighter against him. "Ow," he grunted.

"You were the one who gave me a knife." I bit my lower lip, grinning.

He slid the blade from its sheath and stabbed it into the log above our heads. "I'm surprised you're still wearing it. Figured you'd try to hide it away like the ring."

I traced my thumb over the iron on my finger. "It makes me feel safe."

"More than me?"

I glared at him over my shoulder. "Stop fishing."

"I just want to hear you say it. Is that so wrong?"

With complete lack of inflection, I said, "You're Superman to my Lois with the attitude of Batman. Satisfied?"

He pulled me flush against him, sweeping his nose over my ear. "Close. But you have it backwards. I'm Batman with the powers of Superman, and you are definitely more Selina Kyle than Lois Lane."

My insides throbbed at his references, and I shoved my hands under my head as a pillow. "Goodnight, *Bruce*."

"Goodnight, Catsy," he purred into my ear.

20

I AWOKE THE NEXT MORNING warm and cozy, snuggled within Erimon's jacket, his arms wrapped around me. His even, calm breathing as he nuzzled against the tightness at my back indicated he was still asleep. His chin rested on my shoulder, and his hips pressed against my backside. My eyes flew open.

My heart racing, I shifted myself forward. Erimon murmured, tightening his arm on me.

I could fool myself into thinking I wanted to move—to be anywhere but here. It'd be a lie.

Running my nose over the collar of his jacket, I let the smell of salt and forest tantalize me.

"Are you smelling me?" Erimon mumbled against my neck, pressing a smile to my skin.

"You must've been dreaming." I grinned and bit my thumbnail.

Erimon trailed the tip of his nose across my chin. "Mm. You smell like peaches and prosecco."

"Are you saying I smell like alcohol?"

"Sweet alcohol. And like it—you're intoxicating."

I let out a haggard breath, forcing my focus to a falcon landing on a branch above us.

"I hate to break this up, but it's been sunup for some time," Finn said, poking at the dying fire with a log.

Erimon groaned. "This is why I normally work alone." He uncurled his arm, and a chill replaced the soothing heat, sprouting goosebumps on my arms.

"Well, good morning," a sleepy-eyed Phoebe said. She sat on a log with Patrick, his arm around her shoulders. They both had dopey grins.

Erimon stood and helped me to my feet and squeezed my shoulder before turning away.

"Have a restful night?" Phoebe asked, still grinning.

I dusted off my clothes. "It's called sleeping."

"Sure, sure." She held out a dispenser. "Want a mint?"

Discreetly, I breathed into my palm, and winced. "Yes. Desperately."

Her smiled widened, and she jiggled the box of mints.

"Are we waiting for The Dullahan to grow stronger as we take our sweet time?" Cu leaned on the car with his arms folded.

"I'd ask if you woke up on the wrong side of a dirt pile this mornin', but then I remember the source," Finn said, slapping Cu on the shoulder.

The ring buzzed on my finger, and Erimon walked past, kneading his palm with a thumb.

"Are we all here?" Erimon looked around.

"We're missin' the witch," Cu grunted.

I tossed the mint around in my mouth. "You've noticed her absence. Progress."

"You want to come closer and say that to me again?" Cu asked with narrowed eyes, tapping his finger on the hilt of his ax.

"I wouldn't want to intimidate you." I grinned and moved for the door.

Erimon wrapped his arm around my waist. "Someone woke up sassy this mornin'." He spoke low, his lips hovering near my temple.

"I had a good sleep."

Something feral flashed in his eyes.

"A woman can't take a wazz without you all sendin' a search party?" Mave asked.

"Good mornin', Sleepin' Haggardly," Cu snapped.

"Does anyone know how to perform a silencing spell? I feel it'd benefit the entire group," Mave quipped before climbing into the car.

"I could always cut out his tongue," Finn said, his head already sticking out the sunroof.

Erimon shook his head with a crooked smile and held the door open for me. "M'lady?"

"Don't act like you have manners all of a sudden."

"I wouldn't dream of it."

We saddled up and headed for the cave.

We trudged through the woods, our boots sinking into mud up to our shins. Except for Finn, of course. Occasionally he'd pull us free when our feet stuck.

"What a marvelous path you've taken us on," Cu muttered, using his ax to help pry himself from the mud.

"I never said it'd be easy," Mave grunted with every step.

"Are we goin' to talk about why Ilmarinen has a grudge against Erimon?" Patrick asked, holding Phoebe piggy-back style.

Mave's face turned to stone.

"No. Because it happened two centuries ago," Erimon grumbled.

My foot stuck, and I started to fall forward, my boot sticking in the mud. Erimon caught me under the arm with the grace of a bird. He crouched and pulled my boot free. As he slipped it onto my foot, he made sure to trail his fingers under my pant leg and over my ankle for the briefest of moments.

My throat dried, watching him stand to his full height. "Thanks."

Finn marched past us. "We're immortal. We tend to hold grudges longer, and you know that, Monny."

"Why not Goibniu? Or Hephaestus?" Patrick asked.

"Hephaestus is rarely in the same dimension anymore, and Goibniu no longer has his head." Cu sliced his finger across his neck.

Finn gasped. "I hadn't heard that."

"And why is this guy not in Finland?" Phoebe asked.

"He went into hidin' after several failed marriage proposals," Mave answered.

Finn rubbed Mave's shoulders. "And we're pretty sure he chose Ireland because of Mave."

She sneered.

Cu grumbled, storming ahead of us all.

"He's our only shot at this," Mave added.

"Look. I—*we* can handle Ilmarinen. Keep your wits about ye, and remember why we're here." Erimon held his fist up for us to halt.

We reached a cave entrance. A chill crept up my spine as I eyed the dew forming on the rocks, the smell of sulfur and death wafting from within. A never-ending black abyss, reeling in would-be victims to swallow whole.

Erimon knelt, scooping a pile of leaves into his palm, and held it out to a ray of sun peeking through the tree line. The leaves ignited, and he held a fireball lantern in his palm. He motioned with his head for us to follow him, his fireball lighting the way. I followed on Erimon's heels, half expecting giant spiders to lower from the cave ceiling.

Low guttural growls surrounded us, and claws scraped against the stone floor. I reached one hand for the knife while the other grabbed Erimon's jacket.

"What was that?" Phoebe whispered.

"*Cu Sidhe*," Cu growled, removing his ax from its sheath.

"What?" Phoebe whispered.

"Hell Hounds," Erimon spat.

Creatures pounced from the darkness with bodies like gorillas, moving and running on their knuckles—legs like a horse with hooves but bent backward. Dark thin manes traveled down their spines. Their glowing red eyes blazed as they bared rows of pointy teeth, drool dripping on the floor.

My heart jumped to my throat, and I tightened my grip on Erimon's jacket, pulling it from his shoulders. Without warning, Cu stormed past us, with ax held high. His body contorted, growing and growing until his head bumped the cave ceiling, knocking off bits of rock—the sound of shifting bones resonated off the stone walls. My hand fell from Erimon, the knife hilt limp in my grasp. One of Cu's eyes sunk into his head, the other bulged out of his skull, making him a deranged cyclops. His long red locks fell away, replaced by spikes down his back—a monstrous deformed Mr. Hyde.

Erimon stood still as Cu charged the hounds, ax swinging. "Abby, grab Phoebe and hide out of sight." He pointed behind him.

"But—"

"Abby." He lifted my hand with the knife. "If anything comes at you, you stab until it's dead. Got it?"

My jaw chattered, but I nodded and forced my feet to move—to act.

Phoebe stared at the deformed creature Cu had turned into, frozen with her mouth hanging open.

Erimon's arm swooped left and right, hurling rocks from the cave floor to rise as violent spikes. The hounds' claws gripped the stone, dodging most of them. One hound nicked its side on a barb, and it let out a blood-curdling shriek.

Finn launched forward, removing the hilt of a sword from his jacket. No blade, but a thin line of grey fog formed. Finn swung at one hound, instantly cutting it in half like a laser strike.

Erimon threw up a rock wall in front of us, and I forced

Phoebe to crouch behind it with me.

Patrick faced one of the creatures, his fists clenched at his sides. Liquid gold eked its way over Patrick's hands, traveling down until his whole arm was metal. Patrick swung at the hound, a metallic pang echoing off the cave walls. He swung and swung, but the hound clamped its teeth on his hand. I winced. The dog's teeth broke off once they made contact with Patrick's fist.

Mave fought off another dog in the corner, moving with the grace of a dancer—dipping, diving, and swinging her sword. She cackled, avoiding every bite, snarl, and slash the hound had to offer until finally, it leaped forward. Mave dropped and slid on her back with the sword pointed up. The hound landed on her blade, impaling itself.

Cu's giant hands grabbed one dog, and despite its numerous bites, ripped it in half like tearing bread. Bile threatened its way up my throat, and I clamped a hand over my mouth. Phoebe screamed. A hound clamped onto her leg, and blood oozed down her calf. Patrick plowed his golden fists into the dog's head, making it release her. Finn swung his sword in one quick strike, decapitating it.

Phoebe cried as her hand shook over the gaping wound. Dozens of bite marks eked blood, staining the cave floor. I took off my jacket and wrapped it below her knee. Patrick knelt beside her, stroking her forehead, protecting her from any other hounds daring to get close.

A hound snuck behind Erimon while he was preoccupied with another. I hyperventilated, contemplating my next move. Gripping the knife with my clammy palm, I bolted forward, slamming the blade into the beast's side. Blood as black as ink poured over my hand, and the hound roared. It heaved its head into my shoulder, throwing me to the floor, the knife sliding away. I stared up at the monster, my heart racing.

A stone spike launched from the ground in front of me, skewering it.

When the spike retreated to the floor, Erimon stood staring as if he didn't recognize me. I opened my mouth to say something—anything.

A shrill whistle took my breath, making the dogs run away.

A man slinked from the shadows with a torch in hand, peering at us with coal-black eyes. His long snow-white hair and equally long mustache blended together, falling down the front of his tan robe.

Everyone stood still. Cu's chest heaved as he willed himself back to his more human-looking form. The only sound was Phoebe's whimpers. Patrick sat next to her on the ground, my jacket still wrapped tightly around her leg. Dozens of dead hounds scattered at our feet. Mave tucked her sword into her cloak and took a step forward.

The man cocked his head at her, a smile slithering over his thin lips.

"Ilmarinen, we've come seekin' your help," Mave said, holding her palms up.

"Mave, my dear, it's been far too long. I knew you'd find me one day."

Mave's throat bobbed as she swallowed.

"She's not here for you." Erimon slid my knife to me across the floor with his boot.

I caught it and held it firmly in my grasp.

Ilmarinen's eyes formed slits. "Druid Erimon. You have some gall showing up here."

Finn swore under his breath.

"You can't seriously say you're still hung up on it? It was a long time ago. Times were different."

Ilmarinen let out a low, raspy chuckle. "That they were. Yes. Water under the bridge. But I still can't stand the sight of you."

Erimon glared. "Then I'll stay behind ye."

"We need you to forge something for us out of gold," Mave interjected.

"There are plenty of blacksmiths. Why me?"

"We need golden shackles. Enchanted ones. Strong enough to subdue…The Dullahan." She hesitated before mentioning Death's name.

Ilmarinen's white brows shot up. "The Dullahan, you say? Why do you seek this?"

"What does that matter? Will you forge them or not?" Erimon said.

Ilmarinen's lips curled. "I'll expect payment."

Mave nudged her head at Patrick. He held out his hand, and several gold coins fell into it from an invisible pocket in the air.

"No. I want—" His gaze cut to Mave. "Something else."

"We don't deal people as currency," Erimon growled.

Ilmarinen held a hand out to him behind his back. "This isn't your negotiation."

"Why don't you come out and say it?" Mave asked through gritted teeth.

"I will forge your golden shackles in exchange for your

hand, Mave."

Mave's face paled. "In marriage?"

"I certainly wasn't asking you to lop off an appendage."

"I'm an eternal Queen of a region. I can't marry."

A sly grin tugged at his lips. "I, too, am eternal."

"No. Who do you think you are? Barking orders?" Cu's lip bounced.

"You are the one who barks, *Hound*. I'm simply offering you all a solution. Take it or leave it."

Mave stared at the ground, her fists shaking at her sides.

"Mave," Erimon beckoned. When she didn't look at him, "Mave, look at me. You don't have to do this."

"I don't have a choice. The Dullahan *has* to be stopped."

Finn's face fell. "We'll find another way."

Mave's gaze landed on me, and I frantically shook my head.

"Fine," she said, turning her attention to Ilmarinen.

"No," I screamed.

A dark evil shaded Ilmarinen's eyes, chilling me to the bone. He extended a hand for her to shake, to seal the deal. She lifted her hand and slid her palm over his. A bright light flashed between them, and he yanked her forward.

"After The Dullahan or the woman meet their demise, you're mine."

"The woman?" Mave asked.

"Abigail. She is the one marked, is she not?"

No. No.

Dizziness washed over me, and I backed up as my vision clouded.

Erimon steadied me and snarled at Ilmarinen. "It won't be

her who dies. Make the shackles. Now."

Mave blinked rapidly, frozen in place, once Ilmarinen let go of her hand.

"Follow me. Some of you will want to tend to that girl's leg first, however, before she loses it...or worse. Their bite has a nasty venom in it." He grinned like the serpent he was and slunk into the shadows.

I ran to Phoebe, ripping my jacket from her leg. The bites had turned black, pus-filled, and jagged veins spread up to her thigh.

"Is it bad?" she asked, tears filling her eyes.

"You're going to be okay, Phoebs." Panic swirled through me, not knowing what to do—how to think.

Finn stood near a rock hanging from the cave ceiling, his hands cupped, catching droplets within his palm. After he filled them, he knelt near Phoebe, holding the water to her lips.

"Drink, Phoebe," he implored softly.

Patrick helped her sit up, coaxing her lips to Finn's hands. As she drank, the bite marks disappeared one-by-one until her leg was as pale and unscathed as it was when we entered the cave.

"How did you do that?" I ran my fingers over the healed flesh.

Finn stood, letting the remaining water drip from his hands. "A story for another time. I'm glad she's alright." He patted Patrick on the shoulder before he turned to follow Ilmarinen.

Phoebe leaped up, twirling in circles. I grabbed her and hugged her so tight neither of us could breathe.

"For a moment there, I really thought I was going to lose you, Phoebs."

She peeled away with a smile and tugged my hair. "I'm not easy to get rid of."

She turned to Patrick, planting a kiss so fierce, it toppled them to the ground.

He ran his thumbs over her cheeks. "I know you're immortal now, but the way that venom traveled through ye, I didn't know what to think."

Phoebe sat up, perched on top of him. "I'm what?"

Patrick raised to his elbows. "Immortal. You made an eternal bond with a leprechaun who's immortal. I thought—" His mouth fell open.

"I didn't think about that. I hadn't realized…"

When Erimon had said Phoebe was part of their world, in my gut, I knew that's what he'd meant.

"Would the venom have killed her?" I picked up the tattered remains of my jacket, bloody and stained.

"I don't know. It wouldn't have killed me, just slowed me down a bit as my body fought it off, but—" Patrick stood, bringing Phoebe with him. "I didn't want to take the chance, love."

Phoebe stared at her hands as if they held eternity within them, and they started to shake.

Patrick curled his arm around her waist and kissed her temple. "Come on, Phoebe. We'll talk this through later. For now, I need you to focus. I don't trust Ilmarinen in the slightest." He led her into the shadows, leaving me standing there alone.

Where had Erimon gone?

"That was stupid." His voice gruffed from the darkness.

I whirled around to face him. "Excuse me?"

He pushed off the cave wall and stalked toward me until we stood toe-to-toe. "It was admirable. But stupid."

"Stabbing a Hell Hound, you mean? Like you *told* me to do?"

"If *you* were in trouble not—" He'd raised his voice and paused, dragging a hand through his hair. "I'm a Druid, Abby. Hardly anything in this universe can kill me. Do you understand?"

I rolled my shoulders back. "I'm supposed to apologize for fearing for your life or say I won't do it again?"

"Yes." His lip twitched.

I raised to the balls of my feet, getting closer to his level. "No."

He squinted at me, his eyes roaming my face.

I flopped onto my heels and turned away in a huff.

He grabbed my forearm. "Abby—"

"Don't," I said, yanking my arm from his grasp. He let me. "Let's get these fucking shackles and get the hell out of here."

21

WE'D FOLLOWED THE OTHERS TO a hollowed portion of the cave. Molten lava flowed into a stone pool, casting an orange glow, the heat instantly beading my forehead with sweat.

"I assume the Chaun is providing the necessary materials for these enchanted shackles?" Ilmarinen asked, a hiss flowing from his tongue with every other word.

Patrick looked at Erimon, raising his brow. Erimon folded his hands in front of him and jutted his chin at the vat with a scowl. Patrick rubbed the back of his neck before holding his hand over the pot. Dozens of gold coins fell from an invisible opening, clanging against the metal.

Ilmarinen watched the coins fall in silence, his eyes marking each one. He held his hand up, and Patrick made a fist, instantly stopping the money shower.

"Your donation is much appreciated," Ilmarinen said with a wicked glint in his eyes. He threw his arm up, and flames roared beneath the pot.

Within seconds, the coins melted into liquid gold. Like water defying gravity, the gold floated from the pot, swirling in mid-air until a gold ingot formed on the anvil. Ilmarinen tapped his fingers on it until the metal glowed crimson and sizzled against his touch. Using his own hands as hammers, he brought them down, striking areas of the ingot he wanted to shape. Two circular shackles formed after several more strikes. He paused, rolling up the sleeves of his robe with labored speed.

Cu rolled his eyes and paced.

After he secured the sleeves at his elbows, Ilmarinen dunked the shackles into a vat of oil, making them sizzle and hiss, steam filling the air. He set the bonds aside and summoned more of the liquid gold with a flick of his wrist. It spiraled from the pot and curled through the air, landing on the anvil. Repeating the same steps, he hammered and molded until a gold chain formed. He held the shackles up and slammed them onto the chain, spraying red sparks and bonding them together. He closed his eyes and waved his hand back and forth over the shackles, making them glitter and glow.

Once completed, he opened his eyes and picked them up with one finger by the shackle chain, holding them out to whoever would take them.

Finn pushed forward, taking the shackles, which looked child-sized in his massive hands. "And your enchantment... it'll work?"

"Are you questioning my level of skill?" Ilmarinen didn't look at him as he slid his sleeves back to his wrists.

"Yes," Cu gruffed.

"It will work as can be expected. You realize these shackles will not kill The Dullahan? Simply slow him down." Ilmarinen steepled his fingers.

"We have it under control," Erimon sneered.

Ilmarinen raised a thin white brow. "Do you?"

"Enough of these riddles. We got the shackles we came for. Let's get the bleedin' hell out of here," Finn said, taking wide strides toward the exit, Cu, Phoebe, and Patrick following him.

Erimon glared at Ilmarinen, sliding closer to him. "What exact enchantment did you use?"

"One unfamiliar to Druids. Its intricacies would be lost on you."

"Try me."

The ring felt hot against my skin, making me wince.

Erimon edged closer, and Ilmarinen stood his ground, craning his neck to one side.

"All that was meant to cease will cease. All that was meant to prevail will prevail."

Erimon growled as he pulled lava from the vat, lifting his hand, so it swirled like a tornado above Ilmarinen's head. "You didn't enchant it at all, did you?"

Ilmarinen took one fleeting glance at the magma above him and smirked. "It will do what it's intended to do. How you use them is entirely up to you."

Erimon's lip bounced, and he dropped his hand, letting the lava fall along with it. Ilmarinen swooshed his arm, sending it all back into the vat pool.

"Mave, my dear." A wicked grin curled Ilmarinen's lip.

Mave halted at the exit, not looking over her shoulder at him.

"Do remember our deal. I'd much rather you come willingly, but the universe will bring you to me one way or the other."

"Go to hell," Mave snarled and stormed from the cave.

"Mm. I've been." Ilmarinen's eyes darted to me. "It is not near all it's cracked up to be."

I slid to Erimon's side, hiding behind him.

"Time is running out. The blood moon rises one night from tomorrow. Have you fought him during a blood moon before, Druid?"

Erimon took a harsh gulp, the sound of it echoing through my ear.

"That's what I thought. But you *are* aware how much stronger it makes him." Ilmarinen shook his head. "You've quite the challenge on your hands."

"Come on, Abby. Let's get out of here." Erimon pressed a hand to my back, ushering me to the exit.

"I had something else in mind," Ilmarinen spat.

We appeared in a cube-shaped room with no windows or doors—floor-to-ceiling bright white. A breath loosed from my lungs, and I clung to Erimon's jacket.

"You will find, Druid, that this box is made entirely of human-made materials," Ilmarinen displayed his hand to the room.

Erimon charged forward, grabbing nothing but air. Ilmarinen's body reappeared in the opposite corner.

"Do you think I'd forget you killed my brother? Forgive you?" Ilmarinen scowled at him.

My heart skipped a beat.

"It was war." Erimon balled his hands into fists.

"You had a choice. We always have a choice. And now you'll watch someone you care about wither away in front of you. Perhaps even in your arms as my brother did in mine." Ilmarinen floated past us.

Care.

The ring thrummed against my skin.

"No. I won't. As soon as you're gone, I'm going to rip these walls to shreds. Even artificial materials have natural elements." Erimon's chest heaved, his heartbeat so intense I could hear it pounding in my ears as if it were my own.

"Do you think me a fool?" Ilmarinen pointed to a wall. "These walls are comprised of layer upon layer of varying compounded materials. By the time you'd even get to the center, she'll be dead."

I held back a whimper.

"Oh. And one more thing. This box is above the lava pool. It may get a tad…uncomfortable in here very very soon." Ilmarinen chuckled, raspy and chilling.

"You're a dead man," Erimon snapped.

"No. But Abby is. And once she's gone…Mave is mine." Ilmarinen gave one last blood-curdling laugh before disappearing like mist in the night.

Erimon's hands splayed at the walls, pulling any fragment he could from them. Microscopic bits of coal, salt, and droplets of oil scattered the ceiling, bouncing off his chest and staining his shirt.

The heat from the lava had already begun to seep through the walls, and I yanked off my jacket. "Erimon, what the hell are we going to do?"

He grunted, his hands shaking as he summoned any element willing to succumb to him. "Don't talk. You have to conserve your oxygen."

I furrowed my brow at him and yanked the knife from its sheath. Moving to the opposite wall, I slammed it into the plastic over and over, working away one-inch chunks. Tears stung my sinuses as I stabbed. I'd sprung hope in myself that my end wouldn't come with The Dullahan—dying in a heat box wasn't a death I'd ever thought for myself. I let out all my anger, my frustration on that wall, screaming, stabbing, kicking.

"Abby, Abby, Abby," Erimon repeated, grabbing my arms and turning me to look at him. "What are you doin'? Not talkin' also meant not wearing yourself down."

"This is all your fault." The knife dropped from my hand, bouncing on its hilt as it hit the floor.

"What?"

I tried to pull away, but he held firm. "You killed his brother. We wouldn't be in his mess. *Mave* wouldn't be in this mess if it weren't for you."

The ring sent a static shock from my finger down my arm.

"That's it then, hm? You believe a madman and give me no chance to explain?" His nostrils flared, his grip loosening from my arms.

I stared up at him, peered into those blue eyes. Such burdens rested in his gaze—such tiredness. "I have time."

Erimon snarled and tore the jacket from his shoulders, tossing it aside. "No. I've got to get through this wall." He threw his arms out, weaving them around each other, trembling as

234

he pulled more material out. A bulging vein sprouted in his temple.

I placed a gentle hand on his bicep, taking a moment to trace his Celtic sleeves' intricate designs. "You're right. He is a madman. So, I believe it when he said we're not getting out of here."

Erimon's gaze dropped to my skin touching his, a light moan forming at the back of his throat.

"If I'm going to die, let me at least know who you were, who you *are*."

Erimon grimaced as if he'd been punched in the stomach before he dropped to the floor and leaned his back on the partially destroyed wall. He patted next to him, and I sat, my head already feeling woozy, sweat trickling down my back.

"There was a time in my youth I didn't want anything to do with the order of Druids."

I snorted.

He bumped his knuckle under my chin. "Hey now. No interruptions." He gave a weak smile that faded away no sooner than it appeared.

"In history, they saw us as priests, teachers, judges. And the humans who called themselves Druid, that is exactly what they were. But not us. Not true Druids."

The heat intensified, pooling in my chest, making my head ache. I shimmied out of my pants, not caring that I sat half-naked next to him. Being on one's deathbed threw all scruples out the door.

His eyes darted over my legs, but not in the lustful sense—he studied them, surveyed them like he noted every freckle and groove.

"What is a Druid's true purpose?" I whispered, only parting my lips enough to let the words escape.

"We control nature, therefore control balance. The reason I knew you were marked by The Dullahan Abby before I even told you, is because The Dullahan seeks to throw off that balance. It's my job to restore it."

My eyes lifted to his, and I rested my head on his shoulder. "So, you do your job now?"

"Yes. I have for centuries."

"What made you change your mind?"

My cheek flushed against his heated skin, and I distracted myself from the dizziness pulling at my brain, by counting the number of lines in his tattoo.

"The Elder Druid cursed me for not doing my job. For bastardizing the Druid way." He rested his finger atop mine, following my movements over his skin.

"Cursed?"

He brushed some hair sticking to my damp forehead over my shoulder. "This tattoo is compliments of them. A reminder of what I did. What I'm doomed to endure for eternity."

"What doom?" Words became harder to push from my throat.

"My curse is going day-by-day not knowing what I'm to gain or have taken from me. And not knowing when or if it will ever happen." He nudged me with his shoulder. "Stay awake, Abby."

"Maybe you shouldn't tell such boring stories," I said, my words raspy and strained, but still, I managed a smile.

A quick chuckle fluttered through his chest, and he took the hand with the ring, stroking the iron, cooling it against my skin.

"Being a warrior is against Druid custom, which is why you heard Mave call me a rebel. After the Elders cursed me, it took some time for me to realize if it weren't for the Druids, I'd have none of my power. Wouldn't be the person I am." He sat me up, pulling me away from his shoulder. "I'd told them I wasn't the type to sit idly by and control balance from the shadows. Seeing as I agreed to uphold my end, they granted me the right to be out in the open—amongst mortals—and fight for them."

I winced. Every breath struggled through my lungs, and my throat burned—matching the fiery heat coursing through my skin. "His….bro…ther?"

"Killed on the battlefield like any other man. I couldn't tell you how many brothers, sons, fathers I've killed. It's part of war. I lost my own brother to one but—"

A weak grin pulled at my lips. "You…brother?" I slid down his chest.

He yanked me up, giving me a light shake. "Would ye like to hear about him?"

I nodded, tracing my finger down his perfect nose.

"His name was Abelio, and he was my older brother." He pressed his forehead to my temple. I could tell he closed his eyes from his lashes tickling my skin. "He was born a mortal, unlike me. To this day, I still wished he would've been givin' the gift of Druidism. He deserved it, would've done more with it, I—"

I reached a shaky hand to his face, pressing my palm against his cheek. "I…never thought—" I swallowed and took a shallow breath. "You..were..a bad man."

Erimon took my hand in his and kissed my knuckles. "Don't tell anyone, hm?"

I half-smiled and started coughing.

"Abby—" Erimon pulled me into his lap, resting my back over one arm. "Stay with me. Concentrate on my voice."

I touched his lips, hoping he'd know it was me asking him to keep talking.

"Abelio was the brains. A scholar first, warrior second. As you know, I was the brawn and nothin' but warrior."

I shook my head, parting my lips to counter him.

"Shh." He kissed my forehead. "I know you think I'm more than that, but Abby…" He gazed down at me, his eyes glistening before he pinched them shut. "My brother and I were drafted into battle. I was only eighteen. I'd just begun my Druid trainin', and they had no choice but to let me fight."

I trailed my fingertips over the grooves of the many rings on his hands.

"It didn't matter how skilled I was…" He hugged me to him. "I couldn't stop the ax flying into his back."

I traced his chiseled jawline, forcing my eyes open to look up at him.

"It should've been me. I would've survived it."

I wished there was wind in this box—wished for dirt to sink my hands into so I could talk to him without feeling like every forced breath brought me closer and closer to fading away. Phoebe was the one with the wishes.

"I'd like to blame his death for my rebellious nature, but

Abelio, he'd smack me in the back of the head and tell me, 'Progress over excuses.'" Erimon huffed a short laugh.

He looked *so* different talking about his brother. So human. If only I'd gotten a chance to see more of this side.

"I want you…to…know—" The room spun, and I pinched my eyes shut.

"Don't finish that sentence."

I pushed a finger to his lips, and it went numb, falling back to my lap. "I've…felt…connected to you since—" My throat wheezed. "Since that night…in the forest."

"That bare-knuckle boxing match I so happened to be fighting in?"

I raised a brow.

"Was my first time competin'. I wanted to see you again, to know what I felt for ye was real."

I clutched my chest. "You…feel it…too?"

He pulled me up and nuzzled his nose against my nape. "From the moment you walked into the pub. I felt it. I felt *you*."

Searching for his hand, he offered it to me, and I slipped it over my chest—pressed it against the skin above my heart.

Erimon sneered, no doubt feeling how slow the beats had become.

"I wished—" I sucked in as much breath as my lungs would let me. "At the steps…I wished…" A fire swirled down my throat, and I gulped it down. "I wished…to feel…whole."

Erimon's hand shook against mine. "Do ye?"

Breaths came less frequently and all my limbs felt as heavy as boulders. I wanted to hug him but couldn't lift my arms.

"Bleedin' shite, Abby?" He shook me.

I wheezed.

"Abby." His lips hovered over mine, and he whispered, "Kiss me."

With dried, cracked lips, I pressed my mouth to his as he brought me forward. A tingle traveled down my throat, settling into my chest.

The wall came crashing down around us, fresh air spilling into the room, pouring into my lungs. I gasped, sputtered, and coughed.

"Are you two alright?" Finn boomed, his knuckles raw and bleeding.

Erimon's head shot up. "How did you—it doesn't matter." Scooping me and his jacket into his arms, he cradled my head against his chest, and carried me through the Finn-sized hole.

"Thank you," I whispered to Finn, looking at him over Erimon's shoulder with hooded eyes.

He gave a warm smile. "I just hope you believe me now."

The rest of the gang stood outside panting and sweaty, their weapons scattered across the ground. Patrick's golden fists morphed back to normal, and he blew out a haggard breath.

"What the bleedin' hell happened?" Mave asked, wiping the back of her hand across her forehead.

"Apparently, Ilmarinen still hates my guts." Erimon set me down and pulled his jacket around me.

Phoebe ran over and slammed a hug to my side, almost knocking me over.

Mave wiggled her fingers in the air and arched a brow. "He's lifted the shield."

"That bastard probably left them for dead and ran away like a coward." Cu spat on the ground.

Erimon slid a hand over my shoulder and touched Finn's arm. "Sorry," he said to him.

"For wh—"

Erimon ported us to the car. Finn bristled, slapped a hand over his mouth, and ran to a bush, vomiting.

Erimon brushed a thumb over my cheek. "I'll be right back."

Nodding, I hugged the jacket around me and watched Finn heave and curse between breaths.

After making two more trips, the entire party surrounded the car. We were all silent, staring at the ground or sky. The situation grew more real with each passing moment. They'd all fought mythical creatures for centuries, and yet the uncertainty visible on their faces, in their scowls, had my insides twisting.

"Abby," Erimon said, lightly touching my elbow. He led me off to the side, coaxing me to lean my back on a tree.

"What was said in there—it was hot, I was—" I stammered, biting my lip to keep it from trembling.

He grabbed each side of my face, his fingers kneading behind my ears. "Don't do that. We both meant what we said."

My eyes dropped to his lips, still remembering their brief skim. The tingle that sizzled in my core and instantly tore away the moment he broke contact. My heart boomed in my chest as he slipped his hands over my hips, dropping, dropping, dropping his lips, sinking against me. I tilted my chin to meet him.

"Erimon, we—" Patrick froze. "Oh, I—"

A snarl vibrated in the back of Erimon's throat as he turned to face him. "Has The Dullahan shown up early, or is the world *literally* fallin' around us?"

Patrick cleared his throat. "Ehm…no."

Erimon cocked a brow.

Patrick peeked at me, snapped his fingers, and hopped. "Right. I'll uh—we'll talk later." He scurried away.

"We probably—" I'd barely breathed the words when Erimon's lips crashed over mine.

He swirled his thumbs over my cheekbones, cupping my face with his callused hands. His tongue traced the seam of my lips, and I opened for him, whimpering as he deepened the kiss. His hardness pushed against my stomach, rocking against me, and his fingers tangled into my hair, tightening.

The ring vibrated and hummed in tune with the groan collecting in my throat.

There was no tingle like when he'd kissed me in the box. This was something far different. Primal. Bottled-up emotion. Lust. I wondered if his lips on mine moments from death were a kiss at all compared to this.

He peeled away, dragging my bottom lip between his teeth. I pressed our foreheads together, panting—wanting more but knowing I'd have to wait.

"Does this mean I held up my end of the deal?" A sultry grin tugged at my lips, and I pressed my hips into him.

He traced the tip of his thumb under my bottom lip. "The deal was never about the kiss, and you know it."

Keeping our gazes locked, I licked his thumb, nibbling on it when he slid it past my lip. "Then why use it as a bargaining chip?"

"Because I wanted to see you craving—waiting for it. To wonder...when is he going to take it?" He brushed a soft kiss over my brow, my cheek. "The glances to my lips. The sight of ye pinchin' your thighs together whenever you thought about it. It almost drove me mad."

Tiny fairies beat their wings inside my stomach. "How did you know?"

"The same way you knew I wasn't a bad guy."

My eyelashes fluttered against his cheek, and I smiled at a loss for words.

"Let's get out of here." He interlaced our fingers, leading me back to the rest of the group.

I bit my lip, grinning. "Good. Because I could really use some pants."

His eyes twinkled and he kissed the Claddagh ring. "Not for long."

22

FINN DIDN'T TALK TO ERIMON the entire car ride back, and we had to stop three times for him to puke. There hadn't been much conversation between any of us. We all knew what the next night would bring. An unsettled tension rested between us, and I'd be lying if I said I hadn't thought some of that tension was resentment toward me. Cu had called me a curse when we first met. If I thought about it, he hadn't been too far off. Would The Dullahan have risen to hunt again if he hadn't sensed me? What if I had never stepped foot on Irish soil?

Obviously, Phoebe had a lot on her mind because not once had she noticed Erimon sliding his hand into mine, or the occasional moment I played at the ink on his arm. Then again, she had her own trapped thoughts. Immortality. Eternity. Patrick. She'd crawled into bed like a zombie that night, and for once, I didn't know what to say to make her feel better.

Hey, champ. Look at it this way: You won't grow old and gray like me.

I hadn't seen that going over very well.

Sleep didn't come easy, and my brain only allowed it in spurts. Memories of my own breath dwindling, the heat choking me, my throat closing as I lay in Erimon's arms...dying. I tossed and turned most of the night, praying to any god that would listen that I wouldn't die tomorrow night. That *no one* would die or be injured. I couldn't live with it. I just couldn't.

The ring hummed on my finger, and Erimon's pine scent filled the room.

I sat up, my heart racing, and sprinted to the window. There in the dimly lit alleyway was Erimon, leaning casually on his bike. He waved at me and motioned for me to come outside. I looked at a soundlessly slumbering Phoebe and bit down on my lip. Holding up a finger to him, I grabbed the tablet on the nightstand and scribbled her a quick note. After throwing on some clothes and a jacket, I crept out of the room. When I rounded the corner to the alleyway, my heart sang. So much had changed from the first day we met. I'd never been the type to suggest the concept of love at first sight, but this— Erimon, the bubbling feeling in my stomach—maybe there was something to it.

He held his hand out to me, beckoning me with his hooded gaze. Our palms touched, and I hugged the jacket around myself.

"I want to take ye somewhere and didn't need the others gossipin'." His eyes sparkled as he smirked.

"Worried about my honor?"

He pulled me to him, running the back of his hand over my cheek. "Not if I can help it."

I blinked, and we appeared in a lush forest. Where we'd

left, it'd been nighttime, but here, the sun blazed through the canopy, making animated shadows dance over the leaves. A light fog settled in the air bouncing the sunbeams like ethereal rays. Emerald moss coated nearby boulders, parts of tree trunks and cushioned the dirt beneath our feet. A distant waterfall spilled into a cerulean pool, sunlight reflecting in the cool water, making it glitter. It looked like something straight out of a painting.

"Where are we?" I touched a purple flower petal, letting the dew collect on my fingertip.

"The Bog Garden." Erimon stood still with his hands clasped in front of him, watching me with a sparkle in his gaze.

"I read about that. It's near Blarney Castle but—" A yellow bird perched on a tree branch, the song flowing from its beak like a mystical lullaby.

"The one human eyes can see, yes. The only way to get to this portion, however, is via Druid." His head and gaze followed me as I approached the bird.

Slowly, I raised my finger, and after two small chirps, the bird hopped onto it. "I also read that Bog Garden has fairies living in the flowers."

His arm wrapped around me from behind, his hand splaying over my stomach. "They are if you look close enough." He stroked his knuckle over the bird's crest, taking it from me as I bent forward, surveying the flower bed at my feet.

Two transparent wings like an insect flapped, buzzing, and a small female body no larger than my hand flew up. She was naked save for strategically placed leaves with blonde curls hanging down to her ankles. She gasped when she saw me, and spat but it barely even felt like a raindrop on my arm. After bristling her wings, she zoomed away.

I stared in front of me, unblinking. "That was a fairy?"

Erimon crouched beside me, resting the bird on his shoulder. "I probably should've warned you. Fairies are nasty little buggers. I've been bitten by one—twice."

"I thought they'd be spritely—casting glitter and sparkles wherever they flew."

He traced his fingers through my hair. "And I'm sure you never imagined a Druid to look like me."

Closing my eyes, I groaned as his fingers circled over my scalp. "What's the difference between a fairy and fae then?"

"Fae are normal size just with pointy ears and regional powers." There was a slight bitterness to his tone.

I looked at him with a hooded gaze. "Do Druids and Fae have a beef or something?"

The bird flew from his shoulder, excitedly flapping its wings as a twin yellow bird appeared.

"No. I've just never gotten along with most of them, personally. The society. The courts. Give me the warrior's life with no title any day of the week." He gave a lop-sided grin and took my hand, leading me toward the waterfall.

He swiped his arm up, kicking up flower petals. They fell to the ground in vibrant shades of yellow, pink, and purple—like summer rain.

Slipping a pink petal that'd landed in my hair, I grinned at him—the ring on my finger pulsing against my skin.

"Your connection with the wind, the ground—" He swirled his hand in a circle, creating a spiral of petals. "How do you feel here?"

Closing my eyes, I concentrated on the wind curling over my arms like satin. "I feel I could barely whisper your name, and you'd still hear me."

"Take off your shoes, Abby." He commanded—a fire lit in his gaze when I opened my eyes.

Doing as he asked, I stood barefoot, the soil seeping between my toes.

"And now?" He circled me, studying me.

An invisible current washed over my chest, and I dragged my hands down my throat, over my breasts, and wrapped my arms around myself. "I *am* the earth."

He stood in front of me, and blue tendrils floated from his palm, coiling around my body in shimmers of blue and white. Bit by bit, my clothes disappeared, replaced by a pale blue silk dress twinkling from the sun. The cloth was akin to wearing nothing at all—a cloud hanging from my body to use as I saw fit.

He locked our gazes and with slow, calculated movements, slipped his jacket off, followed by the white tank top underneath until he stood shirtless and barefoot. The wind played through the branches, making music intended for only the two of us to hear. I swayed my hips, the cloth shifting over me like a lover's caress. My hands traveled up my stomach, climbing past my neck and bunching in my hair. I was the lady of the wood and the trees, the flowers, the very ground I sank my toes into, were all my children.

Erimon's strong arm curled over my hips, his hand trussing my dress. My eyes fluttered open to find him devouring me with his stare. He tightened his grip around me, bending me backward. His hand began a torturous trail starting at my lips, meticulously letting a finger dip into my mouth before dragging it down my throat. He spread his hand wide once it reached my breasts, and a swirl of wind enveloped me.

I slid my leg up his thigh. He caught me under the knee, pinning me to his side. As his touch reached my abdomen, a surge of warmth erupted in my core, almost sending me over the edge. Gasping, I went to pull myself up, but he dipped me back again, pressing his lips against the fabric over my ribs. The wetness from his tongue seeped through the silk as he kissed his way between my breasts, circled over my throat, and pulled me upright.

We paused, peering at each other. Nature had always been my escape from the world—a domain. Here, with him—it felt like my *castle*. Ours to mold and control, to let it consume us. The heat from the sun beaming down on us mixed with the soft earth between my toes and those eyes—Erimon's eyes like two gleaming sapphires—had my insides writhing.

I pushed my lips to his, wrapping my arms around his neck. His hardness pressed against my stomach as he pulled me against him, flesh against flesh that had me trembling. He kept one hand curled around me while the other removed his pants in one swift motion. My back hit against a tree trunk, and he cupped my chin, peeling away from the kiss.

"It was *never* about the deal, Abby." His eyes were feral but patient.

I ran my hands up his arms, feeling the tattoo sizzle against my skin. "I know."

A short masculine growl vibrated from his throat, and he cupped my ass, pinning my back to the tree and wrapping my legs around him. His lips crashed to mine, and he thrust his tongue in and out of my mouth as he bunched the dress at my hips. I'd expected the bark against my back to feel abrasive, rough—it softened to my touch, welcoming my skin like it was its own.

He plunged into me, and I cried out, my back arching as I dug my nails into the corded muscle of his back. The straps of the dress fell from my shoulders until the shimmers of cloth were merely an accessory circling my stomach. He worked the wind in tandem with his thrusts, the breeze tantalizing my breasts, making my nipples pucker. My body had answered his woodland call from the first moment our gazes met, and now it pulled me to him, succumbing to whatever force nudged us together.

The clouds parted, spilling more sunlight around us—framing us. Erimon kissed me—deeply, ravenously. The roll of his hips slowed as a searing heat crept up my inner thighs, trickling to my core. The heat built and built until a climax burst through me, making my head fly back, quivering and quaking.

He held me to him, carrying us away from the tree, continuing to kiss me with each step. As he lowered me, he slid the dress down my legs. His hand splayed on a flattened rock, covering it with cushioned moss.

I grinned against his mouth. "A mossy knoll."

"You did say *nothing* but—" He took one of my breasts into his mouth, tongue swirling around my nipple.

Heat ached between my legs—wet, ready, and greedy. I lifted my hips, rubbing against him as a silent plea.

He gave feather-light kisses to my collar bone, lifting to my chin and earlobe. "So impatient."

A white spark lit in his eyes as he drove into me, lifting my knee to his side. The waterfall splashed into the pool beside us, the faint sounds of fairies' wings vibrating like a hummingbird as they migrated from one flower bed to the next.

As he rocked in and out of me, I dug my fingers into the ground, pushing, pulling, transferring my every nerve through it.

You called me to Ireland. You, Erimon.

He froze, and my eyes flew open. Slowly canting his head to the side, a sultry grin tugged at his lips.

"Good girl," he teased, delivering one hard thrust, pushing me further up the rock.

My heart raced, breaths trying to catch up to the swirl of emotions charging through me like a hurricane. I moved against him, and we fell into a rhythm, his girth throbbing inside me. His tattoo pulsed once with a radiant blue glow the same instant the ring hissed on my finger. I sat up, locking my legs around him, and kissed him like it was our first and last night together.

He gripped the back of my head as he welcomed the kiss, delivering it back with equal urgency, his beard tickling my chin. The smell of sea salt settled in the air, followed by a light mist coating my skin. He traced a finger up my spine, heat building with each touched vertebra. I dipped my head back, and he kissed my throat, licking, nibbling, sucking. The trees whistled around us like Irish pipes, and images of myself in that shimmery dress with leaf garland braided in my hair pulsed through my mind.

"What am I, Erimon?"

His rhythm slowed, and he coaxed me back to the rock. His gaze turned weighty as he traced a single finger down the side of my face. "A treasure."

He plowed into me, filling me to the hilt with every thrust. The wind swirled around me, caressing every axon and sending an equal mix of heat and chill pulsing through my veins. It built and built until the universe exploded around me—stars burst against my eyelids, and branches sighed with me as I loosed a breath of release.

My eyes fluttered open, staring up at the hardened warrior with a soft smile displayed only for me. He pressed his forearms on each side of my head, rotating his hips, his taut stomach pushing against me. I pressed my hand to his cheek, and the ring caught the sun's glint, brightening as if in appreciation of our union. He shuddered at my touch and with a moan bordering on a snarl, he reached his own climax.

We lay motionless, breathy, and our skin sheen with sweat. The wind continued to play through my hair, the sun's rays warming my cheeks.

"We have a few hours before sunrise in the *real* world. Would ye like to stay here?" He let my hair fall through his fingers.

"That depends." I walked my fingers up his forearm. "How many more times can we do what we just did?" I was a ravenous tigress. I'd never realized how close to starving I was until Erimon. I'd gotten a taste of the nectar, and now I feared I could never get enough.

He grew hard again between my legs and lazily smiled down at me. "I'd give you forever if I could."

We made love several more times amidst the emerald moss and dipped branches of willow trees, pretending as if eternity were only within arm's reach.

23

WE'D FALLEN ASLEEP NAKED AND curled within each other's arms. The steady current from the waterfall lulled me into some of the deepest sleep I'd ever gotten. A family of squirrels squeaked overhead, chasing each other through the tree branches and stirring me awake. Erimon lay peaceful and silent. I watched the steady rise and fall of his bronzed chest, a calm expression on his face. Looking at him, you'd never imagine him a killer. Never dream of his rough and tough exterior.

I trailed my fingertip over the light beard on his chin and smiled against his shoulder as those sky-blue eyes opened to greet me.

His expression tempered as soon as he caught sight of me staring at him. "Top 'o the mornin'." He gave a lop-sided grin.

"You look so peaceful when you're sleeping." I nuzzled into the crook of his arm.

"You mean as opposed to when I'm fightin' death incarnate or demon dogs?" His lips curved into a lazy grin

Biting down on my bottom lip, I slipped on top of him and

pinned his arms above his head.

"I like where this is goin'." He rolled his hips beneath me.

"I want to know more about what you did to receive such an outlandish curse." I tapped my finger against a Celtic knot in the tattoo.

He frowned. "Can't we just pretend I've always been this upstanding gentleman?"

"I wouldn't go *that* far." I gave a lop-sided grin, pushing more weight on his arms.

"Fine." He closed his eyes and puffed his chest. After opening one eye to peek at me, he said, "You sure you want to hear this?"

"Yes."

He curled his fingers into fists. "I was extremely arrogant." He held up a finger. "I talked back to the Elder Druid more times than I care to admit." Another finger. "I bedded a different woman nearly every day of the week."

I glared at him.

"Hey. You asked. Do you want me to sugarcoat the truth?"

Flicking some hair over my shoulder, I nodded. "Continue."

"I was selfish. As I told you, I didn't perform bondings because I couldn't have one of my own."

"Druids can't be bonded to someone?" Nausea boiled in my stomach, and my gaze dropped to the grooves of the carved muscle above his hipbones.

He slipped his hand from my grasp and pressed his knuckle under my chin, lifting my eyes to meet his. "I never said that. But there was a time I saw it as a 'tie-down,' and when I started thinkin' of the possibility for it, I couldn't find her, so I gave up."

I didn't ask because I feared I wouldn't like the answer and brushed the thought away.

"Anything else?" I raised a brow.

His face turned stone cold. "I've killed a lot of people in my time, but it's always been in defense or battle." His jaw tightened. "But they all stay with me—ghosts. In my mind. My dreams. So, when you say I'm not a bad guy, that tells me I'm doin' my job at never getting to that dark place by letting them all go." His eyes lifted to mine, a gaze yearning to be told it was alright. "As soon as that would happen, I'd cease to be a Druid. And *that* is why the order normally forbids heroism."

I didn't say anything at first, staring down at an immortal man who'd spent centuries harboring what he's done—dealing with it, coping with it, all by himself. I cupped his face and kissed him—tenderly, sweetly—as if to say, you don't have to ride that white horse for me. I accept you as you are.

A groan vibrated at the back of his throat, and as he pulled away from the kiss, he pressed our foreheads together. "Where were you five-hundred years ago, hm?"

I sat back, trailing my finger down the light scattering of hair traveling in a line from his belly button down. "It's odd to hear a mystical entity being anything but perfect."

Erimon snorted, and he traced his fingers up my thighs. "We're expected to be."

"You have free will like us mere mortals. So that's bullshit."

Humor gleamed in his eyes. "I'd love to hear you say that to the Elder."

"Point me at him." I winked.

"What about you, Abby Weber? Ever stole gum from a gas station? Leave a lit paper bag of dog shite on someone's porch? Any flaws at all except for bein' far too beautiful than should be allowed?" He gripped my hip with a snarky grin.

I playfully punched him in the shoulder. "Of course, I have flaws. Take, for example, what I did recently. I stole a puppy from going to the pound."

He blinked once, slow and deliberate. "That's the flaw you come up with? Rescuin' a puppy?"

"It wasn't legal."

He bit back a smile.

"Shut up." I swatted him in the chest, half chuckling. "I've drunk too much, ate too much, and have thought some pretty bad things about certain people in my life."

"Just as I thought." He sat up, curling my legs around his waist. "Perfect."

Sliding my forearms over his shoulders, I interlaced my fingers behind his head and leaned into him. "We've already had sex several times. You don't have to butter me up."

"Mm." He licked the tip of my nose. "I haven't even begun to butter ye."

I scrunched my face, feeling the wetness on my nose but I didn't wipe it away.

"We're going to need to get back." He dragged a finger between my breasts, the callus on the tip of his finger making me shiver.

"Can The Dullahan find me here?"

"No. But you're mortal. Stay too long in a place like this, and it'll drive you mad."

My shoulders slumped. "A small sacrifice."

"I quite like your mind the way it is." He brushed his hand over my forehead and hair.

"Are you going to give a motivational speech to Team Druid?"

"Team Druid?"

I chuckled. "Patrick made it up."

"Of course, he did, the little green bugger." With a brightened smile, he shook his head. "Yes. I believe some talkin' around a fire is in order. Everyone needs to be aware of what we'll be up against. Not to mention the unpredictable factors."

"Any advice on what I should say to Phoebe? The whole immortality thing doesn't seem to be settling well with her."

He pressed his fingertips against mine and held our hands in mid-air. "I was born immortal, but I can imagine for someone becoming one, the idea of watching those you care about dying around you would be the most difficult part."

"Me. She agreed to marry Patrick to help ensure I lived and now will have to watch me die anyway." The words came out hushed and distant.

"You know your friend better than I do, but you need to make sure she understands and to make peace with it." His gaze turned grave.

Erimon silently made his own peace.

"Let's head back, Erimon." I cupped his cheek.

He gave a solemn nod, and, in a flash, we appeared fully-clothed in my room at The Lucky Cove, only to find an empty bed with no Phoebe in sight. Seeing her familiar handwriting scribbled beneath mine on the note, I scooped it into my hand.

"She went to Patrick's."

Phoebe's home was here now. With Patrick. A thought that hadn't crossed my mind until the realization of her being immortal settled in. I had an apartment back in America, a life, a job. To ensnare the euphoria that still fluttered through me from The Bog Garden, I pushed the thoughts away.

"I'm going to let them all know to meet at Patrick's." He removed the archaic pager from his jacket pocket. His thumbs worked wildly, punching in the numbers.

"I still can't believe you use a pager."

Erimon raised a brow. "How else would I get in touch with everyone?"

"Words on a phantom wind?"

"You think that's something I can do with just anyone?"

"Can't you?"

"Interestin'." Without explaining himself, he curled me into a hug, kissed my head, and poofed us in front of Patrick's house.

I'd drill him about it later. Phoebe was at the top of my priority list.

Squeezing Erimon's hand, I didn't have to say a word.

"Go talk to her. Come meet us by the fire when you're done." He gave my temple a quick peck and walked into the woods.

I knocked on the door with my head held low.

Patrick answered with a dimpled smile. "She's in the bedroom."

"Erimon is having everyone meet by the fire." I nudged my head at the woods.

Patrick swiped a scarf from the pegs near the entrance. "Say no more." After squeezing my bicep, he whisked away.

I pressed my palms against the tops of my thighs and rounded the corner to a sulking Phoebe sitting on the edge of the bed, staring at nothing on the floor. "Phoebs?"

Her green eyes lifted, softening when she saw me. "Hey."

"I know this is a stupid question, but are you okay?"

She bunched the sheets in her grasp. "I don't regret my decision at all but am I that dense to not think about the implications of what I'd be doing?"

It killed a sliver of my soul to see her like this. A vibrant, happy woman who I rarely saw sad or even angry. We used to joke about how strong her face must've been from all the smiling.

"You're not dense." I sat next to her, curling her against my side. "I hadn't thought about it either."

"I'm going to live forever."

Hearing her say it out loud made my neck tense. "How many humans can say that?"

"We've both seen movies, Abs." She stared up at me, unblinking. "Unless you're Lestat or Damon Salvatore most of them seem to claim it isn't all it's cracked up to be."

"You've got a lot to offer the world. And now you can do so much more. Make your immortality *mean* something."

She rested her head on my shoulder. "I don't want to watch you die."

"You won't. Not tonight. Not in a week or years. I won't let it happen even if it means not letting you see it." I stroked her hair.

A huge declaration that I had no idea if I could truly keep.

"Did you…sleep with Erimon?"

This was how I got Phoebe back. "Yes."

Her head shot up, her cheeks flush with pink. "You had sex with a Druid?" She said the word "sex" in a whisper like someone else listened to our conversation.

"Yes, Phoebe." I held up three fingers and wiggled them.

She cupped her hands over her mouth and giggled. "Three times?" After slapping my hand, she leaped up, doing one spin in the middle of the floor. "You've got to tell me more."

"Let's save that conversation for after The Dullahan is dead. Give us something to look forward to, hm?" A warm smile pulled at my lips.

She cocked her head to the side. "You seem different."

The ring hummed.

"What do you mean?"

"You've got this calmness to you. You're always wound so tight and worrying over the little things, but now…you're like spaghetti noodles." She beamed.

Something in me had changed in that garden. But I couldn't put my finger on it any more than how I was able to talk to Erimon through the wind and ground.

"Isn't that what they say about great sex?" My attempt at deflecting the conversation elsewhere.

She cackled and pulled me up. "Come on. Let's go join the others. I cannot wait to hear more about this tomorrow."

Yet another reason I loved my best friend. She had no doubts we'd all live to see tomorrow. No doubts that The Dullahan was as good as dead.

The whole crew sat around the fire as grey clouds shadowed the midday sun. Even the sky itself slipped into gloom over what would transpire when nightfall arose. I locked eyes with Erimon through the flickering flames. He sat silently on a log by himself, leaning forward with a set jaw.

Come to me.

His words fluttered over my ear as the breeze wafted past. As I went to him, he stood, and I curled my arm around his waist. He kissed the top of my head, and we stayed in that embrace for several quiet moments. Everything felt so natural, the actions fluid and unrehearsed.

"I see there's been some recent developments," Finn's baritone voice said. He gave me a warm smile, but I somehow couldn't find it in me to smile back.

Mave carved a design into the log she sat on with her dagger. "I called that days ago."

Cu grumbled and kicked his boots in the dirt. Phoebe grinned at me, Patrick even smiling as well, hugging Phoebe to his side.

"Everyone, I have some things to say." Erimon traced his thumb under my jaw before turning to speak to everyone.

"Lemme guess, you suddenly prefer men?" Finn asked, raising a bushy eyebrow before roaring with laughter.

"Very cute, Finn." Erimon's gaze fell to the sparking embers. "I know you all agreed, for the most part, to help because of favors owed. I want you to know that you all fighting by my side tonight pays back those favors tenfold. I also know some of us have never been considered friends."

Cu snorted, digging his heel into the ground.

"But you have my sincerest gratitude." Erimon's eyes shot to me before returning to his warrior band. "The Dullahan's strength has grown. He also has the advantage of the blood moon tonight, which will make him even *stronger*. I need you all to acknowledge—" He paused, peeking a glance at me again before clearing his throat. "I need you all to acknowledge the possibility of injury or…death. He may have the power to do one or both to immortals assisted by the blood moon."

Nerves swirled in my stomach, shooting through my chest and into my throat. "What? You never said anything about that." I stepped in front of Erimon.

"I acknowledge it, Druid. And I'll still fight." Mave gave a curt nod.

"As will I." Finn stood, slamming his fist against his chest.

"Aye," Cu said.

I frantically shook my head, looking around at all the immortals willing to give up eternity for my sake. Whirling to face Patrick and Phoebe, I held up a finger. "Don't either one of you agree to this. Don't."

Patrick gulped and looked past me to Erimon. "You still have my fists if you need them."

Tears pooled in my eyes, and before Phoebe could say anything, I grabbed Erimon by the crook of the arm and hurled him away from everyone. "A word."

Erimon let me drag him and let out a deep sigh once we were by ourselves. "Abby—"

"Don't Abby me." A tear rolled down my cheek. "Why would you not tell me that?"

"Because you wouldn't have let them—let me—help you, if you knew it could mean our lives for yours." He played with his rings, not meeting my gaze.

"You're damn right I won't." I threw my hands in the air, turning my back on him. "I can't."

"There are four immortals over there willing to sacrifice everything for you. For you to be able to *live* your life. Refusing their help is like spittin' in their bleedin' faces."

I spun back to face him, seething. "How dare you."

"Jump down from your high horse one minute, Abigail." He stepped forward, glowering down at me. "And realize this isn't only about you. The Dullahan needs to be stopped. You think it's all over the minute he has your essence? Because it's *not.*"

"Of course, I know this isn't just about me, but I can't stand the idea of people dying for me."

His nostrils flared. "We're all born and bred for this. Don't insult them by takin' that away from them, do you not understand?" He yelled his last word, and a pair of wings sprouted from his back.

My jaw dropped, and I took a step back, eyes bulging at the brown and white feathers, the predatorial shape of them familiar—a falcon.

"Abby? What's the matter?" Erimon squinted at me.

"You have—you have—" I stammered, unable to say the final word.

"Holy shite. Those are new," Finn yelled from the fire, pointing at Erimon's back.

Erimon shot a look over his shoulder, and his brows pinched together. "Wings. I've *never* been able to conjure wings."

Staring up at them in awe, I shuffled forward. "Erimon, I'm sorry. I should be thankful any one is willing to help at all." Tears poured down my cheeks.

He frowned and the wings folded back as he pulled me to him, hugging me. "I'm sorry I yelled at ye. I can't stand hearin' you say you don't want me risking my life to save yours."

Sniffling, I reached over his shoulder to stroke the feathers on his wing. It rustled against my touch. "They're falcon wings."

He flashed a lazy smile. "I thought you hated me there for a minute. And all it took to reel you back in was a pair of wings, hm?"

"They're beautiful. How were you never able to conjure them before?"

He stretched the wings to their full span with a crack of his neck and pulled them back in tight. "My powers have evolved since the day I started my trainin'. Each was a milestone—a marker. The day I decided to rebel, fire. The day I committed to the ways of the Druid, wind. These..." He peered over his shoulder, flaring the wings with a grimace. "I think they're because of you."

A breath hitched in my throat. "Me?"

"Hey, you two. The day isn't gettin' any younger," Finn yelled at us from the fire.

Erimon took my hand. "Some illustrious leader I am, eh?"

A laugh pushed from my lungs and I wiped away the remainder of the tears from my cheeks.

"Bleedin' hell. Please tell me some bird somewhere isn't wingless." Mave stared wide-eyed.

"Not how it works, Mave." Erimon's brow furrowed. "At least I don't think so."

Cu snorted and pushed to his feet. "At least we have an aerial advantage now, hm?"

"Everyone, I apologize for my outburst, and please know there aren't words to describe how grateful I feel for having you all on my side." I pressed my hands over my stomach.

"Even us immortals seek glory in our death because we don't know if we'll ever meet it," Finn said.

Mave nodded as she gazed into the fire. "Yes. You'd be surprised how powerful eternity can be, Abby. Between us all, we've lived for thousands and thousands of years. Far longer than any being should. If any of us die tonight, it would be fightin' for something we believe in—for the greater good. And there'd be no regrets because we've lived for more than one lifetime."

Cu nodded, remaining silent.

"I still hope for victory with no casualties so I can celebrate with you all afterward." A weak smile curled over my lips.

Erimon tightened his arms, making the wings disappear. His jacket now had two torn holes down the back. Grimacing, he flexed, and the wings popped back out.

"Do you know how to use those things?" Patrick asked.

"I'm a fast learner. I need to be."

We all sat around the fire, letting the dancing flames bounce in our gazes. Each of us mentally prepared ourselves in whatever way we needed—a shared silence between a group of people that knew and didn't know simultaneously what was to come.

"I regret the very day I killed my sister," Mave murmured, her eyes glazing over, reflecting the flames.

We all sat up straighter.

"You what?" Cu turned his stony features in her direction.

She didn't dare look at any of us, kept her gaze on the fire as if it'd burn each word that escaped her lips. "It was a very long time ago, but before I wished for immortality. Before I made a deal with a sorceress, I'd been married to the King of Connacht. He was a bastard of a husband, and I left him."

Finn rolled his shoulders, and I curled my arm with Erimon's.

"My father, in turn, married him to my sister. I was so enraged—so jealous. I drowned her." Mave's chest heaved as her hands curled around themselves.

Phoebe rested her head on Patrick's shoulder, a tear rolling down her cheek.

"It's how I became the sole leader of Connacht. And I didn't want to see anyone else on my throne, so I made a deal with the sorceress. A life of immortality in exchange for never bearing children. Life for life."

She still didn't look at any of us, and we made no move to speak.

"I've never told a soul about this. And if I should survive, I trust that none of you will hold it against me because I regret with every waking breath doing what I did." She took a quick breath and shut her eyes. "And if I die, I needed it to be said. To confess."

We all gave solemn nods.

Cu glanced to her, his jaw hardening. "I killed my own son."

Mave snapped her attention to Cu, her nostrils crimson from fighting back tears.

"He came to Ireland to find me. I mistook him for an intruder, and he refused to tell me who he was." Cu threw a rock into the fire. "And I killed him."

A lump formed in my throat.

"Only to find out weeks later he was my son, and his daft mother told him not to identify himself to anyone." Cu snarled, and spit on the ground. "How's that for a confession?" His eyes lifted to Mave, who stared at him with saddened eyes.

Phoebe's whispy voice started to sing. *Óró Sé Do Bheatha Bhaile*. An Irish rallying call.

I recognized it well from all the time's Phoebe had sung it.

Finn chimed in with his rich baritone, and one-by-one, each of us joined with the fire as our only audience, night consuming the world around us with a starless sky, the blood moon beaming down on us with an ominous red hue.

Fog built up around us, but we continued to sing even as the monstrous form of The Dullahan appeared through the smoke mounted atop his fire-breathing steed.

24

WHEN I FIRST LAID EYES on the demonic form of The Dullahan I'd frozen with fear. It wasn't that it still didn't swirl through my body, but now, I had the overwhelming urge to live—to survive. To ensure that the others who were about to throw every skill, every strength they had to stop him—lived along with me.

The headless demon stood still on his horse, its hooves scraping the ground, snorting smoke into the air that mixed with the fiery embers. "You all know why I have come. Spare yourselves and let me have her."

Erimon reached behind me and yanked the seax from its sheath. "I'm goin' to do all I can to keep on eye on ye. But *use* this, Abby. Even if it's a stupid action, use it. Defend yourself if it comes down to it."

I nodded, staring up at him. Praying. Hoping it wouldn't be the last time I'd get lost in the way his eyes sparkled. We barely had enough time. So much left unsaid—so much still a mystery. "It won't leave my hand."

He set his jaw, curled his hand around the back of my neck, and kissed me as he held his other hand out to the elements. The world went silent around us, and our heartbeats thumped in sync. My eyes fluttered open as he pulled away, his eyes searching mine before he turned away, a newly formed sword in hand.

Phoebe stood on the other side of the fire, motionless and rigid despite Patrick trying to get her attention.

"The real question, Dully," Erimon started as he twirled the sword. "Is whether or not you're prepared to die today." He narrowed his eyes. "We are."

The Dullahan let out a raspy chuckle that echoed off the surrounding trees. "Then you all are fools." The horse's eyes burst with a red flame.

"Phoebe," I screamed.

She whipped her head at me, eyes as large as saucers.

"Come here. Now." The words were a command, not a request.

Patrick urged her on, pushing her toward me. She sprinted, and I held out my hand, grabbing onto hers once it was within reach and dragging her behind two trees nuzzled together.

The Dullahan snapped his human spine whip and a shield formed over his forearm. Without pause, he charged the horse forward, jumping through the roaring fire. The fire we'd all sat around singing an Irish song of rebellion. The fire I'd watched cast shadows over every groove of Erimon's face. The same fire that members of our party confessed mortifying deeds around.

Cu stepped from the shadows, roaring in his warp-spasm beast form, swinging the large ax. Dozens of holes formed in the ground, billowing swirling fog as the goblins crawled out. Mave shrugged off her cloak, yanking the sword on her back from its sheath, doing a low spin that lopped off two goblin heads. Finn snarled as he removed the hilt from his jacket, forming his fog sword.

"Flank," Erimon yelled to Finn as he stormed the left side.

Finn ran to the right. Erimon jumped, pushed off a tree with his boot, and winced, pushing those newly earned falcon wings from his back. They flapped once, giving him extra air-time and a chance to deliver a devastating blow to The Dullahan's shield. But he dropped to the ground, grunting as he rolled to his feet.

"What the bleedin' hell was that?" Finn yelled.

Erimon rolled his shoulder. "I'm workin' on it."

"Ye better work faster, lad." Finn raised a thick brow.

Patrick clenched his fists, the gold pooling over them, hardening. A goblin leaped in front of him, and he slammed his fists together, popping its head between them with a *splat* sending green ooze spraying in our direction.

Phoebe slapped her hands over her ears, rocking back and forth with her back pressed against the tree trunk. "How are you so calm right now, Abby?"

I didn't take my eyes off Erimon with the dagger's hilt firmly in my grasp. Crouching behind the tree, I fought every impulse to charge ahead and join them. Even with my leg muscles twitching, pulsing, and urging me onward. "Remember when you told me deciding to marry Patrick was easy. That it felt right?"

"Yes," her small voice squeaked.

"Last night, I made a similar decision. And I plan to make sure it's seen through." I winced as The Dullahan slammed his shield into Erimon's chest as he made another aerial attack that came up short.

"What did you—" Phoebe started to say before a hole opened between us, several hell hounds emerging.

Phoebe screamed and backpedaled away on her hands and heels. Without a passing thought, I slammed the knife into one hound's head, grimacing as I yanked it back out, ignoring the oil-like blood smeared over my hands, my face, my jacket.

"You've got to be shitting me," Mave said, falling on her back as a hound pounced on her. She grabbed its jaws, prying them apart as they snapped at her face.

"Compliments of Ilmarinen I'd imagine." Several hounds leaped on Finn's shoulders, biting and clawing. He threw one into a tree as he thrashed and spun.

Cu's monstrous form stormed for Mave, slamming his shoulder into the dog and sending it flying into the tree branches. Mave sat up on her elbows and gave a single nod as thanks.

"Come on, Phoebe. Move," I yelled, hurrying to another spot.

Phoebe scrambled behind me, and the hounds followed, the sounds of their claws scraping against the dirt pulsing in my ears. My heart pounded so fiercely it made the back of my skull sting, watching the hounds snarl and snap their way toward us. Shoving Phoebe behind me, I held the knife up, unable to stop my arm from trembling.

Two fireballs launched into their sides. Yelping, they landed on the ground in slumps with sizzling holes in their stomachs.

Erimon's hand lowered from across the clearing, immediately turning back to The Dullahan once he saw we were safe…for now. I stared at the small dagger, shifting my eyes to the hounds dead at our feet that each was as big as we were combined.

Closing my eyes, I whispered into the passing breeze, "I need more than this dagger."

"Who are you talking to?" Phoebe asked, tremors lacing her voice.

My eyes flew open. Iron ore began to seep from the ground near us, swirling into the air as wood flew in shards from surrounding trees. "Erimon."

A sword, the twin to Erimon's, fell into the dirt.

Don't cut yourself with it.

After shoving the dagger into Phoebe's limp hands, I scooped the sword into my palm.

"Do you know how to use that?"

I sucked on my lip, the sword heavy yet surprisingly light in my hand. Erimon's wings flapped twice, three times before he fell to the ground. With each attempt, he grew stronger.

"I'm a fast learner," I said, stumbling backward as a hound headbutted me in the ribs. Breaths no longer flowed through my lungs as I held the blade up.

The beast landed on it, impaling itself. Black blood splashed over my eyes and mouth, making me sputter. Wrists burning from the immense weight on the sword, I rolled to my side, slamming the hound into the dirt and using my foot to pry the blade free.

Erimon, Mave, and Patrick focused on Dullahan while the

other two used their hulking forms to keep as many hounds and goblins away from them. Erimon pulled fire into his palm, hurling repeated fireballs in tandem with delivering blows of his sword. Patrick beat his fists into the horse, trying to launch its rider off, but the horse kept kicking him away with its hooves.

Mave used her blade to block snaps of Dullahan's whip, leaping into the air to kick or punch at him and his shield. She landed, blowing out a haggard breath, and the point of the whip slammed into her shoulder.

My throat closed, and I stood still, staring through the smoke at a wounded immortal warrior goddess. Blood poured from the wound. Grinding her teeth, she yanked herself free, glaring up at the laughing horseman. Rubbing her fingers together, she smeared three lines of her own blood down her face—warpaint. She yanked her blade free from the ground and held it above her head with a shrill battle cry.

"Mave," I whispered.

She'll heal. Keep focus.

Phoebe yelped behind me, and it snapped me back into action. Three goblins waddled toward her as she scrambled across the dirt on her butt. I launched forward, stabbing the sword through two of them like grotesque kabobs. I shook the blade to remove the goblins, but they stuck to it like glue. Slamming my boot against them, I pushed, and green sludge slid down the edge.

Another goblin leaped through the air from my side. I turned on my heel and swung my sword, lopping off its feet. It fell to the ground, shrieking, trying to pull itself away with its hands. A dagger with a Celtic pommel slammed into its body.

Phoebe gasped and threw her hands up. "I didn't mean to, I—"

I squeezed her shoulder. "Thank you."

An electric chill shot down my spine. The Dullahan's head, hanging from his saddlebag, stared at me, its eyes glowing yellow, mouth gaping. The horse snorted, eyes ablaze with red. I wanted to back up, to move to another area of cover, but goblins and hounds surrounded us, and the only way was forward.

The horse charged and I stood my ground, grip tightening on the sword's hilt. What I intended to do once The Dullahan got close enough, I wasn't sure, but something was better than curling into a ball and waiting for it to happen.

Dark clouds rolled in, dimming the red light from the blood moon. Thunder roared like an angry Titan in the sky.

Closer. Closer.

Finn and Cu ran from opposite sides. Cu threw his shoulder into the horse while Finn leaped, wrapping his arms around The Dullahan and tackling him to the ground. I'd knowingly held my breath despite the burning building in my lungs and only now found the strength to let it out in shallow bouts.

As Finn wrestled with Dullahan on the ground, grabbing bits of his torn robe, bone, and decayed flesh, Cu wrestled with the horse.

"I'll keep the horse distracted," Cu yelled, slamming his fist between the horse's eyes.

Goblins and hounds had me, and Phoebe surrounded. They walked toward us slowly, deliberately, forcing us to a confined space. Our backs pressed against each other, and we held our blades up.

"Abby, I'm immortal. If they don't kill me, I'll—I'll heal." Her body shook behind me, making my elbow vibrate.

"Don't finish that thought, Phoebe. I'm *not* leaving you." I ground my teeth and sliced a hound that got too close in half. "These things won't kill me."

"What are you talking about? Do you see those teeth?"

"Their job is to slow me down. Make it easier for *him*."

More and more holes opened from the earth. For every two I killed, four more would appear like a hydra.

I tried to stay focused—tried to keep positive but—

Spiky rock walls launched from the ground, killing all creatures who circled us.

Run to the other side. Now. Go.

There was just enough space between the rocks for us to slip through. I grabbed Phoebe's hand and led her away.

Erimon let out a monstrous growl, splaying both hands, lightning flashing in his eyes. The ground vibrated beneath our feet as hundreds of rocks exploded through the soil. His arms shook as more and more rocks plunged through the earth, suspended in the air. Pulling a flashing lightning bolt from the sky, he wrapped each rock in electricity, closed his fists, and the stones flew in all directions.

Goblins and hounds fell in heaps, and those that didn't get hit sizzled and smoked from the lightning coursing through them.

"Do you think that was the entirety of my army, Druid?"

Erimon ignored him, his lip bouncing in a snarl. He crouched and pushed off the ground, flaring those wings, catching the wind as it breezed past. Flapping them, he paused in mid-air, surveying the battlefield. Another flash of lightning crackled, and he threw his fists up, pulling its power to him as it wrapped around his hands. Swooping up, he folded the wings back and dive-bombed at The Dullahan.

"Finn, now!" Erimon roared right before slamming into the ground, sending every bit of that lightning into The Dullahan's chest.

Finn pulled the golden shackles from his jacket and fastened them to The Dullahan's wrists as the lightning held him still but not for long.

Several surviving hounds hobbled toward us, snarling, baring their teeth. One leaped for Phobe, I swung my sword and missed. Golden hands flew into the hound's neck, severing its head from the body.

Phoebe cried at the sight of Patrick and hugged him.

The Dullahan's laugh started low and breathy as the lightning faded away. Erimon's wings twitched as he slid back, holding up the sword. Dullahan pushed to his feet, the chain from the shackles clanking. He ran his bony fingers over the metal, and his laugh grew louder, maniacal.

"Do you think these will stop me?"

"We only need them to stop you long enough for us to kill ye," Mave spat, the wound in her shoulder healed.

Dullahan's tattered robes flapped in the breeze as he splayed his hand at the horse. Cu held the kicking beast on the ground, wrapped in his arms. The hanging head glowed bright orange, and all dead goblins and hounds began to reanimate. Bones cracked and popped as they stood.

Some kind of...zombies.

"Let's see how you handle them when they *can't* die." The Dullahan pushed his fingertips together.

"Bleedin' Christ," Finn mumbled, holding up his fog sword.

"Abby." Phoebe's small fingers grabbed my jacket, making it tighten on my shoulders.

The hell hounds walked on stumps, some of their jaws broken, foam spewing from their mouths.

"She *will* be mine before this night is through." The Dullahan lifted his shackled hands, and all the goblins and hounds launched at us.

So, this is how I died.

25

PATRICK TURNED HIS HANDS BACK to normal, hauling Phoebe away and behind a boulder. I wanted to follow, but I didn't want to hide. Whether it be behind cover or out in the open, this could very well be it.

The zombie hounds let out blood-curdling howls, their pitch rivaling nails on a chalkboard. I covered one ear, wincing as my other eardrum threatened to burst.

"Stay here and don't move, ye hear me?" Patrick asked a worried Phoebe.

She shook her head, tears streaking her cheeks as she reached for his shirt to stop him, but he already turned away.

Dozens of goblins and hounds crawled over Cu, pulling his arms away from The Dullahan's horse. Once free, it leaped to its feet with a shake of its head and galloped to its master. With labored steps, he hoisted himself to the saddle, and pulled the whip into his hand.

A zombie hound charged at me, and I slashed, clipping its shoulder, a mound of flesh flying to the ground. It didn't stop it. Didn't even faze it. I held my blade above my head, ready to strike again as it leaped into the air. Another blade skewered it. Sliced it. Not once, but four times. The remaining pieces wiggled on the ground, still alive but unable to move.

"You're handlin' that pretty well for a zoologist," Mave said, jutting her chin at the blade.

I offered a weak smile, thankful for the brief moment of normalcy, for the jabs we all hadn't near enough time to share.

Erimon used everything at his disposal, launching rocks, fireballs, lightning blasts when they flashed in the sky, warding as many of the zombie creatures away as possible.

The Dullahan charged his horse at Finn. The golden shackles clanked on Dullahan's wrists as he blocked a blow from Finn's fog sword with his black shield.

I stood out of breath, covered in blood, and tired. So. So. Tired. A neverending battle ensued around me, and the wooziness made everything seem to react in slow motion. Regardless of all the immortal powers surrounding me, we were being overrun. Goblins and hounds continued to crawl from the holes and would not die unless sliced into a dozen pieces.

Every time Erimon would seal a hole, The Dullahan would re-open it. Given his weakened state from the golden shackles, it was his only real line of defense. Cu's hulkish form stormed the perimeter, hounds, and goblins scattered over his shoulders, biting and clawing.

Suddenly, none of the goblins or hounds attacked me, but continued to fight everyone around me, distracting them, deterring them. As Erimon locked eyes with mine, I realized I was right. This was The Dullahan's plan, and the shackles made no difference. He never intended to use the goblins and hounds to kill me. That was *his* job. They were merely a distraction. Panic swept up my spine, and I turned on my heel, ready to sprint. A hound slid in front of me, teeth bared, drool sliding down his chin, pooling at the floor.

I kicked it in the head and followed with a swing of my sword, slashing its chest. As I took another step forward, two goblins leaped at my ankles. I bashed one in the skull with the hilt of my sword and kicked the other goblin away and into the trees. Another step.

Erimon flew up, avoiding a launched attack of zombie goblins. One grabbed his foot, and he used a rock to hurl it away. The flaps of his wings were strong and defiant now—worthy of the falcon predator they resembled.

Patrick, ragged and tired, threw golden punches at hounds. Each swing grew slower and packed less force. The power of the blood moon, making even immortals tire, I imagined. A hound leaped from nowhere, slamming its paws into my chest. The sword flew from my grip and I fell with a grunt, blocking my head with my arms. The hound's hot breath misted against my hands, the drool landing on my stomach, and it snapped its jaws at my face, pinning me.

The snapping ceased. As I parted my arms, I saw Finn standing over me. The hound lay in two pieces. If Finn wasn't fighting The Dullahan...I sat up, looking for Erimon. The Dullahan walked toward him, his feet dragging behind him in weakened steps, hands clenched within the shackles. He gripped the human spine whip in his palm, raising it above his head to strike. Hands trembling, I pushed my fingers into the ground, snapping a nail.

"Erimon," I said into the dirt.

We locked eyes as The Dullahan's whip swung past Erimon and came straight…for me. I'm not sure I would've even known what happened were it not for Erimon's pain-stricken face.

Immense pressure built in my chest, and my breathing shallowed as I gasped. I looked down at the tip of The Dullahan's spine whip lodged in my sternum. A crimson liquid stained my already dirtied shirt. Noises drowned out around me, and all I could hear were waves of voices, murmurs. My body went limp, my shoulder slamming against the ground as I fell over.

"Abby. Oh my God," I faintly heard Phoebe's voice yelling from somewhere behind me. My hands numbed. I struggled to peer up at the darkened form of The Dullahan glaring down at me.

He jerked his hand, and the pressure in my chest disappeared. A moist heat pulled over my torso, the taste of copper consuming my mouth.

"You are *mine*, Abigail. A valiant attempt," The Dullahan said, his headless form dipping down to my face. He held the golden shackles in front of me before he stood, laughing at the blood moon. His horse appeared, and as he mounted his steed, all the holes stopped glowing—all creatures disappeared. Tunneled darkness threatened to consume me.

"Fuckin' hell, no." Erimon snarled.

I heard the flap of his wings followed by his knees sliding over the dirt to me. He moved my head to his lap.

I could hear Phoebe's frantic voice, her fists pounding on

something hard.

"Finn, do something. Do what you did for me," she cried. She'd been pounding on Finn's chest.

Finn mumbled something that I couldn't decipher, my vision going in and out of focus.

"Try. Please." Phoebe screeched. She was crying.

Finn crouched in front of me. His hands raised to my lips, filled with a clear, cool liquid. "Drink, Abby," he commanded.

Erimon helped me lift my head. I weakly moved my blood-crusted lips toward Finn's palms, sipping as much as I could. The water felt like daggers going down my dry throat. I waited, expecting to feel something different.

"Why isn't it working?" Phoebe sobbed.

I heard Patrick's voice next and imagined his arm going around her shoulders, attempting to prepare her for my death. "Phoebe—" was all he managed to say.

"I'm—I'm sorry. I can only heal the wounded. She's too far gone. She's dyin'," Finn's voice boomed above me.

"No," Phoebe wailed, her sobs becoming muffled. I pictured her face burying into her new husband's chest.

Death was a funny thing and nothing like how imagined. There was no hand reaching out to you to guide you to an afterlife. No light to walk toward. Only darkness. Pure darkness that eased its way in to lull you to an endless slumber.

I blinked my eyes a few times, trying to focus my vision. Erimon's face looked down at me, clear as crystal. I raised a shaky hand to his cheek, and his hand grabbed mine, planting a kiss on my palm. I could've sworn I saw tears forming in his eyes. His jaw squared off, and his face fell suddenly. A harsh breath pushed from his lungs, and he picked me up, cradling me in his arms.

My head felt fuzzy as it usually did when Erimon ported us. Breath wheezed from my throat, but the view of us on a cliff, overlooking the sea, the night sky blazing with twinkling white starlight, was unmistakable.

He sat on the ground with me draped in his lap, and he moved my hand so I could feel the mound of dirt we sat in against my fingertips. The coarse feel brought a faint smile to my lips.

One palm pressed to my cheek while the other hovered over the hole in my chest. He began to speak, his words hushed and calm. Like whispers on the wind, we'd made our own secret form of communication.

Glac cuid domsa.

Glac cuid de mo anam.

Beo.

Beo domsa mar a dhéanaimid ar cheann.

Beo.

Beo.

A vibration pulsed over my skin, settling into my legs, my arms. Erimon's tattoo glowed blue and bright. His blue eyes were now iridescent pools of white. He opened his mouth, the same light resonating within it. He dipped his head down.

"Kiss me, Abby," he whispered.

As I parted my lips, his mouth claimed mine, his tongue coaxing it further open. A force surging from him into me trickled down my throat, seeping into my chest. My fists clenched at my sides as a mixture of pain, comfort, and static coursed through every nerve in my body—the worst swirling in my chest. A bright light flashed, rays bursting from my chest. My back arched, and Erimon's hand pressed against me, keeping me still and deepening that kiss between us. I fell limp in his arms.

My eyes fluttered open, squinting at a lit sky where the sun had yet to rise. His scent filled the air, and I nuzzled my cheek against his arm, still in his lap. Still on the cliff. I tensed, snapping my hand to my chest. Healed.

"Eri—"

He slipped a finger over my mouth. "Shh, Abby. I've got a lot to explain."

A darkness traced my arm, and I blinked at a Celtic tattoo that started at my wrist, traveling up to my shoulder. I opened my mouth to speak but snapped it shut. Erimon stared into the horizon, tranquility on his face. Green, black, and red blood spattered his face and clothes. But his jaw remained unclenched, his shoulders relaxed.

"It took me far too long to realize what you are. What you *truly* are. And I figured it out at the right moment." His finger trailed down the fresh tattoo on my arm.

"As soon as you walked into the pub that night, every nerve in my body lit on fire. The tattoo *burned* my skin." He let my hair fall through his fingers, panning his eyes over me but never making eye contact. "I knew right then I was to give you something. But I didn't know what. My heart? My soul?

My life?"

My chest heaved, wanting so badly to say something but didn't dare interrupt him.

"It turns out…" He locked our gazes. "I was meant to give it *all* to you."

My heart thrummed, and the ring vibrated on my finger.

"Where are we, Erimon?" A deep part of me knew but couldn't form the words.

He hoisted me up, moving me, so my back pressed against his chest. "The Cliffs of Moher." The very tip of the sun peeked over the cliffs, the sky turning pink and orange. "Where Druids come to be reborn."

My heart stopped.

He kissed my temple as the sun rose. The tattoo on my arm turned a blazing red as dozens of images blasted through my head. They came so fast and overlapped each other in no sense of order, so it was hard to concentrate on them. A white owl flying overhead, endless forest, swirls of dirt, stag horns.

My hands dug into the dirt surrounding us, and for the first time, it whispered back, "Welcome home."

I turned to face Erimon, shoving his back to the ground and straddling him. "You need to be clearer than that."

He stared up at me with feral eyes, his hands trailing up my thighs but stopping. "You have the blood of the Bandruí in your veins. Female Druids. They've always been rare, and I haven't seen one in…I can't even remember. You were born a mortal. Nature found you worthy of power regardless but anything past that…had to be *given* to you." He patted the tattoo on my arm.

I sat back, nature around us speaking to me with every lap of the sea waves, every passing cloud, every earthworm crawling below the surface. "But how?"

He lifted to his elbows. "The Dullahan sought your essence— little did he realize him killing you created his undoing."

"But I would've died if it weren't—" I traced my fingers over the side of his face.

"You said it yourself, Abby. I called you to Ireland. It called you here to be reborn. You're the key to stopping the chaos cycle."

I stared at the tattoo. "What exactly did you give up?"

He rubbed his arm against mine, our tattoos glowing once they touched. "A part of my soul. My power."

"Your power? But how much I—"

He gave a lop-sided grin and cupped my chin. "I have plenty. What's a Druid without power? Whispering to me in the wind would only get us so far. You saw what we're up against."

"What power do I have?" I held my palm up as if something would appear in it.

"The continued joke of the Elder's curse. I have no idea. In time, it'll manifest itself, and when we know what it is, I'll show you how to use it."

It should've felt overwhelming. My mind should've been spinning. But it felt right. With him. Here. All of it.

"When you said all of it. That included your heart." I raised a brow.

His eyes grew heavy, and he kissed me, quick and sweet but just as erotic. "You've had it on a silver platter for days now."

I pressed my forehead against his. "I think you've had mine

before I knew you existed."

Erimon lifted my hand with the Claddagh ring, letting his fingertips scrape against my palm. "May I do the honors?"

I nodded, keeping our heads pressed together as he ever so deliberately slid the ring from my finger and turned the heart to face me. The ring purred against my skin.

"Did you tell the others where you were going?" I let my hands roam his shoulders.

"Ehm…no. They're probably losin' their damn minds by now."

"We should probably let them know I'm not dead."

"We will. But don't think I'm not porting you away so we can…explore this." He rubbed our tattoos together again, shocking us both with a grin.

His arms still had those full sleeves, but I squinted at his back. The tattoo spread across his shoulder blades but from there down was bare unmarked skin.

"This is…yours?" I held my arm out.

"A symbol of my undying devotion. And I'd do it again and again if I had to." He stood and helped me to my feet.

I wobbled at first and his arm snapped around me.

"They're going to have a lot of questions."

I kissed him. "And *you* will answer them all."

He ported us back to the carnage left behind. The crew sat around the dwindling fire, groggy and tired.

"Abby?" Phoebe's voice said sleepily.

Erimon let go of me, poking my back with one finger to go to her.

Phoebe ran over, fresh tears rolling down the dried ones on

her cheeks. "Where were you? I—"

I pulled back and ran my hands over the sides of her face, pushing back strands of auburn hair. "I'm here. I'm alive. And I promise you never have to worry about that happening again." The tattoo pulsed as if in agreement.

"How are you—" She stared at my chest. At the gaping hole in the fabric but no wound in sight. She lifted up my shirt, showing my bra to the world.

I snapped it back down with a snicker. "Erimon healed me."

"I didn't know you had the power to do that," Mave said, picking up my tattooed arm with two fingers. "Either of you care to explain?"

Phoebe gasped and yanked my arm from Mave's grasp, running her fingers up and down the ink swirls.

"I made a transference." Everyone shifted their eyes at each other. "I've told you all about the curse this tattoo represents. It allowed me to *give* part of myself to her—a part of my power.

"The polar opposite of selfishness," Patrick said, rubbing his stubbled chin.

Phoebe pushed past me and sprinted at Erimon, slamming her body into his with a resounding hug. "Thank you. Thank you. Thank you."

Erimon coughed and patted her back. "I kind of have a soft spot for her too, Phoebe."

"You can't simply *give* a mortal power," Finn said, rubbing the back of his head.

"I grew up not knowing where I came from. I never knew my parents. No relatives." I wrung my hands together, willing the wind through my hair to calm me. It answered. "In a past life, I was a Bandruí. It took this place. Ireland. A fellow Druid. And…dying, for me to be reborn."

Cu dropped his ax.

"She's the key?" Mave asked Erimon, pointing at me.

Erimon saddled to my side. "A twist I didn't even know I was creating in this story."

"You forget something, Monny." Finn nudged his head at me.

Erimon narrowed his eyes. "Thanks, Finn."

Pausing to study Finn's expression, I gripped Erimon's arm and turned him to me. "What is it?

"You're not immortal."

My eyes fell shut, a pain forming at my temple. "But how? When Patrick and Phoebe—"

His hands slid over my shoulders. "I performed a bonding. This was different."

"Then do it with us. You've given me part of your *soul*, Erimon. I don't think being eternally bonded with you in the official sense would be a huge step further." The branches overhead rustled as my heart raced.

Cu raised his brows, eyeing the trees curiously.

"I can't do my own. The only one who can is the Elder."

"Then let's go talk to him. You've proven you're not the same Druid. I'm a walking example of it." I turned to walk away like we were to leave in the same instant.

He gently pulled me back to him. "No one's seen him in over five hundred years."

"So, we find him," Patrick said.

Mave slid from the log, tapping her fingernails on her

sword's hilt. "We've got time before the next full moon. Time before The Dullahan realizes he doesn't have her essence. She *needs* to be immortal if we have any shot of destroying him."

"What power did you give up, anyway?" Finn asked Erimon.

"I don't know. And we won't know right away until the power has time to manifest. She's mortal. It has to make sense of its new host." Erimon kneaded my lower back with his thumb.

"And you've never done this before?" Cu asked, folding his arms over his broad chest.

Erimon shook his head. "I don't think I was meant to."

"Abby's still marked. We need to hatch a plan to find the Elder and be prepared," Mave said.

"And we will all talk about it, but first, if you all don't mind. Abby and I need to talk."

Before any of them could protest, he swirled his arms around us, and we appeared back in the Bog Garden.

26

THE BRANCHES OF THE WILLOW trees parted in greeting, the sun beaming brighter than the last time we'd visited. With our hands locked, he led me through the same path we walked before, only this time flowers bloomed beyond every step I took. Several fairies flapped past, not spitting, not biting, merely curious to see me.

"Wait." I stopped and gripped Erimon's hand.

He looked over his shoulder at me with a knowing smile as I took off my boots and socks. A calm coiled through me as my skin touched the moss. My flesh against nature's flesh.

"Tell me something, Druid." I pulled him to me, nuzzling my forehead against his chin.

"Mm, anything."

I trailed my hands down his tattoos, shivering as they reacted to my touch, the lines and knots feeling textured against my skin as I explored. "You said you weren't able to find *her*. This…mystical being you could bond with." I locked our gazes.

"You know the answer to this, Abby." He bumped his knuckle under my chin.

I slid my arms around him, dipping my fingers into the top of his pants. "I just want to hear you *say* it. Is that so wrong?"

He let out a deep masculine chuckle as his hand grabbed my ass and pulled me tighter against him. "Abigal Weber, it's you. Why do you think you're the only one I can talk to through the wind and ground? And just as the universe likes to play its cruel jokes of fate, we had to jump through hoops, and battle hellspawn to figure it out."

The tree branches rustled, the leaves shaking like a chuckling whisper.

He pointed up. "See? Even the trees are laughin' at us."

A gentle breeze wafted over us.

"Kiss me," I said into it, even though my Druid was right in front of me.

He smiled and obliged. As his lips slid over mine, nature sighed around us. The wind surged, mist coated our skin from the nearby sea, the sun beamed its brightest light.

I kept my hands on his face as we peeled away. "You asked me in that godforsaken heat box if I'd gotten my wish. If I feel whole."

His eyes searched, my face and he rubbed his thumb over my tattoo.

"Yes. I walked those steps backward, felt the surge when I reached the top, and wished with every fiber of being *just* to feel whole. I've never had a family. Never known where I came from or where I belonged." I pressed our tattoos together, beaming at the glowing red and blue swirls. "Now I know."

A grin tugged at Erimon's lips with so many emotions overlaying them—but the one that stood out like a sparkling brook was his sense of relief. I'd lifted if but a few of those burdens, the ones he buried deep.

"Since the cliff, I feel such a deeper connection to *everything*." I closed my eyes, listening to the blades of grass rub together like violins in the wind.

He brushed his lips over my ear. "Show me, Bandruí."

The ring thrummed as the word fluttered from his throat.

Moving to the closest tree, I pressed my hand against it, *feeling* its breath like a human's. In-and-out, steady and relaxed. Pinching my eyes shut, I used the same force, the same will when I'd whispered into the dirt to Erimon. Tiny white blossoms sprouted over the tree's branches, and an appreciative hum vibrated against my fingertips through the bark.

Erimon reached up and ran his thumb over one of the newly formed flowers. "I've never even tried to do that."

"I wouldn't have thought flowers to be on the top of a warrior's to-do list." I gave him a lazy grin.

He stepped beside me, grinding against my hip. "Despite my hardened nature, I can appreciate beauty."

I snaked an arm around his waist. "I tried to summon an animal, but it didn't seem to work."

"What are ye tryin' to summon, love?" He pressed the bridge of his nose against the side of my head.

"A white owl." I looked up at him.

His eyes sparked to life, and he turned me to face him. After interlacing our fingers, he held our hands in front of us. "Use me as a conduit. Try again."

"I'm not dumb. You're going to do it and make me think I did."

"I've never once thought or called you dumb. I'm serious. Try it." He kissed the tip of my nose.

I closed my eyes and instead of pushing the power through my hands, I pulled it from him. Picturing white feathers flapping through the sky, the large brown eyes, its head swiveling.

Hoot.

Erimon rubbed my palm with his thumb, and I slowly opened my eyes. A majestic white owl rested on a branch of the tree I'd communicated with. My heart galloped at the sight of it.

"I can't thank you enough for this," I whispered in the owl's direction.

Erimon tugged my hand. "Are you talkin' to the owl or me?"

Tears filled my eyes, and I laughed, jumping into his arms and wrapping myself around him. "You, you idiot."

"Never thank me for this again. Ever. Ye hear me?" He grabbed under my thighs, supporting my weight against him.

I peeled back. "Why?"

"This was meant to happen, Abby. I played my part, and I've told you I'd do it again in a heartbeat. I've spent most of my life wonderin' if I could even lead a selfless one. You showin' up told me I can and will. So, thank *you*."

I smiled and bit down on my lower lip as I twirled my hand behind him.

He gave a coy grin and squinted at me. "What are ye doin'?" He started to turn his chin, but I grabbed it with my free hand.

"Ah, ah. Just wait."

After pulling enough water from the sparkling river, I balanced it over our heads and let go. It fell over us like a shimmering bucket of water.

We both sputtered and laughed.

"If ye wanted to be kissed in the rain, you could've just asked." Water beads dripped from his spiky locks and collected on his eyelashes. "There's something I need to talk to you about, and I've been hesitatin' on bringing it up. You're so happy."

I tightened my thighs on his ribs, making him wince. "Is what you're about to say going to make me *un*happy?"

He cleared his throat and averted his gaze to the owl I'd summoned. "Probably."

"Erimon," I groaned, sliding down his body.

Erimon took one of my hands in his and drew absent circles on it with his thumb.

He licked his lips, unable to look at me. "I want you to go home, Abby. Go back to America."

Hurt, fury, and confusion tugged at my heart. I yanked my hand from him, taking a step back. "You what? What do you mean? Why?"

"You have a lot of loose ends to tie up. Your job. Your life." The corners of his jaw bobbed.

"You've already told me how many times never to be alone. How is me in a completely different country helping anything?"

He rolled his shoulders. "You wouldn't be alone. I'm asking Phoebe to go with ye. She has her own life to wrap up."

I pinched the bridge of my nose. "She's of this world. Her alone wouldn't stop him from showing up."

"Finn will be going with you too. He doesn't know it yet. But he's goin'. Big babby wouldn't want to port once, let alone dozens of times anyway."

"Finn? In my apartment?"

He gave a cheeky grin. "Funny thought, huh? You'll have to take photos."

I smiled, but it didn't last long.

He gripped my shoulders with a deep sigh. "Dully's power is greater here. And he won't even realize he doesn't have your soul for some time. Give me some time to figure out a plan while you figure out everything you need to do to start a new life. Not to mention I'll be portin' all over the universe in search of answers. I don't know who I'll encounter."

It killed me inside, twisted a knife in my gut to know he was right. Not to mention that he'd even thought to give me a chance.

"When you're not around me, Erimon, it's like—" I gulped, playing with the Claddagh ring. "A piece of me is gone."

"Hey. Look at this way. An *actual* piece of me is gone whenever I'm not around ye now." He half-smiled, trying to make me smile too, but all he received was a smirk. "I'm not askin' you—I'm begging you. Please." He stared down at me, the skin between his brows wrinkled.

"What am I supposed to do when my power manifests? Roll with the punches?" I bit down on my lip to keep it from trembling, and a single tear streamed down my cheek.

Erimon lifted a hand to brush the tear away. I closed my eyes, committing the way his skin felt on mine to memory. "You'll see me again before that happens. I'll be there for you.

Did you think this was goodbye?"

"I don't even know what to think anymore. This past month has been—" I started, but his lips pressed against mine, halting my words. I opened my eyes, staring up at that sparkling blue gaze.

"Abby, please? I'll be able to do more if I know you're safe, and you can always, *always* talk to me."

The wind gust blew past us, chilling my wet skin.

On a phantom whisper. Remember?

I wrapped my arms around him, burying my face against his neck, breathing him in. "Promise you'll come back to me. I want your word."

"I promise, Abby." He brushed his lips against mine.

And a Druid holds his word above all else.

I kissed him so deeply it was as if I tried to pull more of his soul into me, to harbor more of him to hold onto it while he was away. Our tattoos brushed over each other, rippling a vibrating coil that shot through my core.

Gasping, I pulled away. "What the hell was that?"

Erimon's chest pumped up and down as he looked from one arm to the other. "I haven't the foggiest."

The ring sizzled on my finger, and I dug my fingers into the back of his head.

"Make love to me before you leave me."

It wasn't a request, and by the way he hoisted me up with a dominating growl…he knew it.

We all sat at the table in Patrick's house. Erimon had done what he could to repair the destruction within the woods—filled holes, sped up the decay of corpses to feed the earth. But it still remained an eerie sight knowing what we'd all went through, how we fought.

"We learned a valuable lesson durin' this battle," Erimon started.

"That we lost?" Cu interjected.

"We lost because we thought The Dullahan was our only concern."

"He's right. The shackles only slowed him down. It didn't stop the creatures from escapin' those God-forsaken holes." Finn pounded his fist so harshly on the table it almost flipped over.

Patrick widened his eyes at Finn, who slouched forward like a scolded puppy.

"Perhaps the Druid should've been quicker to seal the holes," Cu said, venom lacing his tone.

Narrowing my eyes, I leaned forward. "He sealed them as fast as he could, all the while summoning rocks, hurling them all over the place, and not once hitting any of us. Not to mention The Dullahan constantly advancing on him, no doubt trying to keep him away from me. Everyone in this room put everything they had into that fight to the point of exhaustion. Don't start the blame game." My chest heaved up and down, the tattoo blazing red as I flopped back to the chair.

Erimon squeezed my thigh underneath the table as Mave and Finn exchanged grins.

Lips twitching, nostrils flared, Cu stood from the table, knocking the chair to the floor behind him. "I'll be outside.

When you all have come to some sort of an actual plan, come find me." The creature he turned into during his warp-spasm was easier to get along with.

"Are you sure it was only your *power* you transferred to Abby?" Finn asked Erimon with a twinkle in his eye.

"We can't expect Erimon to seal all the holes. Like Abby said, he moved faster than I'd ever seen him move before. We're goin' to need another strategy," Mave said.

"What powers does he have on the water?" Patrick chimed in, his one arm around Phoebe's shoulders, the other resting on the table, absently picking at the woodgrain with his fingernails.

Mave stared at the ground, and her lips were the only thing that moved when she spoke. "The Otherworld Islands."

Finn traced his fingers down his long mustache. "That might work. If we could break the Ninth Wave." He looked at Erimon.

Erimon scratched at the light beard on his chin. "It's a long shot, but if we could make the break and take The Dullahan with us, we'd have supreme power over him."

"Do you think the other gods would help you? Poppin' into their sanctuary such as it were?" Patrick asked.

"The last thing they'd want is The Dullahan showin' up, wreaking havoc on their misty paradise land." Erimon shook his head. "It's our best bet. Not only do we need to find the Elder before the next full moon, but we'll also need a ship, information, whatever else we can find as a means to lure The Dullahan."

"Do you think he's figured out a way to get the shackles off yet?" Patrick snickered.

"More importantly, do you think he's figured out why Abby's soul hasn't appeared?" Mave asked, her expression not near as amused as Patrick's.

"May I ask what the Otherworld Islands are?" I interjected.

"The Otherworld Islands are similar to the Underworld, or Heaven and Hell. Manannan is a sea deity who serves as the ferryman, but since none of us wish to arrive in the Otherworld in such a way, we will have to break the Ninth Wave ourselves," Mave explained.

"And how do we do that?" Phoebe asked.

"That's what we need to figure out," Finn said, looking between Mave and Erimon.

Erimon rose from his seat, pressing his fingertips into the table. "We all know what we have to do. When you know of something, alert me immediately." Mave, Patrick, and Finn nodded. "And would someone inform Mr. Grumpy Pants outside of our plan?"

Finn grumbled, pushing against the table to stand up. "I'll do it."

"Actually—" Erimon lifted a finger. "I need to talk to you, Finn." His gaze turned to Mave. "Would you please?"

She raised a thin red brow. "You're serious?"

Erimon plastered a fake grin.

She rolled her eyes with a sigh. "Fine. We're going to break the Ninth Wave together, might as well learn how to be civil at some point." She stood up, biting back a smile before she exploded in a fit of laughter on her way out the door.

"You wanted to talk?" Finn crossed his burly arms.

Erimon pressed his hands together like he was praying. "I want you to go back to America with Abby."

Finn's gaze moved to me before snapping back to Erimon. "America? Me?"

"My apartment's not big, but I have a couch, and it's relatively quiet most of the time." I gave a meager shrug.

"Oh, I see you've two already talked this through, hm?" Finn's hands moved to his hips.

Erimon moved closer to him. "We're going to have to port over a dozen times to get the answers we need. You'd serve me better by keepin' an eye on her. If she calls for me, I can come, but I'd feel better knowing someone is there to handle the seconds it'd take me."

Finn scratched the back of his head. "Porting over a dozen times, ye say?"

"Mmhm."

I wrapped my arms around myself, still feeling uneasy about Erimon not being with me.

"Alright, fine. I'll escort your lady love."

My heart hummed at the label.

"Thank you, old friend." Erimon slapped Finn's shoulder and then gripped it. "It goes without sayin', but if anything were to happen to her…"

Finn shook his head. "Aye, yes. You'd have my hide. I got it, Monny." He brushed his hand away.

We walked outside hand in hand. Absently kicking a pebble on the ground, I shoved my other hand in my pocket. Patrick and Phoebe sat on a nearby log. They looked as if they'd had about as fun a conversation as we did. Phoebe walked toward us with her hands pressed to her sides.

"Ready to go wrap things up in New York, Phoebs?"

Finn awkwardly trailed behind me.

"Mhm. And Patrick is coming with us," Phoebe said.

"You are?" Erimon raised a brow at Patrick.

"I thought it only right I meet her parents given the uh… circumstances." Patrick made a toothy grin.

Erimon pulled me into his side, kissing the top of my head.

"We'll have to call the airline, see if they're willing to exchange our tickets since we missed our flight," Phoebe said.

Sniffling, I lifted my head from Erimon's shoulder. "Missed our flight? Our flight is tomorrow."

"Our flight was actually two weeks ago," she said, staring at me like a deer in headlights.

"Two weeks—I—I must have lost track of time." My voice trailed off in thought.

"Abby, you better get goin'." Erimon sniffed once, running a knuckle under his nose.

Blood drained from my cheeks, and nausea boiled in my core. I turned to him, his hands finding my hips. I snaked my arms around his neck and brushed my lips against his, ignoring the tenderness building from the light scratch of his beard. I wanted the kiss to last forever, but he pulled away, pressing his forehead to mine.

"Go, Abby," he said curtly, digging deep to find the strength for both of us. His hands slowly began to push me away from him.

I fought back tears as his hands dropped to his sides. He sniffed again, running a hand down his face, his beard. He motioned with his head as a taxi van cab approached. Phoebe slipped her phone into her pocket, and Patrick wrapped his arm around Phoebe's shoulders.

"I mean it, Finn." Erimon squared his jaw, pointing at him, plead in his gaze.

Finn paused mid-way to crouching into the van. "Erimon, you have my word on my mother's grave. I'll protect her with my life."

More promises of life for life.

I slid the van door back and peered over my shoulder at him one last time. My tattoo sent a light burn across my skin.

"Go," he said more sternly.

And I climbed into the van, unable to look back for fear I'd jump out the window of a moving vehicle if I saw him watching me roll away.

If Phoebe or Finn talked to me during the ride to the airport, I didn't notice because I'd gone into autopilot for the trip duration. I remembered Phoebe shrugging a hoodie over my shoulders to cover my blood-stained shirt. I remembered absently removing my shoes and placing what little belongings I had with me on the conveyor belt for security. I even remembered the feeling of the kid kicking at the back of my seat on the airplane, but it wasn't until I arrived at my apartment that I regained consciousness.

My humble abode filled with all my possessions. Dozens of photos of varying animals I cared for through the years littered the walls, enough plants to call half of my apartment a forest, a bookshelf filled with nothing but animal science books.

Finn had eyed my couch, mumbling something about not being able to fit his arse on it and opted for the floor. I'd piled the area rug with all of my extra blankets despite his claims of sleeping on plenty of stone slabs in his youth.

Dragging my feet into my bedroom, I felt for the light switch, somehow forgetting its location. I pulled my cell phone from my pocket, fumbling with the charging cable on my nightstand. The battery was drained, and I knew that I'd have a slew of messages from work, so I left it off. Crossing the room to the window of my reading nook, I opened it a crack.

As I made my way to the bathroom, I took off my clothes, leaving them in random places in a trail. I stared into space, turning the knobs for the shower, waiting until the water was so hot that the steam fogged the mirror, marring my reflection. Letting the warm water trail over my face, I sputtered and turned my gaze down. The water spiraled into the drain, and I wondered what dangers were involved with breaking through the Ninth Wave.

Pushing my palms against the tiled wall, I moaned as the water flowed down my neck and back. As I lifted my head, I traced the new tattoo on my arm. Designs that only days prior I had trailed my finger over on Erimon's back as we lay in a mystic wooded wonderland. The Claddagh ring glowed and hummed. My heart ached, already missing him. I pictured his snarky face if and when I'd ever tell him that it didn't even take twenty-four hours. The thought made me smile, but it faded away soon after.

A cool current wafted from my bedroom, flowing from the window I'd purposely left ajar. It would become a habit as a constant means to keep in touch with him—my Druid.

"I miss you," I whispered against the water as it trailed down my face.

I knew you could never get enough of me.

I laughed and sobbed at the same time.

"How long until I see you again?"

I don't know, love.

Silence on my part.

But I promised ye, remember? I gave you my word.

"A Druid's word is everything."

Yes. And now…so are you.

EPILOGUE

ERIMON'S JAW TIGHTENED AS HE watched the yellow taxi drive off, kicking up dirt from its tires.

He sniffed several times, fighting back the tears he knew wanted to escape. The last thing he wanted to do was send Abby away. Giving part of his soul to her caused his very being to feel incomplete—a piece of him was about to be thousands of miles away, and even though it'd drive him mad, he'd shove it down and deal.

He *had* to send her away. There wasn't a choice. Not only would he be porting across the known universe, through other dimensions, and encountering some of the most lowlife scum in existence to get answers…it was what he might have to *do* to get those answers. Torture. Killing. Threatening. A darkness he didn't need Abby seeing so early on. Not yet. Let the glitz and glamour of their newfound Druidic entanglement shine before dousing the flame.

He ground his teeth together as he stormed into the woods, ready to destroy anything in his path only to repair it afterward.

307

Growling, he split trees in half and forced them back together, summoned water from beds buried in the soil to splash over his face—to drown him.

He knelt to the ground, making it vibrate against his touch, pulling iron ore through the earth at his command. Swirling his hand around, molding the ore, flashes of the whip plowing through Abby's chest plagued his mind. He snarled as he slammed the newly formed iron ball into the ground. He tore off his jacket, tossing it away. It'd been soiled in goblin blood. Hound blood. *Her* blood. He'd almost lost her and now he knew he'd tear magma from the earth's core if it meant keeping her safe. It wouldn't happen again.

He stared at the tattoo on his arm, glowing radiant blue, pulsing, burning from being so far away from its counterpart. He pictured Abby's slender arm with the same design—his tattoo on her, wondering if she felt the same and hoping she wasn't in pain because of it.

His nostrils twitched, smelling sulfur and death in the air. Over his shoulder, dark mist and clouds formed. An older man emerged, his fingers steepled, his face stony.

"Crom, you're in rare form. To what do I owe this pleasure?"

"You cannot keep her from me."

Erimon noticed his lack of golden shackles and started to walk in a circle around The Dullahan in disguise. "Have you ever dealt with a Druid?"

"Of course, I have."

"Have you ever dealt with a Druid…in love?" Erimon's jaw popped, continuing to pace, fists clenched as he thought about Abby lying near lifeless in his arms.

"Druids cannot fall in love, I—" Crom started before his lips parted, watching Erimon circle him. "Did you fall for the mortal? How *did* you manage to save her? I felt her life force draining second by second."

Erimon stopped directly in front of him. "I gave her part of my power." He paused, wishing to take in every inch of Crom's expression.

Crom's face faltered only slightly, his hands clasping tightly behind his back. He shook his head emphatically. "No Druid has that sort of power."

"And you want to know the real kicker?" He grinned, watching Crom's face grimace. "*You* made it possible."

A wave ran across Erimon, and he attempted to ignore it if only momentarily. Abby called for him, and he had every intention of answering her, reassuring her.

"You created your undoing by killing her. And together, we will *destroy* you." Snarling the last words, Erimon leaned his face into Crom's.

Fist's shaking violently at his sides, Crom let out a monstrous roar into the wind. The very same wind that caught Erimon's wings as they flared out, and carried him into the beckoning horizon.

TO BE CONTINUED...

Additional Information and Pronunciations:

Erimon (ehre-mahn)

Bandruí - (ban-dree) In ancient Celtic society, female Druids composed an intellectual elite, whose knowledge and training placed them as priests of the Celtic religion. They studied literature, poetry, history, Celtic law and astronomy. They also preformed sacrifices, and interpreted omens. Their legacy: WITCHES

Banshee - (ban-shee) A female spirit in Irish folklore who heralds the death of a family member, usually by wailing, shrieking, or keening.

Cu Chulainn - (Coo Cullen) Hound of Ulster, an Irish mythological demigod who appears in the stories of the Ulster Cycle. Born Sétanta, he gained his better-known name as a child, after killing Culann's fierce guard dog in self defense and offering to take its place until a replacement could be reared. At the age of seventeen he defended Ulster single-handedly against the armies of Queen Mave of Connacht in the famous Táin Bó Cúailnge ("Cattle Raid of Cooley"). It was prophesied that his great deeds would give him everlasting fame, but his life would be a short one. He is known for his terrifying battle frenzy, or ríastrad (translated by as "warp spasm"), in which he becomes an unrecognizable monster who knows neither friend nor foe. He fights from his chariot, driven by his loyal charioteer Láeg and drawn by his horses, Liath Macha and Dub Sainglend.

Druids - (droo-uhd) A druid was a member of the high-ranking class in ancient Celtic cultures. Druids were religious leaders as well as legal authorities, adjudicators, lorekeepers, medical professionals and political advisors. Druids left no written accounts.

The Dullahan (Crom Dubh) - (doo-luh-han) is depicted as a headless rider, usually on a black horse, who carries his own head on his arm. Usually, the Dullahan is male, but there are some female versions. The mouth is usually in a hideous grin that touches both sides of the head. Its eyes are constantly moving about and can see across the countryside even during the darkest nights. The flesh of the head is said to have the color and consistency of moldy cheese. The Dullahan is believed to use the spine of a human corpse for a whip, and its wagon is adorned with funeral objects: it has candles in skulls to light the way, the spokes of the wheels are made from thigh bones, and the wagon's covering is made from a worm-chewed pall or dried human skin. The ancient Irish believed that where the Dullahan stops riding, a person is due to die. The Dullahan calls out the person's name, drawing away the soul of his victim, at which point the person immediately drops dead. There are rumors that golden objects can force the Dullahan to disappear.

Finn MacCoul - (fin mək-KOOL) Also spelled, MacCool. A mythical hunter-warrior in Irish mythology, portrayed as a giant. The stories of Finn and his followers, the Fianna, form the Fenian Cycle (an Fhiannaíocht), much of it narrated in the voice of Finn's son, the poet Oisín.

Ilmarinen - (ilmɑ-rinen) The Eternal Hammerer, blacksmith and inventor in the Kalevala, is a god and archetypal artificer from Finnish mythology. He is immortal and capable of creating practically anything, but is portrayed as being unlucky in love.

Kelpie - (kel-pee) A kelpie, or water kelpie, is a shape-shifting spirit inhabiting lakes in Irish and Scottish folklore. It is a Celtic legend; however, analogues exist in other cultures. It is usually described as a black horse-like creature, able to adopt human form.

Leprechaun - (leh-pruh-kaan) A leprechaun is a diminutive supernatural being in Irish folklore, classed by some as a type of solitary fairy. They are usually depicted as little bearded men, wearing a coat and hat, who partake in mischief. It's said that every leprechaun has a pot of gold that he hides deep in the Irish countryside.

Mave (also spelled Maeve) - A strong and independent ruler of the Connacht, with a knowledge of magic and sorcery. She never shirked her duty, and knew well how to encourage and lead her followers. She was always depicted as very beautiful, yet dressed for war! She could be harsh, jealous, vicious, scheming and domineering. Always willing to go to great lengths to assert her rightful status. The name Maeve is said to mean 'she who intoxicates', perhaps alluding to her role as a sovereignty Goddess. In modern times her legend lives on and she is often represented as a symbol of the power of women over men in terms of sexuality, of cunning and of courage.

Oisín - (uh-SHEEN), or Osheen, Regarded in legend as the greatest poet of Ireland, a warrior of the fianna in the Ossianic or Fenian Cycle of Irish mythology. He is the son of Fionn mac Cumhaill and of Sadhbh, and is the narrator of much of the cycle and composition of the poems are attributed to him. Sadhbh - (sive) was the mother of Oisín by Fionn mac Cumhail (Finn MacCoul). She was enchanted to take the form of a doe for refusing the love of Fer Doirich (or Fear Doirche), the dark druid of the Men of Dea (Tuatha Dé Danann). She held this form for three years, until a serving man of the Dark Druid took pity on her and told her that if she set foot in the dún (fort or castle) of the Fianna of Ireland, the druid would no longer have any power over her. She then traveled straight to Almhuin (Fionn's house) and was found by Finn while he was out hunting. Since Sadhbh was a human in animal form, she was not harmed by Finn's hounds Bran and Sceolan, as they too had been transformed from their original human shape.

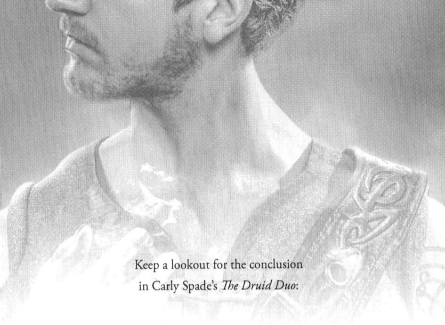

Keep a lookout for the conclusion
in Carly Spade's *The Druid Duo*:

ETERNALLY
YOURS

COMING SOON

Catch the first book in the Contemporary Mythos series:

HADES

The King of the Underworld may have found a woman
truly capable of melting his cold, dark heart.

HADES (Contemporary Mythos, #1)
BUY IT ON AMAZON

Catch the second book in the Contemporary Mythos series:

It's not easy being a *true* rock god.

APOLLO (Contemporary Mythos, #2)
BUY IT ON AMAZON

ACKNOWLEDGEMENTS

This is the second edition of the first book I ever published and I remembered the way my hands trembled the first time I was thinking up acknowledgements. If you're taking the time to read this, know that an author's path is never-ending. Power of Eternity was an idea that manifested in a dream and though I'm still even proud of that first edition because I WROTE A BOOK, I knew as my skills improved it could use a vast improvement. I'm so deeply in love with this story, its characters, and Erimon is the hero I've always wanted a written. If this is the version you've read, thank you. If you've read the first version and gave this one a chance too, THANK YOU.

Firstly, thank you to my husband. Your patience and love continue to astound me on a daily basis. Thank you for being my reference for what men would *really* do in certain situations and for giving me suggestions to make the hero even more bad ass. And despite having no interest in romance novels (and that's totally okay, LOL), you still listen to my ideas and offer input. You're amazing.

To my parents for always believing in me and encouraging me to follow my dreams.

To Rochelle, thank you for taking the time to read this new version of the story frontward, backward, and all in between and loving Erimon as much as I do. (I still called dibs first because I wrote him…fair is fair.)

Thank you to Jilly, my first ever beta reader, A LOT has changed in this book since you and I first worked together, but I'll always remember you were the first.

To Kristen B, who inspired me to write original works after cheering on my FanFiction for over a year.

To AK, my kick ass critique partner for helping me to improve my writing ten-fold, being honest while also being a cheerleader. You read through this new story, somehow remembering the original and gave me that boost of confidence I needed to know all the sweat and tears (literally) was worth the revisions.

Lastly, to all the readers who took a chance on this book. I can't thank you enough! And if you've come so far as to make it to the acknowledgements section, your name deserves to be immortalized in marble.

STAY TUNED!
WWW.CARLYSPADE.COM

Made in the USA
Middletown, DE
17 April 2021

37802587R00194